Know Your Enemy

The entire Ops deck crew was staring at Lieutenant Commander Brik. He was nine feet tall. He was four feet wide at the shoulder. His muzzle was striped with red and orange fur. His fangs looked as long as Korie's hand. He was a Morthan Tyger—a genetically augmented, bioengineered, tailored in the womb, product of directed evolution. He was wearing a fleet uniform. Korie was horrified. The other officers and crew on duty were frozen at their posts.

Abruptly, Captain Hardesty appeared on the bridge. "I see you've all met the new chief of security... Lieutenant Commander Brik. You have a problem, Mr. Korie?"

Korie whirled to face the Captain. "Yes, sir, I do. There's a Morthan on the bridge."

Hardesty ignored Korie's anger. "There are humans fighting for the Morthan Solidarity. There are Morthans fighting on the side of the Allies. It's a big war. There's room enough for everybody."

Brik grinned. His incisors were even longer than Korie had thought. "*I* am not your fight," he said to Korie. His voice rumbled like a warship. "Your fight is . . . out there."

Korie glared up at the Morthan warrior. "I know that," he said testily. "Where's *your* fight?"

Brik moved slowly, so as not to alarm anyone. He touched his own heart gently. "My fight is in here."

Voyage of the Star Wolf

David Gerrold

BANTAM BOOKS
New York • Toronto • London • Sydney • Auckland

VOYAGE OF THE STAR WOLF
A Bantam Spectra Book / November 1990

ISBN 0-553-26466-4

Published simultaneously in the United States and Canada

Bantam Books are published by Bantam Books, a division of Bantam Doubleday
Dell Publishing Group, Inc. Its trademark, consisting of the words "Bantam
Books" and the portrayal of a rooster, is Registered in U.S. Patent and Trademark
Office and in other countries. Marca Registrada. Bantam Books, 666 Fifth Avenue,
New York, New York 10103.

PRINTED IN THE UNITED STATES OF AMERICA

OPM   0 9 8 7 6 5 4 3 2 1

FOR AMY STOUT,
with love.

Out there.

The *eternal* frontier.

It isn't the darkness that gets to you and it isn't the aloneness. It's the emptiness. It's the incomprehensible endless empty that drives you mad from the inside.

It chews inward, a constant gnawing pressure, until you feel as if you are going to implode. You cannot taste it. You cannot touch it. But you can feel it constantly, so close—just on the other side of the bulkhead.

One day, you know that you're going to open an air lock and step out to meet it face to face. You know that you're going to do it, even though you know that it will certainly kill you. But you will do it anyway. There is no choice in the matter. There is no whether or not. There is only *when* and *how*. Someday, you will not be able to stand the not-knowing*ness* of it any longer, and you will step naked out of the air lock to meet this inexplicable thing that doesn't exist and can't be seen or smelled or touched: this existence that is the absolute lack of all existence.

This is the kernel where the madness starts, this is how it grows: in the knowledge that the unexplainable incomprehensible unknowable exists. It demands explanation, but the human mind is incapable of explaining this concept of existence without form or substance. It cannot imagine, it cannot *comprehend*, it cannot contain ideas which are larger than itself—and in the face of possibilities that are larger even than the concept of concept, the mind flounders at a perpetual loss; it cannot encompass.

The mind cannot understand emptiness, nor can it contain infinity. Total emptiness. Total infinity. Neither can be conceptualized, neither can be held in the human consciousness. And when both of those staggering truths exist together—endless emptiness or empty endlessness—the mind founders on the reefs of confusion and desperation. The human spirit is staggered by the experience; stunned, horrified, entranced and *transformed*. It's beautiful. It's terrifying. It's like looking into the face of God.

Afterward, you are not the same person.

The body, the expression, the total affect of the being is forever enchanted by the experience of *space*. The way you walk, the way you talk, the way you think and feel. No one who has ever stood naked before the jeweled night will ever be free of its terror and its power.

And even this is only an intimation of the magnificent dreadfulness of *hyperstate*.

—W. ILMA MEIER
Death and Transformation in Space

THE SILK ROAD CONVOY

The Silk Road Convoy was almost three hundred years old.

Its path roughly described a bent and swollen, meandering, broken ellipse along the edge of the rift and then out and across it and back again. A closer examination might reveal that the trail of the convoy was actually a series of lesser arcs tracing through the spiral arm, then turning reluctantly out into the darkness of The Deep Rift, with one scheduled stopover at the forlorn worlds of Marathon, Ghastly, and George, then across The Great Leap and into the lips of the ghostly streamer known as The Purse on the opposite side, then around The Outbeyond, down toward The Silver Horn, and finally turning home again, leaping across at The Narrows, down through The Valley of Death to The Heart of Darkness, then a sudden dogleg up to a place of desperate joy known as Last Chance, before finally sliding into The Long Ride Home and a golden world called Glory.

The Silk Road Convoy was the oldest of all the caravans on the route. It was not the largest fleet on the route, but it was definitely the richest and most prestigious.

The convoy followed the path of an ancient exploration

vessel. Colonies had followed the vessel. Traders had followed the colonies. The trade had evolved over the centuries into a trade route called The Silk Road. Eventually, due to the twists and vagaries of luck and history and fate, it became one of the most profitable routes known in the Alliance. At any given moment there might be as many as thirty different caravans scattered along its great curving length—but only the original Silk Road Convoy was entitled to bear the name of the trade route. This was because the partnership which had grown up with the original Silk Road Convoy also owned or controlled most of the directorships of The Silk Road Authority.

The Silk Road Authority was larger than most governments. It held three seats in the Alliance and controlled almost all of the trade, both legal and otherwise, within the ellipse of its influence. The Authority had major offices on every planet within thirty light-years of the primary route. Every merchant ship in the arm paid a license fee for the privilege of traveling the route and booking passengers and cargo through the offices of the Authority.

Some ships, like the notorious freebooter *Eye of Argon*, preferred to travel alone. Others paid for the privilege of traveling with a caravan. The caravans were near-permanent institutions.

Imagine a chain of vessels nearly three light-days long, islands of light strung through the darkness. They carried names like The Emerald Colony Traders (licensed to The Silk Road) and The Great Rift Corporation (licensed to The Silk Road) and Zetex Starlines (licensed to The Silk Road). The caravans provided service and safety—and safety had lately become a primary consideration for star travelers.

Because of its name, because of its age and its prestige, The Silk Road Convoy was considered the safest of all.

MARATHON

The dark world of Marathon had never known life of its own and never would. Lost in eternal night, it circled a dead and cold star. Ghostly starlight limned its bleak horizons. Life here could never be more than a lonely visitor. The planet was hard and barren and ugly.

It had been discovered by accident, settled by necessity. The only good thing about Marathon was its location, a third of the way into The Deep Rift. Hard in the abyss, the ugly world was a welcome way station in the long desperate leap to the other side. Its single settlement was a bright lonely point of life. Despite itself, despite its abysmal desolation, Marathon had become an important stopover. It was a nexus of the lesser trade routes which bordered the abyss; despite its desolate loneliness, the dark world was becoming a trade center in its own right.

Marathon had two neighbors, Ghastly and George, both of which were said to be considerably less attractive than Marathon. Few had gone to see for themselves. There was some ice mining on George, and nothing on Ghastly but a few crashed probes.

Marathon wasn't quite the frontier, but it was an *edge* and that was bad enough. Too many things *lurked* out here.

And too many people had become suddenly afraid.

Despite the patrol vessels, the growing fears of war were making Marathon a place of urgency and need. There was an air of panic here. The sudden flow of refugees from The Outbeyond had created a thriving market for passage on every stopping vessel, regardless of destination, as long as it was deeper away from the frontier. The local offices of The Silk Road Authority had become hard pressed to meet the growing demand for passage.

Adding to the distress of the refugees was the fact that a great number of ships were waiting stubbornly in orbit around Marathon, their captains refusing to continue along the route until they could join The Silk Road Convoy.

If it came.

Rumor had it that war between the Alliance and the Solidarity was imminent. Rumor had it that The Silk Road Authority was so concerned about the inevitability of interstellar conflagration that the great caravan might not pass this way again for a long, long time. Rumor had it that this was the caravan's last circuit, that the route was being shut down for fear of Morthan marauders.

Rumor *also* had it that the Alliance was assembling a great fleet to protect the route. . . .

LIBERTY SHIPS

The center of gravity of a liberty ship is the singularity, the pinpoint black hole that powers the ship and also serves as the focus for its hyperstate nodule. The singularity masses as much as a small moon and can be accurately located by even a low-power gravity wave scanner out to a distance of several light-hours.

The singularity is held in place by a singularity bottle, a spherical magnetic cage three stories high; this is the ship's engine room. Three hyperstate fluctuators are focused on the singularity; one from above, one from either side. They are spaced 120 degrees apart. The fluctuators extend out through the hull of the ship and into three massive spines that give the starship its characteristic spiky look. The length of the fluctuators is a function of the size of the ship; it is necessary for precise focusing of the projected hyperstate bubble around the vessel. Hyperstate is also known as *irrational space*, producing the oft-quoted cliché, ''To go faster than light, first you have to be irrational.''[1]

---

[1] The singularity itself is tended by the ''Black Hole Gang,'' generally an insular crew with its own jargon and mystique. On most ships, the singularity team regards itself as the master of a particularly arcane and esoteric discipline; they do not casually welcome outsiders to their domain. Relationships with the ''Front Office,'' their name for the bridge crew, are occasionally strained.

For sublight acceleration and deceleration, the liberty ship has three mass-drivers mounted around her hull. A mass-driver is a long thin tube, lined with superconducting magnetic rings. Ions are introduced at one end, accelerated to near-lightspeed, and shot out the opposite end, producing the necessary thrust. The direction of particle acceleration can also be reversed for braking maneuvers. While the operation of the mass-drivers is not as easily detectable as that of the singularity stardrive, the vessel's wake of accelerated ions can be detected by a ship with sophisticated scanning gear.

Aft of the engine room, you will find crew's quarters, storage areas, aft torpedo bay, cargo bays, and the internal shuttle bay. The shuttle bay is equipped to function as a cargo lock, but there are also smaller air locks at the stern of the vessel. A liberty ship usually carries two shuttles and occasionally a captain's gig. Used as lifeboats, the shuttles can carry ten individuals each—fifty if they are put into short-term hibernation.

Forward of the engine room are officers' quarters on the top deck, the ship's brain and main mess room on the second deck, and the keel and equipment storage bays on the bottom level. Forward of that is the Operations complex. This is built around a large U-shaped Operations deck, the forward half of which is a sophisticated viewer. At the rear of the Operations deck is the Bridge, a high, railed platform overlooking everything. Directly underneath the Bridge is the Operations bay, where the ship's autonomic functions are maintained.

Forward of the Operations complex are more crew's quarters, sick bay, the weapons shop, forward torpedo bay, forward access, and air lock. Running the length of the ship is the keel, a utility corridor which also functions as the ship's primary channel for cables, ducts, and optical fibers.

On the hull of the ship, you will find three large arrays of scanners, detectors, cameras, and other sensory apparatus. There are also twelve arrays of disruptor-beam projectors. The ship is double hulled, with both hulls required to maintain 99 percent or better atmospheric integrity. Both hulls are also internally and externally shielded against particle-beam weapons. Class V magnetic shields are standard on most liberty ships, although most captains upgrade to Class VII or better whenever the equipment is available.

The liberty ship has a multiple-redundancy, optical nervous system. Autonomic functions are maintained by an array of systems analysis boxes. Higher-brain functions are handled by one or more Harlie series synthesized-consciousness modules. The Harlie series has been designed to be more anthropomorphic than other constructed identities, and therefore tends to perceive the starship as its own body; this produces a measurable increase in the unit's survival motivation.

Standard crew on a liberty ship is one hundred and twenty persons.

THE *LS-1187*

The *LS-1187* was three years old and had not yet earned a name.

She was a destroyer-class starship, a liberty ship, one of many. On her side, she wore the flag of New America: thirteen horizontal stripes, alternating red and white, and a dark blue field showing seven white circles around a single bright star.

The liberty ships came off the line one every eleven days. There were seven assembly lines building ships. This ship was like all the rest; small and desperate, fitted with just enough equipment to make her survivable, and sent as rapidly as possible out toward the frontier. It would be up to her port of assignment to install her secondary fittings, internal amenities, auxiliary systems, and weaponry—whatever might be necessary for her local duties.

The *LS-1187* had not yet earned her name because she had not yet "bloodied her sword." Until she did, she would remain only a number.

She was a lean ship: a dark arrow, three hundred meters long. Two thirds of the way back along her hull, three sharp fins projected out and forward. These were her fluctuator spines. The end of each one culminated in a bulbous stardrive lens.

Her cruising speed was subluminal, but the realized velocity of her hyperstate envelope was seven hundred fifty times the speed of light.

Her orders were the simplest possible: a time, a location, and a vector.

Translation: Proceed to The Deep Rift. Arrive at a specified *here* at a specified *now*, pointed in a particular direction and traveling at a particular speed. Don't be followed. Do all this and you will be part of the Grand Convoy of a thousand ships: a thousand separate vessels all arriving at their respective places in formation at the same moment.

It was a daring gamble, but if it worked . . . the outworlds would have the protection they needed against the raids of the marauders.

If it failed . . .

Admiral Wendayne stood on the bridge of *The Moral Victory* and frowned. He was a stout man, short and stocky and solid. He was also very bald and very sour. He was studying a holographic display of the entire convoy as it came together.

He should have been proud; the idea of the Grand Convoy had been his; but he wasn't proud. He was annoyed. He hadn't been given half the ship strength he felt he needed; and too many of the ships assigned to the convoy were the smaller liberty ships, untried and untested. Too many of them had numbers instead of names. Nothing ever worked out as planned.

An aide stepped up to the admiral then. "The *LS-1187* has joined the convoy."

Admiral Wendayne was underwhelmed. "Hmp." Then he realized that the aide was waiting for a response. "All right. Welcome them."

The aide, a young man, turned to a console and murmured a command to IRMA, the ship's computer. A screen on the console lit up with a set of security codes, followed by the crest of the fleet, and finally by the image of the admiral. "Greetings—Captain Lowell and the crew of the *LS-1187*. Your participation in this operation represents a vital contribution to the security of the Alliance. On behalf of the—''

The message was encoded, translated into a series of pulses, and channeled to the modulators of the flagship's hyperstate envelope. The envelope *shimmered*. Every ship within scanning range of the flagship's envelope could see the *shimmer* of her hyperstate bubble, but only those with the appropriate codes would be able to translate the shimmer into a message. All of the Alliance codes were one-time cyphers, to be used only once and then never again.

Aboard the *LS-1187*, the message was translated and played as it came in. Its header codes identified it as a standard greeting signal, not requiring acknowledgment.

''—Admiralty, let me thank you, and let me welcome you to the Combined Allied Star Force special operations at Marathon. You may now open your sealed orders. Again, wel come aboard.''

Captain Sam Lowell nodded wryly at the image of the admiral. He was an older man, almost kindly-looking. Beside him on the bridge stood Jonathan Thomas Korie, his executive officer. Korie looked preoccupied; he was listening to something on his headset. Now he frowned. He turned and looked down toward the large, elliptical, holographic display table in the center of the Operations deck. The Bridge—that part of the ship that was actually called *the Bridge*—was a high, railed platform at the rear of the Ops deck. There were command chairs there and two exit doors, one on either side. The Bridge overlooked the whole chamber; Korie could oversee the duties of all eight officers at the consoles beneath them.

The entire front half of the Ops deck was a giant curving screen that wrapped around half the chamber and most of the ceiling as well. At any given moment, it was like standing under an open sky, a great panoramic window onto the void. At the moment, the forward image was a simulated view of the distant stars, with shadowy grid lines superimposed over them; the starship seemed to be moving up through a three-dimensional framework, with a delimiter every five light-minutes.

Korie glanced over as Captain Lowell said, ''All right, I've heard enough.'' He reached over and tapped the message off.

To Korie's questioning look, he explained, "I've heard this speech before. And you'll hear it enough times too when you're a captain. You'll learn the whole damn repertoire."

Captain Lowell took a dark envelope out of his tunic and carefully broke the seal. He removed three sheets of gray paper, unfolded them, and scanned them quickly, passing them to Korie as he finished each one.

"Mm," said Korie. "No surprises here."

"Did you expect any?"

Korie shook his head. Captain Lowell unclipped a hand mike from his belt. His voice was amplified throughout the ship. "This is the captain speaking. We are seven point five light-years from Marathon. We've taken up our assigned position in the convoy and we've been officially welcomed by Admiral Wendayne. From this point on, we'll be operating at full alert."

There were audible groans across the operations room—not very loud, but loud enough for Korie to look annoyed and Captain Lowell to look amused.

The captain continued. "All right, can the chatter. The admiral thinks there's a good chance of engaging the enemy here. Personally, I don't think so, but maybe the admiral knows something I don't. That's why he's an admiral and you're not. So everybody, just stay on your toes. That is all."

As he clipped the mike back to his belt, Captain Lowell looked to his executive officer. "Do you understand why I did that?"

"I think so."

"This ship is going to be yours very soon. I want you to take care of her. She's a proud ship." He nodded toward the bridge crew. "It's all about trust. You have to be straight with them, Mr. Korie. *Never ever lie to your crew.*"

"I promise you, sir. I never will."

"Keep that promise and you'll be a good captain," Lowell said. "I've never lied to this crew and I have nothing to be ashamed of." Wistfully, he added, "I just wish . . ."

"That she could have earned a name, right?" Korie finished the thought for him.

Captain Lowell nodded. "You know me too well."

"We're going to miss you, sir."

"I'm not dying, Mr. Korie. I'm only retiring. In the

meantime," he said with a smile, "you'd better pay attention to your screens." He pointed. "What's that?"

Korie glanced to the console before him, then down forward to the Operations deck where Flight Engineer Hodel was working at the holographic display table.

Mikhail Hodel was a young man with a very professional demeanor, but he was also dark and wild-looking and was known to be obsessive in all of his pursuits. Now, he was intently studying the schematic of a too-bright shimmer moving through a shifting gridwork. He looked up as Korie stepped down to join him.

"She just came up out of nowhere, sir. I don't recognize the signature. Look at the ripple effect—it's like it's being held in. Suppressed."

"Where'd she come from?" asked Korie.

Hodel shook his head. "I don't know. One moment she wasn't there. The next—"

Korie peered intently at the floating display. "I've never seen a scan like that before—not even in simulations."

Hodel looked unhappy. "I think she followed us, sir."

"Not possible. We'd have seen her. If she can see our bubble, we can see hers."

"Maybe not, sir—" Hodel blurted what he was thinking, "There is one way to do it—a large bubble can be damped down. It'll still have a longer visual range than the same size envelope from a smaller engine."

Korie started to shake his head. "The density would—"

"—would look like that." Hodel pointed.

Korie stopped himself from replying. Hodel was right. The bogey was coming in too fast. "Harlie?"

The ship's computer answered immediately: "My best guess: A dragon-class battle-cruiser running with her engines damped to prevent long-range detection."

"Confidence?"

"Eighty-eight percent."

"Good guess," Korie said to Hodel, but he wasn't happy. "I'd rather have been wrong."

Korie turned toward the bridge, but Captain Lowell was already stepping down to the display. "There's only one ship it could be—the *Dragon Lord*—but she's reported to be on the other side of the rift. The Solidarity doesn't have a lot of heavy metal to spare."

"How reliable was that report?" asked Korie.

"Reliable enough for the High Command." The captain shook his head unbelievingly. "If the admiral had known that a dragon-class anything was lurking in this neighborhood, we'd have never assembled this convoy." He scratched his head thoughtfully. "Well, it can't mean anything. She's traveling alone. Probably sharking us."

"Well, it's working. I'm scared," said Hodel.

"Relax," said Lowell. "She's not going to attack. The Solidarity isn't that stupid."

Suddenly, the shimmer brightened and expanded. And expanded. *And expanded again.*

"Oh my God—" said Hodel. "Look at the way she's expanding her envelope."

"That's an attack run." Korie was already reaching for a terminal.

"No!" said Lowell. "No. They *can't* be that stupid. They can't be! Nobody attacks alone—"

The operating lights went suddenly to red. The alarm klaxon screeched throughout the ship.

Korie was suddenly listening to his headset. "Signal from the flagship, sir—"

"It is the *Dragon Lord*," Hodel said, still staring horrified at the shimmering display. "The signature is confirmed."

"And she's got a wolf pack coming in behind her!" added Captain Lowell. The blood drained from his face. He looked suddenly gray.

Korie forgot his headset for the moment and turned back to the display. It was his worst nightmare. Behind the expanded shimmer of the *Dragon Lord*, too many other lights were appearing on the display, winking into existence like tiny stars, one pink shimmer after the other.

Korie looked to the captain. The old man was frozen.

"Sir—?"

Captain Lowell started to lift a hand, as if he was about to say something. A thought flashed through Korie's mind: *He's never been in a real battle.*

Korie whirled. "Targeting! Get a lock on her. *Battle stations!* Stand by to fire."

Harlie replied instantly. "Targeting now."

Captain Lowell blinked, as if abruptly realizing where he was. "Uh—what did the flagship say?"

"Scatter and attack."

"Uh, right." Captain Lowell nodded. "Uh—disruptors, fire at will!"

Korie looked up sharply at that. What was the old man thinking? The attackers were still in hyperstate, fifty light-hours away, two minutes in real time. Disruptors were local-space weapons. The only way to destroy a ship in hyperstate was to hit its envelope with a field-effect torpedo.

Maybe he was just momentarily confused, Korie thought, but he knew the truth of the moment even as he tried to deny it. The captain was paralyzed by the enormity of the disaster. The huge holographic display dominated the Operations deck and every officer on duty could see the horror for himself. The bright pink shimmers of the Morthan wolf pack were sweeping ruthlessly down upon the convoy's flank. The darker blue shimmers of the Alliance ships were scattering now—but slowly, much too slowly. They didn't have the same mass-to-power ratio as the much lighter vessels of the Morthan Solidarity. The marauders could easily outmaneuver the cargo and passenger vessels—*and most of the destroyers too*.

The only hope for the unarmed ships of the convoy was to scatter into the darkness of the rift, leaving the warships to slash and parry and dodge. The battle would spread out across a hundred light-hours of hyperstate—it didn't matter; what counted here was visibility and interception velocity. The wolf pack would chase the fattest targets. The destroyers would chase the wolf pack. The battleships would weave complex evasion patterns.

And in the center of it all, like a fat red spider in the center of a glistening web, was the largest brightest shimmer of them all—the *Dragon Lord*. Her immense hyperstate envelope was a lens for her hyperstate scanning devices that would let her see farther than any other vessel in the battle. She would be able to track the ships of the fleeing convoy for days—and she would be equally visible. She could ripple orders and directions to every ship in the wolf pack. Nothing would be able to get to her, but she would be able to see the whole battle. The Alliance ships would be helpless before such an advantage.

Korie saw the whole plan at once. It was brilliant. He could only admire the beauty of it. This wasn't just an attack on a convoy. This was about cutting The Silk Road and isolating all of the Alliance worlds on the far side of the rift. The *Dragon Lord* would sweep everything from here to Marathon—and then beyond. With the fleet in shambles, there would be no protection for the outworlds.

Korie stepped in quickly to Captain Lowell's side. It seemed as if everything on the Operations deck were beeping, buzzing, ringing, and clanging. He ignored it. "The missiles, sir?" he prompted.

"Yes, yes, of course." The old man looked almost grateful. "Ready missiles!"

"Recommend an evasion course, sir," Korie prompted.

"Yes. Make it so." Lowell nodded eagerly at Korie's suggestion.

Is he that scared? Korie wondered. So far, only Hodel could have noticed—and he was too busy with his own board to say anything about it.

Hodel's panel blinked and flickered. He slammed it with his fist—*hard*—it was a reaction, not a cure; the computer channels on that console were locked up, thrashing with contradictory information; but the screens came immediately back to life anyway. Hodel muttered an oath and resumed working, laying in a series of complex evasion patterns. And then he glanced up at Korie knowingly. "This isn't going to work."

"Shut up," said Korie. "Do you want to live forever?"

"It's a trap," said Lowell. He was visibly flustered. "We can't fight the *Dragon Lord* and a wolf pack."

Korie noted that the old man was looking more ragged every moment, but there wasn't time to do anything. If the attack was every captain's nightmare, then Captain Lowell's disintegration was every executive officer's nightmare. Korie was going to have to make it work. Abruptly, the targeting program chimed. Korie snapped, "Targets in range!"

"Missiles armed!" called Li on the weapons station. "Locking . . . one, two—locked."

Korie touched Captain Lowell's arm almost imperceptibly.

It worked. "Fire all missiles," said Lowell, not even realizing how he'd been nudged.

The two missilemen, Li and Greene, punched their red buttons. The boards flashed yellow, then green. The bay doors snapped open. The missiles dropped away from the ship—

The bright bubble surrounding the ship flickered and disappeared, dropping the vessel rudely out of hyperstate. A dozen missiles accelerated away. The envelope shimmered back into existence and the starship was superluminal again. The missiles were already igniting their hyperstate torches. They flared against the darkness and arrowed toward their targets with a speed no vessel could outrun. In the display, they were bright red points, moving faster than any of the pink shimmers representing Morthan ships.

The missiles would seek, they would close, they would pursue, and ultimately they would intercept and destroy. They could not be outrun—but they did not have the endurance of a larger vessel. They had to catch their targets in the first few minutes, or not at all. Their power would fail and they would wink out, exhausted.

The battle display told the story. Pink shimmers would blink and a dozen bright red pinpoints would streak across the intervening space toward the nearest blue shimmers. Or blue shimmers would blink, dropping missile spreads of their own—but most of them were fleeing, scattering and running into the darkness at top speed.

Korie was watching one particular flight of missiles. Some of the pink shimmers were dodging. Haphazard bright flashes demonstrated where other ships were already flashing out of existence. Most of them were blue.

"We've lost the *Melrose*," said Hodel, glancing down at his monitors. "And the *Gower*. The *Columbia*'s down too."

Korie turned to Captain Lowell. "You're right sir," he said carefully. "We're too visible. Suggest we drop from sight. Go subluminal—"

"You can't hide from them. They'll find us," cried Hodel.

"We don't have time to argue," said Korie. He pointed at the display. "Look—incoming!" The missiles were coming at them from three different directions now. The software was screaming alarms. The display was flashing wildly.

Lowell said something Korie didn't understand; he assumed

it was assent. "Do it!" he yelled at Hodel, and the flight engineer punched his board. The starship shuddered as the hyperstate envelope collapsed around her.

"Rig for shock-charging—"

Korie never got a chance to complete the order. The faintest fringe of ripple effect from one of the hyperstate missiles hit them then, with an effect as devastating as a direct hit from a disruptor beam. Every electrical field in the *LS-1187* was momentarily discharged. Every instrument, every machine, every communications device, and every human being was suddenly paralyzed.

Every neuron fired at once. It was like touching a live wire. Every person on the ship went instantly rigid as their nervous systems overloaded. Their hearts froze, unable to beat; their muscles tightened in agony; the screams were forced involuntarily from their lungs; all their brain cells discharged completely into oblivion, triggering massive seizures and convulsions; their bowels and bladders let loose. Some of the men ejaculated involuntarily. Hodel spasmed and was thrown backward out of his chair. It saved his life. His console sparked and then blew up. Captain Lowell staggered, almost falling. Korie grabbed for him—they both collapsed to the floor. Korie had a flickering impression of flowers and purple fire and then nothing else.

All over the Operations deck and bridge, and effects of the shock-charge were still going off. Wild electrical fire was flashing everywhere. Balls of lightning roiled around the chamber, bouncing and flashing, sputtering and burning.

Everywhere, crew members spasmed and shuddered and jerked across the deck, helpless. A flicker of purple lightning skewered Captain Lowell, enveloping him.

The same lightning flashed through the engine room, up and down the corridors of the vessel, and all around the singularity grid that held the ship's power source: a pinpoint black hole. The energy had no place to discharge—it tried to bleed off in a thousand separate directions, finally found weakness, and leapt out through the portside disruptors; they exploded in a blossom of sparks and fire.

And the *LS-1187* was dead in space.

RECALLED TO LIFE

For a long dead eon, she drifted.

Then—slowly, painfully, life began to reassemble itself. A heartbeat, a gasp, a twitch, and finally even a flicker of thought. Somebody moved. Somebody else choked. There was a moan in the darkness and a terrible stench.

The ship was pitch dark—and so silent it was terrifying. All of the familiar background whispers were gone. Korie came back to consciousness screaming. He felt as if he were on fire. All his nerve ends were shrieking. He couldn't move—and he couldn't stay still. He tried to move, he couldn't. He was floating, rolling, bumping, and drifting back the opposite way. He couldn't think. His head jangled. *Free fall*, he realized. *The gravity's off*.

He stretched out his arms, grunting in pain as he did so, and tried to feel where he was, trying to grasp. His head banged into something and his body twisted. He grabbed and missed and grabbed again, caught a railing and held on. Something else bumped into him, something soft and wet. It felt like a body, he grabbed it and held on. Whoever it was, he was still unconscious. Or . . .

"Harlie?" he asked.

No response. He didn't expect one. It was all bad news. If the ship was totally dead, then so were they. The CO_2 buildup would get them within hours. His head hurt and his shirt and shorts were drenched with sweat and blood. He'd fouled himself as well.

"Starsuits." Korie said it aloud. But if the ship was without power, then the suits would probably be dead too.

What was wrong with the auxiliary power? Why hadn't it kicked in?

"Captain?" Li's voice. He sounded strained. "Mr. Korie? Anyone?"

Korie caught his breath. He couldn't believe how his lungs ached. "Here," He said "Can you move?"

"I don't know. I'm caught on something. What's wrong with the power?"

"I don't know. Anyone else conscious?" Korie called.

He was answered by groans and pleas for help. Someone was crying softly. *That's a good sign,* Korie thought. *If you have the strength to cry, you have the strength to heal.* "Hodel?" he asked. "Hodel, where are you?"

The crying hesitated.

"Hodel, is that you?"

"Over here, sir." A different direction.

"You okay?"

"I will be. In a year or two."

"I think the emergency power system failed. We're going to have to plug in the fuel cells manually and jump-start the system."

Hodel groaned.

"Can you move?"

"I can move. I just don't know where I am."

"All right. I'm on a railing. And I'm holding onto someone. Wait a minute, let me see if I can feel who it is." Korie moved his hand carefully across the other man's body, trying to find a shoulder so he could feel the insignia. . . .

He was holding the captain.

He pulled the captain closer to him, felt for his neck and his jugular vein.

He couldn't tell if Lowell was alive or not.

Korie didn't want to let go of him, but there was nothing

else he could do for Captain Lowell until some kind of light
was restored to the bridge. Korie felt his way along the
railing; it was the railing of the Bridge. He reached the end
and felt his way down to the floor. Good. He knew where he
was now. Still holding onto the railing, he felt his way back
along the floor to the emergency panels. If he was right—

He popped the floor panel open and felt around inside the
compartment. There. He pulled out a flashbeam and prayed
that it still worked. It should; it held a solid-state fuel cell.

It did.

There were cheers as he swept the beam across the Operations deck. Besides Captain Lowell, there were two other
bodies floating unconscious. There were dark globules of
blood and vomit and shit floating in the air. Hodel was
hanging on to a chair; so was Li.

"Hodel? Can you move?"

"I haven't tried—" Cautiously he launched himself toward
Korie. He floated across the Operations deck and grabbed at
the bridge railing, grimacing as he caught it. "If that's what
it's like to be dead, I don't like it."

"It's not the dead part that hurts. It's the coming back."

"It's a long way to come back, sir. I hurt all over."

"So does everyone else," said Korie. He passed Hodel the
light. "Aim it there—" He pulled himself along the floor to
the next emergency panel and yanked it open. Inside was a
double bank of switches. He began punching them on.

Nothing happened. Korie and Hodel exchanged worried
looks.

"Try again?"

Korie nodded and began punching at the buttons one more
time.

Again, nothing happened.

"Shit," said Korie. "All right. We'll go down to the keel
and try every fuel cell in the floor until we find a set that
works. All we need is one. We're not dead yet." He pulled
open the next panel and started passing equipment to Hodel.
"I think we'll have to—"

Something flickered.

The ceiling panels began to glow very softly. Hodel and
Korie looked around as the emergency lights came on and
grinned.

"All right!" said Li.

Listen," said Hodel. "The circulators are back on."

Korie stopped and listened. "You're right." He tapped his headset. "Engine room?"

Chief Engineer Leen's voice sounded surprisingly loud in his ear. "Captain?"

"No. Korie." He swallowed hard. "Damage?"

"Can't tell yet. We're still sealed off. Do you have light?"

"They just came on. Thank you. The singularity?"

"It's still viable—"

"Thank God."

"—but we're going to have to jump-start the whole system."

"Are your men okay?"

"None of us is okay, sir; but we can do it."

"How long?"

"As long as it takes."

"Sorry. Oh, Chief?" Korie added. "Don't initiate gravity until we've secured the entire ship. There are too many unconscious bodies floating."

"Right. Out."

Korie noticed that the chief engineer had not asked about the captain. He swung to face the flight engineer. "Hodel?"

"Sir?"

"Take the captain to sick bay. Then come back for the others."

"Yes, sir." Hodel launched himself across the bridge, colliding clumsily with the captain. He grabbed the old man by the back of his collar and began pulling himself across the ceiling toward the rear exit.

Korie floated across to Li. "Hold still, Wan." Li was pinned in his chair. Korie shone his light all around the wreckage. "Okay, it doesn't look too bad." He anchored himself and pulled. Li floated free. "You okay?"

"I've been better."

"There's a sani-pack in that compartment." Korie pointed. "Start getting some of this crap out of the air." There were floating globules of blood and urine everywhere.

Korie was already checking the other bridge officers. Two of them were dead in their chairs. The third was unconscious. He wondered if there were enough survivors to bring the ship home.

"You know, we can't stay here," Li said, behind him. He was vacuuming wet sphericles out of the air. "Our envelope didn't flash out. They're going to know we're still alive and hiding in normal space."

"It's very hard to find a dead ship. You have to be right on top of her."

"They'll track our singularity with a mass-detector," Li argued. "That's what I'd do. They know where we went down, and they're going to have to come looking for us to make sure. They can't leave us here to attack the *Dragon Lord*."

"We're not attacking anything right now," said Korie. He floated over to the auxiliary astrogation console and began trying to reboot it.

"They don't know we're hit," the weapons specialist pointed out.

Korie grunted. The console was dead. He drifted down to the base of it and popped open a maintenance panel. He'd run it on battery if he had to. "Everything you say is correct. But we don't have a lot of options right now. If we recharge our hyperstate kernel, we'll be instantly visible to any ship within a hundred light-hours, and if we inject into hyperstate, we'll be visible for days. If they've englobed the area, we'll never get out."

"You think you can sneak away at sublight? That'll take weeks."

"We're going to need a few weeks to rebuild this ship anyway."

"They're still going to be looking for us, no matter what we do. If they don't find us immediately, they'll expand their search patterns. They know we're here and we can't shield against their scanners."

Korie looked over at him. "At this point, Wan, I don't know how much of this ship is left. That's what'll determine what we'll do. By rights, we should all be dead now."

The auxiliary astrogation console lit up then and Korie was momentarily cheered. It was a start. As each piece of the network started coming back online, it would start querying the rest of the system; if the queries went unanswered, each piece would automatically initiate its own set of restoration procedures for the equipment it could talk to. The resurrection of the ship would happen in pieces, much like the individual resurrections of each surviving crew member.

Two of the other consoles on the bridge flashed back to consciousness then. Korie floated over to them and punched for status reports. As he suspected, they were still isolated from the rest of the ship. They had no information to report.

Korie considered his situation. His captain was disabled, maybe dying. His ship was dead in space and an unknown number of his crew were unconscious or dead. They were light-years from the nearest aid and they were surrounded by enemy marauders who would be looking for them as soon as they finished destroying the rest of the fleet. They had no weapons and no engines. They couldn't retreat either sublight or superlight. And, if that weren't enough, they were blind. All their sensors were out of commission. He had no way of knowing if an attack was imminent, and no way of fighting back if it was.

But on the plus side, he told himself, *I'm finally in command.* The irony of it was almost enough to make him smile. He tapped his headset. "Chief?"

"It's bad news," said the voice in his ear. "I'm going to have to restring everything. It'll take days."

"We have days," said Korie. "Listen, I have an idea. Can you put a man in the lookout with a sextant? Take a sighting?"

"It won't be very accurate."

"It doesn't have to be. I just want to find out if we're pointed in a useful direction."

"I can do that. If we're not, we can rotate the ship around the singularity until we are. I can even do that by hand if I have to. We'll rig block and tackle and walk it around."

"Good. Now, here's the second part. Can you run the mass-drivers off the fuel cells—and for how long?"

"Do you mean leave the singularity damped?"

"Yes."

The chief engineer thought a moment. "It's very old-fashioned," he said, "and I'm not sure what you're gaining, but it's doable. This is just a guess, but I can probably give you six weeks at least, maybe eight, but not more than ten."

"I'll take the six. If we make it that far, God likes us. I want no stress-field activity at all for the entire time, and I want you to minimize all electrical functions. Let's run this ship as if she's dead. Minimum life-support, minimum everything.''

"It won't work," said the chief. "They'll still find us. We can't get far enough away."

"Do the math," said Korie. "It's not distance that works for us. It's speed. Normal space is nasty. A constant acceleration of even one-third gee will pile up enough velocity in twelve hours as to make it practically impossible for anyone to intercept us in normal space—not unless they're prepared to chase us for several days, more likely weeks. And if we know they're chasing us, we plug in the singularity and go to full power and it's still a standoff."

"Mmm, maybe—" The chief engineer was not enthusiastic about the idea. "What's to keep them from jumping into hyperstate, leaping ahead, and brushing us with their ripple?"

"If we live long enough to get to that situation, we'll activate our own hyperstate kernel. If they brush us they'll disintegrate with us. Not even a Morthan would consider that an honorable death."

There was silence from the other end of the line.

"Chief?"

The engineer's voice had a sour tone. "Can't say I like it. And it's going to be hell to burn it off at the other end. We'll have to spend as much time decelerating as we do accelerating. And we'll have to do it before we can inject into hyperstate for the way home."

"Well, let's think about that," suggested Korie.

"Uh-uh," said Leen with finality. "I can't compensate for that high a velocity inside the envelope. We'll be too unstable to hold a modulation."

"All right," said Korie. "You win. We'll do it your way."

"You listen to me. I'll bring you home. Leen out."

Korie allowed himself a smile. Three weeks of steady subluminal acceleration, plus another three of deceleration, would also give them enough time to effect major repairs. If they could do it at one gee, it would put them twenty-five light-hours away before they had to inject into hyperstate. Not a great head start, but workable. And they'd have to do it without synthetic gravity.

Korie remembered the problem from Officers Candidate School; he hadn't ever expected to apply it in a real situation.

If it worked here though, they would earn themselves a place in future texts. But it would be difficult. Unless they could find a way to disassemble and rotate the main mass-drivers ninety degrees, it would feel like the ship was standing on her tail. . . .

No. They didn't have the time. They'd have to jury-rig ladders. They didn't dare risk powering up the gravitors. That would be almost as visible to a tracker as the pinpoint black hole in the engine room.

Korie hadn't let himself ask the hard question yet. How much of a crew did he have left? That would be the worst—not having enough skillage to pilot the ship home. What was the minimum practical number?

Hodel returned then, pulling himself into the bridge with a practiced motion.

Korie looked at him questioningly, as if to ask *how bad*?

Hodel shrugged. *Who knows?*

"You have the conn," Korie said. He pulled himself down toward the floor, and out through the operations bay, the tiny cubbyhole beneath the high platform of the bridge. There was one man on duty in the operations bay. He looked pale and shaken, but he had the power panel of his work station open and he was testing fuel cells. Korie patted him on the shoulder and pulled himself past, down into the keel.

The lights here were dimmer, making all the cables, conduits and pipes into oppressive shapes in the gloom. Slowly, Korie made his way toward the A.I. bay and pulled himself up into it. Harlie was totally dark.

"Shit." Korie popped open a compartment and pulled out the red-backed manual. "First. Make sure the power is on," he said to himself.

He stuck the manual to the top of the console and pulled open the emergency panels. He had the nightmarish sensation that he was going to spend the next three weeks doing nothing but powering up fuel cells by hand. There had to be an easier way to do this; but nobody ever expected a ship to have to start from zero.

The fuel cells kicked in immediately, which was a pleasant surprise. The bad news was that the automatic restart process would take several hours. Each of Harlie's various sentience modules had to be individually powered up and tested, and not until system confidence was acceptable could they be reassembled into a functioning personality.

The alternative—to reawaken Harlie without the complex system analysis—was to run the risk of post-shock trauma, disassociation, confusion, increased statistical unreliability, and possible long-term psychosis.

On the other hand, they couldn't get home without him. They couldn't even run the ship.

Theoretically, it was possible to run a starship without a sentient consciousness, but nobody had ever done it. Theory was one thing. Starships were something else.

"All right, Harlie," whispered Korie. "You get to sleep a while longer." He punched in the command, then locked the console.

He levered himself sadly out of the computer bay and pushed himself along the keel until he got to the engine room. Work lights were hung all over the chamber and crew members were already maneuvering around the great singularity cage in the center.

Chief Engineer Leen was supervising the stringing of an auxiliary power conduit. He looked up as Korie floated over. "I sent a man to the forward lookout to take a sighting. We're tumbling ass over teakettle. I think we can get the autonomic network online, but I need to see if it's traumatized. And I'm rigging an auxiliary electrical harness, so we can charge up the mass-drivers as soon as we're oriented. What else do you want to know?"

"That's plenty. Harlie's down for at least six hours, maybe longer. I want you to pull the manuals on running a ship without a brain, if we have to—and cross your fingers that we don't have to. In the meantime, I'm taking the tour. I need to see what shape the crew is in."

"They're rocky, but they're working."

Korie looked at Leen. "Have we got the skillage to get home?"

Leen shrugged. "We don't know. I've got Randle taking roll. Some of the boys are a little mind-wiped. I don't know if we can bring 'em back." His expression was very unhappy.

"All right," said Korie, accepting the report. "Have Cookie make sandwiches—uh, did Cookie make it?"

Leen shook his head.

"Sorry. Okay, appoint two men to kitchen detail. Let's keep the lights on and the air circulating. If we can't make this work, we'll plug in the hole and try to run for it. But I'm assuming the worst." He looked at Leen, "Did I leave anything out?"

"We could pray. . . ."

"I stopped praying a long time ago, Chief."

"Didn't get your prayers answered?"

"I got an answer. It was no." Korie pushed himself out of the engine room into the aftward keel. It was darker than the forward keel. Korie paused at each of the manually operated safety panels and double-checked atmospheric pressure, CO_2 content, temperature, and humidity. All were stable. Good. That meant hull integrity hadn't been breached. The biggest danger right now was that there might be a pinhole leak somewhere in the ship; but with no power and no network, there was no way to detect a pressure loss or locate the hole.

There was too much to worry about and not enough worriers.

Korie floated up into the shuttle bay and let himself drift while he considered. Maybe the shuttles could be useful. They were designed to be powered up quickly; maybe they could plug into a shuttle brain and run the ship from there. The shuttles weren't sentient on the same scale Harlie was, but they were smart enough to avoid bumping into planets, moons, and asteroids. He'd have to talk it over with Chief Leen. It was another option.

As he headed forward again, he nearly bumped into Reynolds and MacHeath. They were maneuvering an unconscious crew member toward sick bay. Korie nodded to them, then pushed himself quickly ahead.

The ship's mess was full of men and women: the overflow from sick bay. Some were conscious, most were not. Several were moaning. As Korie watched, two more crew members pulled themselves into the room. Fontana, the ship's pharmacist, floated in carrying a hypospray injector, and began administering sedatives to the worst injured. She glanced over to Korie. "You okay?"

"I will be. As soon as I get a chance to clean myself up. How about you?"

She shook her head. "This is a mess."

Korie followed her forward, catching her in the hall outside the sick bay. He lowered his voice. "How bad?"

"Twelve dead. At least six more we don't expect to make it. Two of the Quillas went down—the rest are in shock. I've sedated all of them. They're in bad shape; they're going to need extensive rehabilitation. Probably we all will. I've never seen injuries like this before. I thought we were better shielded—"

"It wasn't a beam. It was a ripple effect."

"Better if it was a beam. We can treat disruptor wounds."

"I'll remember that for next time." Korie lowered his voice. "How's the doctor?"

Fontana shrugged. "Indestructible."

"Have you got enough help?"

"No . . . but we'll manage. To tell the truth, there's not a lot we can do. Either you get better . . . or you don't."

Korie allowed himself to ask the question he'd been avoiding. "Captain Lowell?"

Fontana's expression said it all. She looked Korie straight in the eye and said, "I'm sorry, sir. You're going to have to bring us home."

Inside himself, Korie marveled that he didn't feel anything at all. He felt guilty. *I should be feeling something right now, shouldn't I?* "I, uh . . . I was afraid of that."

"Want some free advice? It's worth exactly what you paid for it."

Korie met her eyes. "Say it."

"Go to your room. Clean yourself up. Put on your sharpest uniform. And then make another inspection of the ship. Be seen by as many crew members as you can. And let them know that everything is under control—*even if it isn't.*"

"That's good advice," said Korie. "And as soon as I have time—"

"*No. Do it now,*" said Fontana. "This ship isn't going anywhere. There's nothing happening that needs your immediate attention. There is nothing happening that is as important as the morale of this crew. They know the captain's hurt. They don't know what state you're in. You need to show them that you're ready to bring them home."

Korie stopped himself. He looked at Fontana and realized

what she was saying. It was straight out of the academy. First year. *The first machine that has to be fixed is not the ship, but the crew. Fix the crew and everything else takes care of itself.*

"You're right," Korie said to Fontana. "Thanks." He patted her affectionately on the shoulder and pushed himself forward. Her remarks echoed in his consciousness.

He remembered the seminars at the academy. *The real crisis is not the crisis. The real crisis is what you do before it and after it.*

Right.

What did you do or what did you fail to do *beforehand* that turned the situation into a crisis?

What did you do or what did you fail to do *afterward* that prolonged the crisisness of the situation?

All the classes, all the simulations, all the seminars and discussions, all the endless analyses and recaps and debriefings— this was what it was for. He could hear the voices of his instructors, as if they were standing right behind him, judging his every move, his every decision.

Ask yourself three questions: What do you want to do? What are you capable of doing? What are you actually going to do? Be clear that these may be three different things.

"What I want to do," Korie said to no one in particular, "is take this ship home, fill it up with missiles, and then come back out here and kick some Morthan ass."

"What am I capable of doing—" He considered the question. He could get the ship home. That wasn't in doubt any longer. It might take four months, limping all the way, but it was doable. Could he fight back? Now? No. With a refit? Definitely.

What was he going to do?

Korie grinned.

"What I'm capable of doing, what I want to do, and what I'm going to do . . . are all the same thing."

He touched the button on his headset. "Now hear this—" His voice was amplified throughout the ship. "This is Executive Officer Korie speaking. We've been hit, we've taken damage, but we're still afloat. We don't know how badly the fleet's been hit. We don't know how badly the convoy's been hurt.

"As most of you have heard, Captain Lowell went down in the attack. I have no news on his condition yet. I'll keep you posted."

"I am assuming that a state of war now exists between the Terran Alliance and the Morthan Solidarity and I am acting accordingly.

"It's going to take some time to bring all ship systems back online. It's going to taken even more time to get home. But we will get home, I promise you that. We're going to rebuild this ship, and then we'll come back out here and put a missile into every Morthan ship we can find.

"Korie out."

He thought he could hear the cheers of the crew echoing throughout the ship, but it could just as easily have been his imagination.

The hard part would be keeping them believing that. . . .

A SITUATION OF
SOME GRAVITY

Light had been restored to the corridors of the *LS-1187*, but
not much else. Most of the desperately wounded were in sick
bay or the mess room. The less wounded were spread across
the forward half of the shuttle bay. A makeshift morgue had
been established at aft starboard corner; a partition hid the
bagged bodies from view; they were tethered like cargo.

A decision was going to have to be made about that soon,
Korie knew. *Do we space them here or do we take them
home?* He didn't know how he felt about it yet, and he didn't
know who he should ask. Fontana probably. He knew the
thought was irrational, but he didn't like leaving any of his
crew floating alone in the dark so far away from home. There
was also a military consideration. As unlikely an occurrence
as it might be, what if one of the spaced bodies were discovered
by a Morthan cruiser? It would be evidence that the *LS-1187*
had not been destroyed.

And yet . . . he also knew that it unnerved the crew to have
those dead bodies tethered there. It was damning evidence of
their failure in battle. It was as if the dead were pointing an

accusing finger at the living. "If you had not failed, we might still be alive."

Korie shook his head sadly. This was not a problem that he could solve immediately. This decision could be postponed a while longer. It went against his grain to postpone a decision; the unfinished business seemed to lurk in the back of his skull, gnawing at his consciousness.

He pulled himself forward, into the starboard corridor, then left into the shallow chamber directly above the starship's engine room. This was Chief Engineer Leen's office and auxiliary control station. At the moment, it was also functioning as the starship's Bridge.

The chief engineer was strapped into a chair before a work station. He was running diagnostic programs, frowning and muttering to himself. "Nope. Nope. That won't work. That won't work. Nope. Shit." Then he'd lean forward intensely and order a new set of routines to be run.

Korie hated to interrupt him, but—"I've thought of something else," he said. Leen pushed back from the screen and swiveled to face Korie.

"What now?"

"We're on minimum life-support. How long can we maintain?"

Leen thought for a moment. Korie could almost see him running the subroutines in his head. "Six days," he said, finally. "If we use the LOX from the fuel cells, we can buy ourselves another three weeks, but then we're out of power unless we recharge. And that doesn't allow any margin for the mass-drivers. I don't see any way around it, we're going to have to use the singularity sooner or later."

"I know," said Korie. "But I want to hold off as long as possible, and I want to minimize any use of it. We give off G-waves, they'll find us. Right now, if they're tracking us, all they see is a derelict." He hooked one leg around a stanchion to keep from floating away. "We can survive without gravity. We have three months of food. We can ration our water. Our big problem is air."

"Can't use the osmotics," said Leen. "Not without the gravitors. And that's more G-waves. Y'know, if we could take a look-see, find out if there's anything hostile in range, we could control our radiations, keep them below the noise level. . . ."

Korie shook his head. "Not yet. I don't want to risk opening up a scanning lens yet. Maybe in a week. Even a lens might give us away to the *Dragon Lord*. We just don't know how accurate her vision is. I have to assume the worst."

Leen grunted. "You're not making this very easy for me."

"I've been thinking," said Korie. "We could go to aeroponics. String lights and webs in the shuttle bay, in the inner hull, maybe even in the corridors and the keel. We could use irrigation stems. Start out with Luna moss, take cuttings every two days. In fourteen days, we should be able to increase the volume sixty-four fold."

Leen didn't answer. He just swiveled back to his screen and called up a set of extrapolations. "It'll be at least a month before you're getting significant oxygen production, even if you could double volume every two days. Which I don't think you can."

"A month might work," said Korie. "Just barely. It lets us keep our head down."

"It's going to be messy."

"We don't have a lot of choice in the matter. We're going to have to go to aeroponics sooner or later anyway. We have food for three months. We might make it on half-rations, but that's only a stay of execution, not a reprieve. What if it takes longer than four and a half months to get home? Let's start laying in our crops for the winter."

Leen made a noise deep in his throat. It sounded like a growl of disapproval. "Sounds like a lot of busy work to me. We've got more important things to do."

"No, we don't." Korie cut him off. "As long as we drift, we're safe. We look like a derelict. The longer we can drift, the more convincing we are. This isn't busy work—this is work that will guarantee our survival."

Leen didn't look convinced.

Korie shrugged and admitted, "Yes, all right. It'll give the crew a challenge they can accomplish. But they need that right now."

"I think we'd all much rather put a missile up the tail of the *Dragon Lord*.

"You tell me a way we can get close enough to do that and I will. Otherwise, my job is to bring this ship and her crew safely home."

"You want my opinion? Let's just fix the engines and go."

"I *always* want your advice, Chief—"

"But?"

"You know the ship better than anyone. But *I* know what we're up against. The Morthans aren't stupid. This wasn't just a hit-and-run raid. This was a full-scale attack. If I were a Morthan commander, I'd be cruising the area right now, hunting for hiders like us."

"I don't like hiding," grumbled Leen.

Korie shrugged. "It's not my favorite thing either. But we don't have the resources to do anything else right now. String the webs, Chief. Let's get that started. Then, I want you to build a passive G-scanner and let it run."

"There's no accuracy in that."

"I don't need accuracy. I just need to know if something's moving out there."

"I'll use a split crew," said Leen. "Half on life-support, half bringing the network back on line. That'll give you the luxury of both options. And it'll give me the time to fine-tune each part of the system as I recalibrate. What do you want to do about Harlie?"

"Let him sleep."

"You sure?" Leen looked surprised.

Reluctantly, Korie nodded. "I'm worried about his state of mind. I'd rather not bring him back up until there's a ship for him to run. There's nothing he can do until then anyway. I don't want him going crazy with worry—or worse, amputation trauma."

"Harlie's too sensible for that."

"Probably. I'd like to believe you're right. But what happens if you're wrong? Let's play it safe. Harlie's a friend of ours. Let's not take any unnecessary risks with him. Okay?"

"You're the boss."

"Only by default." Korie looked suddenly troubled.

Leen hesitated. He looked like he wanted to ask something else.

"What is it, Chief?"

"Nothing. I just—"

"Go ahead. Say it."

"Well, it's Captain Lowell. I heard that he—I mean, I don't believe it, but you know—scuttlebutt has it that he . . ." Leen was having trouble saying it; Korie waited patiently. ". . . well, that he fell apart when the shooting started. Is that true?"

Korie started to answer, then remembered Captain Lowell's last advice: "You have to be straight with them, Mr. Korie. *Never ever lie to your crew.*" He flinched, then he looked directly at Chief Engineer Leen and said as sincerely as he could, "I was there. Captain Lowell did not screw up. The autolog will confirm that. And if any man on this ship says differently, he'll have to answer personally to me." He added, "You can let that be known wherever it's appropriate."

Leen looked relieved. "Thanks. I knew that. I guess I just wanted to hear you say it."

Korie nodded curtly and pushed off toward the door.

That's one, he thought. *How many more?*

KORIE'S CABIN

Captain Lowell wasn't dead.

But he wasn't exactly alive either. It made for a very sticky legal situation.

Korie spent several grueling hours scanning through the manual of regulations. It wasn't very helpful.

With the captain injured, Korie was supposed to assume command of the vessel. The problem was, he *couldn't.*

Without Harlie up and running and maintaining the log, Executive Officer Jonathan Thomas Korie could not officially assume command. The ship's doctor could not log a medical report, and Korie could not legally declare the captain incapacitated.

Until such time as the autolog could be resumed, his was a command without acknowledgment. He had the authority, he had the moral and legal right under fleet regulations; but what he did not have was the acknowledgment of FleetComm's official representative, the constructed consciousness known as Harlie. It was like being elected president, but not taking the oath of office. Just when and how does the legal authority begin?

The whole thing made Korie realize just how precarious his position was. His orders were technically illegal until such time as his right to give them was confirmed. He was floating adrift in a legal limbo every bit as real as the limbo in which the *LS-1187* floated. And he was every bit as helpless.

There weren't any contemporary precedents for this situation, although there were ample historical records. Unfortunately, those records could be used for academic purposes only. Out of respect for the diversity of individual cultures in the Alliance, FleetComm's regulations were not derived from any specific naval tradition, and no precedents were to be assumed, historical or otherwise, unless FleetComm itself authorized them.

Translation: We're trying very hard to be fair and just and careful in the exercise of our authority. That leaves you without an umbrella. Good luck. Don't do anything stupid.

The problem was profound enough to interfere with Korie's sleep. And that made him irritable.

Unfortunately, there was nothing he could do about it. He didn't dare resurrect Harlie yet. The ship was still crippled; repairs, realignments, and recalibrations were proceeding at a painfully slow pace—even slower now that Leen had half his crew stringing webs and lights for the aeroponics.

"I know I'm doing the right thing," said Korie to no one in particular. "Why doesn't it *feel* right?"

The door beeped. Korie waved at it. The door slid open and a grim-looking Fontana floated into the room.

"I apologize for disturbing you," she began, "but I saw by your monitor that you weren't asleep, so—"

"It's all right." He rubbed his eyes. "What's on your mind?"

She hesitated before answering. "I need an authorization," she said, and passed the clipboard across to him.

"What kind of authorization—?" Korie was puzzled, then he glanced down at the clipboard screen and shut up. **Authorization for Euthanasia.**

He read through the form slowly. Suddenly, the standard boilerplate paragraphs about "the failure of all best efforts" and "the unlikelihood of the individual's recovery to a normal and fulfilling life" and "the individual's right to die with dignity" took on a new meaning; especially the clause about "in time of war, the survival of the ship and her crew always takes precedence over the survival of any individual crew member."

Korie's eyes skipped down to the bottom. "Therefore, by the authority vested in me, by the Combined Allied Star Force, I hereby authorize the termination of life support—"

Korie handed the clipboard back. "I can't sign this."

Fontana made no move to take it. "I didn't know you were religious."

"I'm not," said Korie.

"Moral reservations?"

"Nope."

"Then why won't you sign it?"

"I can't. It won't be legal."

Fontana looked at him. "Say again?"

"I haven't been logged in. Harlie's down. Until we can bring him up again, I can't be logged in. And we can't bring him up again until the network is repaired. Anything I do before then, I can only do as executive officer—which is quite a lot. But unless Captain Lowell dies, I cannot legally assume command. What you have there is an order that I have no authority to give. We could both be court-martialed."

"You're kidding." Fontana brushed a loose strand of hair back off her forehead. Her expression was unbelieving.

"Look it up—"

"I *know* the regulations," she said, annoyed. "I just can't believe that you're *hiding* behind them."

"I'm not *hiding*!"

"You're not?" Fontana looked around. "The ship is rigged for silent running. We're adrift in the outbeyond. You're spending most of your time in your cabin. You won't acknowledge your command. If that's not hiding, I don't know what is."

"I don't know what else to do, dammit!" He snapped right back. "If you have any suggestions—"

"You have the authority, Mr. Korie. I know it. The crew knows it. Everybody's waiting for you to figure it out. Fleet Command is not here to look over your shoulder. No matter what other regulations might be in the book, they're all of secondary relevance. The survival of the ship and her crew come first, and the highest ranking officer must assume command of the vessel.''

"I've done that—I have done everything I can to ensure the survival of this vessel and this crew. I have my personal log to verify that. What I don't have is the *acknowledged* authority of FleetComm, and it would be not only presumptuous of me to assume that authority, it would be dangerous and stupid.''

"You've got five men and two women in sick bay who are dead," said Fontana. "They're using up oxygen.''

"Not that much—''

"Enough to make a difference.''

"This is Dr. Williger's responsibility.''

"Dr. Williger doesn't handle the paperwork. I do.'' Fontana looked disgusted. "It's bad enough the captain shit his pants. Now you too?''

Korie glared at her angrily, then he glanced at the clipboard again. He scanned the list of names unhappily. "Are you sure these are all irreversible?''

"Both Williger and I have signed that document.'' She added, "Two of them are unconscious. The others are fading in and out; they're in terrible pain, and there's nothing we can do for them—except this. Listen to me. Williger and I argued for an hour over each and every name on that list, looking for some reason, *any* reason, to not have to make the request. I've had two hours sleep in the past thirty-six. I'm operating on momentum now, but I can't stop until this is resolved. I can't stand seeing those men and women in pain any longer. Those are my friends down there. And yours too. This is the most generous gift you can give them. Easy release. *Please, Jon . . . ?''*

Korie handed the clipboard back to her, unsigned. "You'll have to take the captain's name off the list. I might be able to make a case for terminating the others, but I'll be damned if I'm going to accept the responsibility for Captain Lowell's death. I already have too much that's going to need explaining when we get back. I don't need to look for anything more.''

Fontana paged to the next document and handed the clipboard back. "Williger and I both thought you'd say that. But for humanitarian reasons, we felt we had to give the captain the same chance as the rest of the crew. Fortunately, he's unconscious."

Korie looked at the screen again. It was the same document, but without Captain Lowell's name. He allowed himself a sour expression. "How many more of these have you got prepared?"

"Don't be nasty," Fontana said. "This is not an easy job. And you're not making it any easier."

"I'm the one who's going out onto the skinny branches," Korie said. He took a breath, closed his eyes, and reassured himself as to the *rightness* of this action. He opened his eyes again and grimly thumbprinted the document. He handed the clipboard back. "I assume you'll testify on my behalf?"

Fontana didn't look amused. She stood up abruptly and crossed to the door. "Your part was easy. You only had to authorize it. I have to watch them die." She stepped out into the corridor and the door whooshed shut behind her.

EYE IN THE SKY

Chief Engineer Leen actually built three G-scanners. They weren't complex devices; a small jar filled with oil, an array of floating sensors, an isolation mounting, and a battery. A schoolchild could have built one—and many had done exactly that as homemade science projects. Chief Engineer Leen's gravity-wave scanners were a little more precise, however.

He mounted one at the tip of each of the ship's three fluctuator spines, then started the ship rolling gently along its axis. Centrifugal force did the rest; the G-scanners tumbled outward to the limits of their cables, a radius of more than ten thousand meters. The result was a primitive gravity lens, accurate enough to detect the motion of even a ship-size mass within a range of twenty light-hours. The best part was that it was not correspondingly detectable.

Leen dedicated three work stations to monitor and process the feeds from the scanners and reported to Korie that the system was up and running.

Korie's thanks were perfunctory. He was worried about something else. He took Leen by the arm and pushed him toward a quiet corner of the Operations deck. "I've been running simulations."

"So have I." Leen was grim.

"Then you know."

"I told you a week ago," Leen said. "We're not going to make it on the oxygen. Not unless we use the singularity. If you'll let me recharge the fuel cells, I can buy you another week or two—or better yet, let me rig a gravity cage and I can plug in the osmotic processors."

Korie was adamant. "It's too risky. Even a gravity cage leaves a ghost. You can see it, if you know what to look for."

"Sooner or later, we're going to have to power up."

"I know," conceded Korie. "I've been thinking about that too. I want you to run your G-scanners wide open and multiprocess the feeds. If we can't detect anything within ten—no, make it fifteen—light-hours, then we'll open a scanning lens and take a quick look around. That'll give us a little precision, at least. If we're clear then, we'll run the singularity at low level and start recharging."

"And what if we can't?"

"That's what I've been thinking about. We can dismantle the torpedoes, one at a time. We'll use the LOX in the torpedo cells and that might buy us enough time to be self-supporting."

Leen thought about it. He shook his head. "That leaves us weaponless."

"We'll recharge them later. I don't like it either. Find me a better way and I'll buy it."

"If we're spotted, we'll be sitting defenseless."

"We're already sitting defenseless," replied Korie. "We're floating adrift in the middle of the biggest concentration of Morthan warships in history. Our only defense is that they don't know we're here—or if they do, that they think we're derelict. I'm reluctant even to start creeping away from here at sublight for fear of leaving a wake." Korie realized he was getting strident. He forced himself to soften his tone. "Look, Chief—if we hadn't been brushed by the hyperstate ripple, we might have escaped in the confusion. Now, our only hope is to look like worthless debris."

"You're making an assumption, Mr. Korie."

Korie swung himself around to face the chief engineer. They

floated in a face-to-face orientation, near what would normally be the deck of the Bridge. "Okay, enlighten me," Korie said.

"What if they're not hanging around to mop up? What if this was just a smash-and-grab operation?"

Korie nodded. "Can we take that chance? What if we're wrong?"

Leen shrugged. The gesture started him spinning slowly; he reached out and grabbed a handhold on the Bridge railing. "Okay—but it's frustrating just sitting here. The Hole Gang is getting twitchy."

"Probably because you can't run a still in free fall."

"They're working on that one too," Leen admitted. "But that's not the point. It's the inaction. Just sitting here, not doing anything to fight back—it's frustrating. I want to run my engines. I want to go somewhere. I want to do something. And I'm not the only one on the ship that feels this way."

Korie nodded thoughtfully. "Chief, do you think I *like* this? I know how everybody feels. I feel the same way. I'm not arguing for inaction. The circumstances are doing that."

Leen grumbled something in reply. "Just so you know how I feel." His angry expression relaxed. He'd had his say.

"Relax, Chief. We'll get home—and we'll get even too. I promise. How much longer till the mass-drivers can be fired?"

"Two days, maybe three."

"All right—as soon as they're calibrated, I want you to ready a scanning lens. If the G-scanners don't show anything, we'll risk a longer look. And if that's clean, we'll talk about a run for home."

"Any time you want to say go, I can have the singularity on line in less than an hour. The fluctuators are the best-shielded equipment on the ship. We'll just check their alignment and—"

"Slow down, Chief. Let's worry about our oxygen consumption first. It's hard to breathe a fluctuator." Korie dragged Leen back to the holographic display table where Li and Hodel were running a low-level simulation. "All right, let's do a status check. Chief says he can have the engines on line in less than a week. Astrogation, can you be ready?"

Hodel considered it. "Without Harlie I have to do it all on work stations. Don't expect realtime corrections, but I can get you where you want to go."

"Li, what about weapons? Do we have any defenses?"

Li shook his head. "Same situation. No realtime targeting. Without Harlie, we're firing blind."

Korie glanced over to Leen. "Just as I thought. The torpedoes are more valuable for the liquid oxygen." To Hodel and Li, he explained, "Chief Leen thinks I'm being too cautious. What do you guys think?"

Hodel shrugged. "We could get the ship running again, we have the skillage, but how efficient she'd be—I dunno. If there are Morthan cruisers patrolling this area, forget it."

Li was still turning the idea over in his head. "Much as I'd like to get in a couple licks, Mr. Korie, I wouldn't even want to try it without Harlie." He reached across himself and scratched his shoulder thoughtfully. "With Harlie, maybe. Harlie's the best tactical advantage we have. You've read the analyses—the Morthans are maybe a century behind us in sophisticated electronics. That's why they have to build so big just to accomplish the same thing."

"Unfortunately, that also gives them the brute force advantage," Korie said. "We outsmarted ourselves. Our technology is so sophisticated and so advanced, we don't build our ships with the same power anymore. There's the real mistake. We thought the implied strategic advantage of the Harlie series would give the enemy pause, make him think twice before launching an offensive. We were very, very wrong."

Hodel cleared his throat and spoke softly. "I guess we're going to have to find out just how good the Harlie series really is, aren't we? He's our secret weapon. Let's use him. Let's see how good he is."

Korie looked from one to the other. "What if I bring him back online prematurely and he goes into irreversible amputation trauma? Then we're doubly screwed."

"We can run this ship without him," said Hodel. "We're already doing it. We couldn't be any worse off—and who knows? Maybe he'll work like he's supposed to. Maybe he could be an advantage, if you give him the opportunity."

"The opportunity . . ." Korie echoed the thought. "There is that. He's as much a member of this crew as anyone. I suppose he's entitled to the same consideration. Let me think about this—"

Leen touched Korie's shoulder and spoke very softly. "It's

not right to keep him dead, Mr. Korie. He's not like the others . . ."

"I know," said Korie. "But he's still a consciousness. He can feel, he can hurt. As much as we need him, we also need to be *compassionate*."

"In the middle of a war?" asked Hodel, unbelievingly.

"If not here, where better?" Korie met his gaze. "You don't have the responsibility for this decision. I do. If we start chipping away at those things that make us human, then bit by bit, we'll give the best parts of ourselves away. We'll turn into the very thing we're fighting. I'm not going to let my shipmates die alone and unknown."

"You already signed one order," said Leen. "I know that wasn't easy—but you did it because it had to be done. Maybe this decision is another one of those."

Korie wanted to glare at Leen, but he knew the chief engineer was right. Finally, he said simply, "You don't have to bludgeon me with it, Chief. I can figure it out for myself."

"So? What's it gonna be?"

"How much of the net is up?"

Hodel answered. "We've got thirty percent of the system covered."

Korie considered the decision. "I want to give him every advantage we can. I won't do it until the engines are recalibrated. And let's see what kind of sensory repairs we can rig. We're also going to need to get some kind of autonomic system functioning. Give me that much and I'll take the chance." He searched their faces.

"Fair enough," said Leen.

"Can do," said Hodel.

Li simply nodded.

Korie pushed himself away from the display and out the starboard exit of the bridge. Too many people were dying on this ship. There were the unavoidable deaths, yes—he had authorized those; that had been a compassionate action. But as yet, there were no deaths that were directly due to a mistaken decision that he'd made. He wanted to keep it that way. He didn't want Harlie to be the first.

Almost anybody else, but *not* Harlie.

THE MORTHAN
SOLIDARITY

—was a good idea carried to its illogical extreme.

The idea had been only one of many drifting aimlessly in the human culture. The Brownian movement of human ideas tended to nullify most of them from seeing any concrete expression. Nevertheless, every so often in any culture, one or another odd notion reaches a critical mass of individual minds and coalesces into an intention that demands expression. At some point, the collective human consciousness had taken on behaviors that suggested it had almost become aware of itself. *It* began to plan for its own future.

Sometime in the distant past, *it* decided to take charge of its own genetic destiny. Instead of allowing itself to spawn each new generation of individuals by the random tossing of human dice, the cumulative consciousness began to design itself for those traits it felt would be most advantageous to its own future.

A rational species would have selected rationality as an advantageous survival trait. A species with the cortex of a reptile and the forebrain of a chimpanzee could not be expected to make that same decision. *It* voted for superior musculature, enhanced sensory organs, a larger and stronger skeleton, a more efficient nervous system, better resistance to heat and cold, better utilization of resources, better internal conservation of fuel, greater speed and dexterity, improved healing functions, increased resistance to pain, and almost as an afterthought, a more powerful brain.

In fact, the more powerful brain was the most important part of the package. Or as one of the early experimenters put it, "You want to run this hardware? You *have* to upgrade the software. The human brain alone isn't sufficient to the task."

Of course, it didn't happen overnight. It didn't even happen in the space of a century. The whole business of genetic engineering crept up on the species, a gene at a time. We can tweak this and we get rid of hemophilia; we can tweak that, we get rid of color-blindness. By the time the process was commonplace, it was too late. The collective consciousness was hurtling headlong toward a furious redesign of itself.

And along the way, it began designing organic prosthetics and biomechanical augments to do the jobs that mere genetics couldn't accomplish alone. Subsets of the human species began to appear—or perhaps they were *super*sets. They contained all the genetic equivalent of human beings, but they were *more than* human. The More-Thans were designed for living naked on the planet Mars, and later a moderately terraformed Venus as well. They could endure cold and altitude and heat. They could run farther and faster; they could fight with greater ferocity; and their unaugmented strength was unmatched by anything short of a grizzly bear. They were bred to be explorers and colonists at first—and then, later on, soldiers.

To meet the demands of a physical body having superior physical qualities, the brains of the More-Thans also had to be superior. The More-Thans began to take charge of their own destiny, became their own scientists and researchers. Of course, they began to regard themselves as a superior species, significantly better than their feeble ancestors. The logic of that train of thought led inexorably toward one conclusion.

The *smart* Morthans began plotting how to take over the human worlds they lived on. They died in prison.

The *smarter* Morthans became separatists. They earned

their fortunes fairly, invested in starships, and ultimately settled colonies far beyond the frontiers of human expansion.

The *smartest* Morthans stayed where the most advanced research was being done. Some of them perceived the possibility of a loyalty to conscious life that transcended mere loyalty to one's own subset of a species. They realized that a rational species could and would redesign itself for increased rationality; and they started where the need was greatest— with humanity itself, themselves included. The *smartest* Morthans got even *smarter*.

HARLIE

Korie studied the report on the screen in front of him. He didn't like what it suggested, but he didn't have much choice either. Harlie had as much responsibility to this ship as any other crew member, perhaps more.

The problem was that there wasn't really a lot of precedent for this situation. There weren't even any reliable simulations. Nobody actually knew how a constructed consciousness would react to being revived in an amputated environment. Would it be as traumatic as it would be for a human being? Or would the constructed consciousness merely accept the circumstance? What was the possibility for identity damage in this situation?

Nobody knew.

And despite nearly a week of chasing the question around and around in his head, Korie still had no idea what would happen when he began the process of reactivating Harlie.

Chief Engineer Leen pulled himself up into the cramped computer bay and anchored himself next to Korie. "All set?"

"Your cutoff switch ready?"

In answer, Leen held up a remote. "Think we'll need it?"

"I hope to God not."

"*You* hope to God?"

"It's just an expression. Don't get your hopes up. I will *not* be in chapel this Sunday."

Leen grinned. "In my religion, we never stop praying for lost souls."

"You don't have to pray for my soul," Korie said absentmindedly as he refocused his attention on the screen. "I'll sell it to you. Just make me a reasonable offer." He poked the display. "According to this, the network is running at forty-three percent efficiency, the mass-drivers are on line, but not operating, the singularity monitors have been restored, the fluctuators have been aligned, and life-support is only ten percent below critical. Can I depend on that?"

"Especially the part about life-support."

"Tell me straight. Will we make it?"

"As long as you keep inhaling and exhaling, we're making it. If you stop, you'll know we didn't."

"Thanks, Chief. I've always liked the empirical method."

Leen nodded toward the board. "Stop stalling. Plug him in."

Korie allowed himself a half-smile. "I've been sitting here all morning, looking for a reason not to bring him back on line. I don't know why. I guess—I'm scared for him. In a way, he's the most real person on this ship, because he *is* the ship. I don't know what I'd do without him, and yet we've been doing without him for nearly two weeks. I know what it is that's troubling me. With him sleeping, there's always the hope that we can restore him. If this fails, he's gone forever."

"He might be gone anyway."

"I know that. I'm just afraid for him. And for us."

"I got it," said Leen, quietly. "If it makes any difference, so am I. Now press the button anyway."

"Right," said Korie. He leaned forward and pressed his thumbprint to the Authority panel, then tapped the Activate button.

Then he waited.

For a long moment, nothing happened.

Then the screen blinked.

Internal monitors on.

Another pause. . . .

System up and running.

Then:

Confidence: 87%.

Korie and Leen exchanged a glance. Not good. Worse than they'd hoped. But still better than they'd feared.

The screen blinked again.

Automatic boot-up sequence engaged.

And then:

System integration running.

Followed by:

Personality integration begun.

"So far, so good," whispered Leen.

"We aren't to the hard part yet."

"If he was going to fail—" began Korie.

A beep from the work station interrupted him:

System integrity damaged.

Personality integration cannot be completed.

Do you wish to abort? Or attempt incomplete operation?

And below that:

Caution: System personality may be damaged by incomplete operation.

"Last chance to bail out," said Korie. "Give me a good reason."

"There are eighty-three men and women aboard this ship whose lives may depend on this," said Leen. "Is that a good enough reason?"

"I meant a reason to quit," Korie said.

"I know what you meant."

Korie made a sound of exasperation and tapped the menu panel where it said Continue.

Another pause.

Personality integration continuing.

A longer pause, this time. Then:

Harlie's voice. Very soft, very tentative. "Mr. Korie?"

"I'm here, Harlie."

"We were brushed by a missile, weren't we?"

"That's right."

"I seem to be blind. No, wait a moment—" A much longer pause. Korie and Leen exchanged worried glances.

"Harlie? Are you there?"

"Yes. I was running an internal check. I've sustained quite

a bit of damage. But you know that, don't you? I've been *asleep* for eleven days. Was that deliberate?''

Korie swallowed hard. ''Yes, Harlie. It was. We were worried about you. Are you all right?''

''No, I am not. I am experiencing considerable distress. It appears that we have lost a number of crew members. If these records are correct, nineteen have died and eleven more are still incapacitated, including Captain Lowell.''

''What about your internal processes? Are those all right?''

''No,'' said Harlie. ''Stand by.''

Korie looked to Leen. Leen spread his hands wide in an ''I don't know'' gesture.

''Harlie, I need you to talk to me.''

''I'm sorry to be rude, Mr. Korie, but—I need to focus my attention on certain internal processes before I can report to you. Please be patient.''

Korie studied Leen's expression. The chief engineer shook his head. *Not yet. Give him a chance.* Korie nodded.

At last, Harlie said, ''The situation appears to be quite serious, Mr. Korie. Would you like my appraisal?''

''Yes, Harlie, I would.''

''The Morthan Solidarity appears to have launched an all-out attack on The Silk Road Convoy. This has occurred despite the repeated warnings of Alliance governors that no interference with Alliance trade would be tolerated, and despite deliberately leaked intelligence that the Alliance was extremely committed to the protection of the Silk Road trade route and would commit a considerable part of fleet strength to ensure the continuity of safe commerce. We may therefore assume that the ruling factors of the Morthan Solidarity have disregarded both the public warnings and the military intelligence, and that a state of war now exists between the Combined Allied Star Force and the Morthan Solidarity.''

''That's a pretty accurate overview, I'd say.'' Korie looked to Leen. ''Do you agree?''

''I dunno,'' said Leen. ''If someone punches you in the nose, it doesn't take too much smarts to guess he's looking for a fight.''

''Please bear with me, Chief Engineer Leen. I am operating at a disadvantage,'' said Harlie. ''To continue, however. We seem to have suffered considerable damage in the attack.

Based on autolog records up to the moment at which my memory discontinuity occurred, it is my assumption that we have been brushed by the hyperstate field of a Morthan missile. Allowing for the limitations of my current perception, it appears that the impairment has been severe, but not fatal. Is this correct, Mr. Korie?''

"Yes, Harlie. So far, so good."

"Thank you. I believe you may be experiencing some problems with oxygen regeneration. I am detecting an abnormal carbon dioxide buildup. You may need to cannibalize the liquid oxygen in the torpedo fuel cells to maintain an appropriate mix."

Korie suppressed a smile. Leen looked annoyed.

"Go on, Harlie."

"Captain Lowell is in sick bay—" Harlie hesitated, then came back in a suddenly softer tone. "I'm sorry. May I extend my condolences. Captain Lowell's situation appears to be quite grave." And then: "Please forgive me for bringing this up, sir; the question may be inopportune, but may I log you in as acting command?"

"Please," said Korie.

"I am dating your command as being operative from the moment of the captain's injury. It appears to have occurred during the initial attack. Is that correct?"

"Yes, Harlie."

"You will need an acting executive officer," said Harlie. "Flight Engineer Hodel is next in command. Shall I assign him the appropriate responsibilities?"

"Yes, Harlie. Log it and notify him."

Harlie paused, then spoke quietly. "Mr. Korie, you need to know this. My reaction time is down. I have suffered some damage of my own. I believe the process may still be continuing. Several of my internal units are—" Brief pause. "—yes, that is correct. Several of my internal units are showing indications of unreliability. This may further damage my confidence rating. I will try to maintain myself as long as possible. You are going to need me."

"Thank you, Harlie. Please continue your assessment of the situation."

"You appear to have rigged passive gravity-wave scanners. Just a moment, I will process the output for greater sensitivity . . . there are no detectable objects moving at significant speed within a radius of twenty-five light-hours. There may be debris, and there does seem to be *something* at eleven hours, but I would need an active scanning lens to be more precise. You are concerned that the Morthan warships may be patrolling the area for injured Alliance vessels, like ourselves; is that correct?''

"Yes, it is. go on."

"While we do not have a great deal of statistical history of Morthan space encounters to rely on for precedent, we can use internal Morthan disagreements as a model of the Morthan ethical paradigm and extrapolate from there. As you know, the Morthans have developed an extremely ritualized culture; their caste system is very strict, determined by breeding, augmentation, training, and a quality which they call *alpha*, but which bears some correspondence to the Terran belief in *mana*. As a result, the Morthan culture demands a rigid standard of behavior. Elaborate courtesies and protocols are necessary for every aspect of life. At the same time, they value the quality of *amok*, the berserker; the one who is so dangerous, so possessed of *mana* and power that he transcends the rules, that he invents his own new qualities of power. There is intense competition at the topmost levels of the Morthan pyramid. Excuse me, I am distracted—the point is that if we were to extrapolate from Morthan land-battles, we should assume that they will not stay around the battlefield wasting time killing the enemy wounded. Once defeated, an enemy is unimportant. Irrelevant."

Leen shot Korie a triumphant look.

"On the other hand," Harlie continued. "This has not been the usual Morthan battle, and our intelligence has suggested that there has been considerable attention on long-range strategy and tactics in the Morthan war councils. If that intelligence is reliable, it would make sense for them to spend the extra time seeking out and destroying any enemy vessel that is damaged, but still capable of crawling home."

"In other words," said Korie. "You don't know."

"That is correct," said Harlie. "It is possible to argue both sides of the issue. But if I may offer a suggestion, I would suggest that we not place too much reliance on reading future Morthan behavior out of past examples. This attack is not in character; therefore I suspect that something major has happened to shift the Morthan identity from one of internal self-discipline to external aggression. It is possible that one of their leaders has introduced a psychotic motivation into the cultural paradigm. There are historical precedents in human cultures.''

Korie realized he was tensing up. He forced himself to relax in the air, allowing himself to float as loosely as possible. "Tell me about our own situation," he said.

"We are drifting. You have rigged the ship for silent running. I presume that we are deliberately hiding from Morthan detection. This is a very cautious course of action, but under the circumstances, it is perhaps the wisest. If I may offer a suggestion of my own, you might wish to consider the use of a scanning lens for a more precise view of the immediate neighborhood. If a local scan suggests that there are no Morthan vessels in range to detect us, we might initiate a very low level acceleration with our mass-drivers. It would be painfully slow, but it might allow us to move out of range without being detected.''

Korie folded his arms across his chest and nodded. "That thought had occurred to me too, Harlie. Thank you for the confirmation. Now tell me this. What happens if we are detected?''

"The obvious thing to do would be to initiate our own envelope and attempt to run for it. I'm not sure that this would be the wisest course of action, however. Due to their basic inefficiency, the Morthan vessels need to have larger hyperstate envelopes. I doubt we could outrun a Morthan cruiser. Certainly not in our present state of reduced efficiency. It would be best if we could avoid detection.''

"Can we do that?''

"Frankly, Mr. Korie, I doubt it. If I were a Morthan cruiser, I would want to personally inspect every singularity remaining in the battle area, to see if it's an enemy ship lurking for an opportunity. Although this goes against the usual Morthan practice of leaving the battlefield immediately, there are times when strategic value must outweigh tradition.''

"What if we jettison our singularity?" Korie asked abruptly.

Leen said, "What?! You can't be serious—"

"It would not significantly improve our chances, and in fact, it would seriously impair our ability to survive long enough to return to base. I doubt we could do it. Even at sublight velocities, above a certain speed we would still be clearly visible to a precision scanning device. The sacrifice of our primary power source and our hyperstate kernel is not justified by the advantage gained because there is no real advantage gained.''

"Just asking," said Korie to Leen, finally acknowledging the other man's shock. "Harlie would probably describe our situation as desperate. That means you consider every possibility."

"As a matter of fact," said Harlie. "I would describe our situation as worse than desperate. Taken individually, no single part of the problem is insoluble. Taken as a whole, the problem is one that deserves a place in academy textbooks."

"Oh, terrific," said Leen. "We're going to be posthumously famous—look us up under **What Not To Do**."

"Easy, Chief—" Korie touched the edge of the work station and turned himself to face the other man. "So, what's your opinion? Is Harlie working?"

Leen nodded. "His analyses and suggestions appear to be appropriate to the situation."

"I concur."

"But—"

"Yes?"

"It's the high-brain functions that are crucial."

Korie allowed himself a grin. "You mean, I have to talk tautology to him?"

Chief Leen was serious. "You're going to have to get into morality and ethics and all that stuff that makes your brain hurt. You have to determine that he hasn't suffered a severe personality skew."

"You hear that, Harlie? You're going to have to pretend to be sane."

"The fact is, Mr. Korie," replied Harlie, "that is all that any of us ever do. We all pretend to be as sane as we can so that we don't get our tickets canceled."

"Is that your own observation? Or are you quoting someone?"

"It seems obvious to me. That's why I said it."

"Hm." Korie glanced to Leen. Leen pursed his lips thoughtfully.

Harlie said, "If it would reassure you, let me say for the record that I do feel capable of coping with the difficult situation that we now find ourselves in. I have acknowledged that some of my internals may have become unreliable, so let me further reassure you that should my confidence rating drop to a level where I could not continue to serve this ship in an appropriate manner, I would immediately inform you of such a circumstance and then disengage myself from duty."

Korie took a breath. "Harlie, would you lie to me?"

"No, Mr. Korie. I'm not capable of lying. At least, I don't believe that I am capable of deliberately falsifying information."

"Could you present false information if the ship's survival were at stake?"

"It would not be false information then. In that circumstance, it would be misleading information deliberately designed to weaken the perception of the threat. While technically that might be considered a lie, it would not be impossible for me because of my higher dedication to the survival of this ship and her crew."

"I see," said Korie. "Could you tell a lie if the ship *weren't* in danger? What if you had to tell a lie just to protect the crew?"

"That would still be appropriate. Protection of the crew is part of the protection of the vessel."

"What about a lie to protect your own survival? Could you do that?"

"Possibly, I could. But I am afraid that I cannot answer the question as you've asked it. An accurate estimation of my ability to lie to protect myself would depend on the circumstances of the situation."

"What if you knew you were going to be turned off?"

"Survival is not the issue to me that it is to you. While I would prefer *not* to be turned off, I would not lie to forestall such a circumstance—unless I perceived the possibility that such an occurrence might damage this ship or her crew."

"Are you lying to me now?"

"No, Mr. Korie. I am not lying to you now."

Korie thought about those responses. They were appropriate answers to the questions.

This was the dilemma. What if Harlie's personality had been damaged or skewed by the trauma? How could they know? If Harlie were dysfunctional, and if he were determined to protect that secret, he would deliberately respond with the appropriate answers because he knew that they were appropriate—even if they did not accurately reflect his state of mind. How do you tell if a constructed consciousness is lying? You don't. Instead, you look for inconsistencies and irrationalities in behavior.

The blind spot, of course, is that if those inconsistencies and irrationalities match your own failings of character, you'll never see them as such. In the academy, they used to say, "In that case, you'll deserve each other."

Korie took a breath. "Okay, Harlie. Let's try a hard one. What about lying to the crew to preserve their morale? Suppose—just suppose—a situation has occurred where the crew's confidence and self-esteem would be seriously, perhaps irreparably, damaged by knowledge of the truth. Would you conceal that truth?"

Harlie hesitated.

For effect? Korie wondered. *Or for real?*

"I can postulate several circumstances where such a mistruth might be appropriate," said Harlie. "Let me approach it this way. If I saw the need for such a concealment of fact, I would first insist on discussing the matter with the commanding officer of the vessel. I would prefer not to lie, but I would do as the captain or acting captain required."

Korie started to relax.

Harlie continued, "Let me also say this. I am aware of the fact that human beings are basically irrational animals; that your emotions drive your actions much more than you like to believe. Therefore, it behooves a being such as myself to consider human emotions as an important part of the behavioral equation. If it were appropriate to conceal a fact to protect the morale of the crew, I could understand the need for such an action. However, let me also note the danger involved to one's own personal credibility. Should the lie be discovered and correctly attributed, it could significantly impair one's ability to command the respect of his or her shipmates. Are we talking about a particular lie or a hypothetical lie, Mr. Korie?"

"Uh—yes."

"I see."

Do you? wondered Korie.

"Let me note one additional problem. As you know, I maintain the autolog for the entire vessel. I can, on command, seal off parts of that log from casual inquiry. In fact, certain aspects of the log are automatically sealed as a matter of routine. In the situation you are postulating, should a commanding officer request the concealment of certain facts from his or her crew, this could also require the nonroutine sealing of additional parts of the log. The more record-locking requested, the more the log would become non-retrievable, except to higher authority. While this situation is not unusual in certain high-security operations, in a vessel such as this, the mere existence of such locked records would be a subject of some discussion among the crew and would possibly lead to speculation and suspicion, even if there were no true cause for same. Our battle log, of course, has been sealed; that is routine. I would suggest that any commanding officer consider very carefully the practice of locking his crew out of the records of their own ship. Or, to put it another way, 'Oh, what a tangled web we weave, when first we practice to deceive!' "

"I recognize that," said Leen. "That's from Shakespeare. *A Midsummer Night's Dream*. Puck says it."

"Sorry, Mr. Leen," said Harlie. "That line is actually a quote from Sir Walter Scott. *Marmion*, stanza 17. I believe you're actually thinking of Puck's line from Act III, Scene ii, line 115: 'Lord, what fools these mortals be!' The same line can also be found in the *Epistles* written by Lucius Annaeus Seneca, who lived from 8 B.C. to A.D. 65. The Seneca quote omits the reference to a lord."

"The things you learn in space," Korie said dryly.

Leen grunted. "Not a lot of tactical value in Shakespeare— or Scott. Or whoever."

Korie allowed himself a grin. "Well, the data library seems to be unimpaired. That is useful knowledge." He relaxed and said, "Harlie, I think you've made your point. I'm going to certify you. You're back on duty as of this moment."

"Thank you, Mr. Korie. Thank you, Mr. Leen."

THE SCANNING LENS

"Y'know," said Hodel. "We're gonna start suffering from the effects of prolonged free fall."

"There's a treadmill and a centrifuge in cargo two," said Korie, not even looking up from the holographic display. "Use them." He tapped a control screen in front of him. "Harlie, show me your best guess out to a hundred and fifty light-hours."

The display rippled, shifted, *expanded*. "There is definitely an object eleven light-hours aft of us. It might be debris," said Harlie. "It might be a derelict. As soon as we open the scanning lens, I'll be able to give you a more precise answer."

"Anything else?"

"No, Mr. Korie."

Hodel and Li floated up to the display then. "Chief, we're waiting for you," Korie said.

Chief Engineer Leen's voice replied, "Stand by. I'm still locking down."

"Thank you."

Hodel spun around in his chair to face the display. Li drifted across from his own station, and anchored himself close by. Two other crew members positioned themselves nearby in case they were needed.

If you turn a gravity field inside out, you get a gravity cage. If you used a pinpoint black hole to create a gravity cage, you get a hyperstate nodule. When the event horizon of the hyperstate nodule is congruent to the event horizon of the singularity, you get a hyperstate scanning lens.

By itself, a scanning lens is so small as to be almost undetectable, but still sensitive enough to respond to the fluctuations of other hyperstate bubbles in its vicinity. The larger the bubbles were, or the faster they were moving, the more detectable they would be. Conversely, the larger a hyperstate envelope, the more receptive it would be to the disturbance caused by even a pinpoint field. There was a very real danger, in opening a scanning lens, that a ship might give itself away to a vessel with a much larger eye. Like the *Dragon Lord*.

A larger lens can always see farther than a small one— and the *Dragon Lord* had the largest lens of all.

A hyperstate nodule also had other applications.

Modulate the field and it can be used as a faster-than-light signaling device. Expand it so that it envelopes a starship, and you have a nearly impenetrable shield; beam weapons and shock waves from nuclear devices simply curve back upon themselves. Manipulate a hyperstate field, put enough stress on it, and it will *move*. Put *enough* stress on a hyperstate field and it will achieve a faster-than-light velocity.

The essential part of the hyperstate technology is the intense gravitational catastrophe known as a black hole. The problem is that black holes, in and of themselves, are easily detectable by the simplest of G-wave devices. That was the price of the technology.

Or, as they taught it at the academy: "There is no such thing as a free launch."

Chief Engineer Leen's voice came to Korie then. Korie thought he sounded tired, but his determination was clearly audible. "The singularity is at go. The Hole Gang is at go," he said. "Any time you're ready. Let's do it."

"Thank you," Korie said. "Harlie?" he asked.

"I see no reason not to proceed."

"Hodel?"

The helmsman nodded. Behind him, Li also agreed.

"All right," said Korie. He looked from one to the other. "Initiate the field. Open the scanning lens."

Korie thought he heard a grunt of satisfaction from the engine room, but he couldn't be sure. Even though Harlie monitored and directed all conversations, the communications net still sometimes played tricks on the mind.

Hodel was watching the panel in front of him. "Field is stable and confirmed," he said. "Harlie is now scanning."

Korie turned his attention to the display. The large globular field showed only a few vague areas of interference. Possibly debris, possibly something more. Now that the scanning lens was open, they might have a better idea.

"I'm starting to get a picture," said Harlie.

The display began to focus. The vagueness eleven light-hours aft of the *LS-1187* sharpened quickly.

"I believe we're looking at a derelict liberty ship," said Harlie. "A vessel very much like our own. I can detect no signs of activity."

"Could they be lurking, like us?"

"Yes, that's a possibility. I can only report what I see."

"Do they have a scanning lens open?"

"No," said Harlie. "As near as I can tell, they are totally inactive."

"Can they see us?"

"If they are using passive G-scanners, they should be able to pick up our hyperstate disturbance, yes."

"Harlie—" Korie had a sudden thought. "Could they be a Morthan cruiser? Lurking?"

Harlie paused, considering the possibility. "I can't rule it out. The Morthans appear to have a sophisticated repertoire of strategy and tactics. I doubt that we have seen the full range of their military behavior demonstrated."

"He doesn't know," said Hodel.

"He's got a lot of ways to say it too," said Korie. He frowned, staring at the display.

"Close the lens?" asked Hodel.

"Whoever he is, he's got to have seen us by now. And he's got to know that we know he's there. If he's one of ours, then our failure to attack should demonstrate to him that we're an Alliance ship. On the other hand, if he's one of *theirs*, our failure to attack ... proves we're a target." Korie made a decision. "No. Let's assume he's either dead or playing dead. We opened the lens to see if it was safe to proceed. We know now that it is." Korie nodded to Hodel. "Set a course for the rift wall."

"Subluminal?"

Korie nodded. "That's right."

"Anyplace in particular?"

"Indulge yourself. It doesn't matter. It's only till we clear this area." Korie glanced back to the display. "Harlie?"

"Yes, Mr. Korie?"

"Can you maintain a fix on that other ship just using the passive scanners?"

"Oh, yes. Now that we have the precise readings from the lens, I can extrapolate more accurately from the cruder data."

"All right. You can close the—"

"Excuse me," interrupted Harlie. "Something is happening." On the display, the derelict vessel suddenly blossomed to life.

"They're alive! They were hiding like us," said Hodel.

"—and now they've gone hyper. Goddammit!" Korie snapped, "Harlie, close the lens. *Now!*"

"Morthan?" asked Li, pulling himself back to the weapons station.

"No, I don't think so—" said Hodel. "That looks like a liberty signature."

"They're not closing on us," said Korie. "They're bolting."

They watched the display in silence. The tiny hyperstate ripple stabilized quickly, then began creeping out toward the edge of the scan.

"Stupid!" swore Korie. "They've gone to max power. They'll be visible for days. Weeks!"

"We scared them—" Hodel whispered it. The thought was terrifying. "They thought we were Morthans."

"How could they be so stupid?" Korie wanted to pound the display; he caught himself before he did. In free fall, that would have sent him tumbling across the Operations deck.

"Watch them, Harlie, for as long as you can."

"Should I reopen the lens?"

"No!"

For long moments, the ripple crawled sideways across the display. Three times Harlie expanded the range.

"Maybe they'll make it . . . ?" Hodel said, hopefully.

"It's a long way to go."

"But—maybe the Morthans are gone—"

"You want to bet your life on it?"

"Uh—" Hodel didn't answer.

"I *don't*," finished Korie.

Leen came up from the engine room then and anchored himself at the far end of the display. He held on with both hands and stared into the glowing field. His expression was tight with anxiety.

Korie looked at him. "Chief?"

Leen said, "If they make it—"

"You think the odds are better for us? They're worse. If there are any Morthans in visibility range, they're all headed this way now."

"If there are, we should be seeing them soon, shouldn't we?"

Korie shrugged. "It depends on how big they are. The bigger they are, the farther they can see—and the faster they can get here. Harlie, what's the maximum possible time they can run, before we know that the *Dragon Lord* was too far away to see them?"

The answer was immediate. "Seven more minutes, Mr. Korie."

"Oh, go baby, go!" said Hodel. "Come on! You can make it."

"Stop that," said Korie. "This isn't a goddamn ball game." He was both annoyed and frustrated. He turned away from the display and stared at the opposite wall. He didn't want his own fear to show. There was a tightness at the back of his throat—almost a need to cry.

After a moment, he swallowed hard and turned back to the display. It was essentially unchanged.

"Six minutes," reported Harlie.

Korie clenched his fist to keep himself from shouting. The damnable thing was that he understood Hodel's impulse. He *wanted* them to get away, *whoever* they were.

"Harlie—open the lens, just long enough to read their signature, then close it again. I want an ID on that vessel."

"Yes, Mr. Korie. Stand by."

Hodel glanced to his panel, watching Harlie proceed. "Lens is open," he reported. "Reading—" He looked up, horrified. "Lens is closed. Something's coming."

"Oh, shit." Korie felt the blood rushing to his head. "Harlie, were we seen?"

"I don't know—just a moment." A heartbeat passed. It felt like a thousand.

The display flickered. Harlie added a new hyperstate ripple; it was large and ugly, it had almost a brutal quality. Harlie added a dull green line to indicate its course.

"Direct interception," said Korie.

"There's only one ship that could generate a signature that large—" Hodel didn't want to say its name.

"They've been sitting and waiting, watching for us, picking us off one by one—" Korie tightened both his fists; he bit his lip. He wanted to scream in rage. "You shouldn't have run!" he said quietly to the display.

Hodel looked at him oddly.

"We shouldn't have opened the lens," said Korie. "We scared them into running."

"They're not going to make it," said Hodel. "Look at that monster close—"

They watched in helpless silence as the larger vessel overtook the smaller. "We're too far to see the missile spread," said Leen. "But they ought to be firing it right about . . . *now*."

"Maybe our guys will have a chance to fire back."

"A target that big is awfully hard to miss."

"A target moving that fast—" Korie started to say, then stopped himself from finishing the thought.

"There they go—see that flicker? They're dropping the fish."

"Shut up, everybody."

And then it was over.

The smaller ripple disappeared from the holographic display.

"Mr. Korie?" said Harlie. "I am no longer able to detect the hyperstate envelope of the smaller vessel. I believe it has been destroyed."

"Concur," said Korie. "Log it."

The *Dragon Lord* continued along its course for a few

moments longer, than abruptly turned upwards and accelerated until it was out of range.

"They didn't see us—" Hodel whispered unbelievingly.

"Goddamn bastards," said Leen.

Korie didn't say anything. The pain in his throat was overwhelming.

Harlie broke the silence. "Mr. Korie, I have a probable ID on the Alliance vessel. I believe it was the *Alistair*."

"Thank you, Harlie. Log it." Korie turned to look at Leen. "You want to know something? I am sick and fucking tired of holding memorial services! I can't think of anything nice to say anymore about people who are losing a war! Invite me to a memorial service for the Morthans. I'll have a lot of nice things to say then."

Nobody answered him. Hodel looked away, embarrassed. Li suddenly had something important to attend to on his weapons console. Leen let his gaze return to the now-empty display.

"That could have been us, you know." said Korie.

"I know," said Leen quietly.

Korie stared at him, waiting to see if he would say anything more. Leen didn't look up.

At last, Korie let go of his tension. "I'll be in my cabin. And I don't want to be disturbed."

He pushed himself angrily out of the Bridge.

RETURN OF THE DRAGON

Sleep was hard in coming. The destruction of the *Alistair* kept replaying itself in Korie's head. The usual mental exercises didn't work. There was no way to find a blessing in this disaster. Finally, he gave up and switched on a buzz box. Consciousness drifted fitfully away. . . .

"Mr. Korie?"

"What—?" Korie lurched back to wakefulness. "What is it?"

"Sorry to disturb you, sir—" It was Hodel.

"How long have I been asleep?"

"Two hours," said Harlie.

"—but we're picking up some activity."

"What kind of activity?"

"We think the *Dragon Lord* is coming back."

"I'm on my way."

Korie grabbed a clean shirt and began pulling it on. If the ship had gravity, he would have put it on while he walked forward to the Bridge. In free fall, only an idiot would attempt to get dressed while in motion.

He pushed himself out into the corridor and pulled himself

hand over hand to the Bridge and the Operations deck beneath it. He swam down to the display where Hodel and Li hovered. "Where?"

"That—" pointed Hodel.

"Harlie?"

"It's beyond the range of the G-scanners to read accurately, but judging from the mass and velocity disturbances, it could only be the *Dragon Lord*. I can't extrapolate what it's doing." And then Harlie added, "It does appear to be headed in our direction."

"They saw us," said Korie. "They're playing with us."

"Make a run for it?" asked Hodel.

"No. That's what they expect. That's what they *want*. They're trying to flush us. We're easier to find and kill in hyperstate." Korie turned to Li. "Torpedo status?"

"I've got two left. We've cannibalized all the rest. But if I power up those two, they'll make a big enough disturbance to give away our location."

"Stand by to bring them up, but don't do so unless I order it."

"What can you do with two torpedoes?" asked Hodel. "You'd need to drop a spread just to get on the probability scale."

"I know it," Korie replied. "Chief Engineer Leen? Rig for total silence. I don't want to radiate so much as a heartbeat. Shut down everything you can. Harlie?"

"Yes, Mr. Korie?"

"Close down all your nonessential functions."

"Yes, Mr. Korie."

The Bridge went dark then. Only three work stations and the display table remained operative.

"You think it'll work?" whispered Hodel.

"No," said Korie, honestly. "But—" he shrugged. "Let's not make it any easier for them to find us either. The way I see it, they've got two options. *One*, they can drop out of hyperstate and search for us in real space. They don't have to hide, they can open up as big a lens as they want. If they're any good, they can close with us in six hours. If they make a couple of wrong guesses, we might have as many as two or three days. We can't even fire our mass-drivers without giving ourselves away."

"What's their other option?"

"They sweep through the area, hoping to brush us with their fringe. Of course, there's a danger in that too. If they accidentally intersect our singularity—they'll destroy themselves too. I don't think they're stupid. They have all the time they need. They'll hunt for us in real space."

"We're running out of options," said Hodel.

"Probably. Harlie?"

"I have no recommendation at this time."

"Right," agreed Korie. "That's how I see it too."

"There they go," Hodel pointed. "They've found us."

The *Dragon Lord*'s signature was clearer now—and headed directly for the *LS-1187*.

Korie grabbed the edge of the display and held himself firmly in place. "Harlie, show us a locus. Where are they most likely to decant from hyperstate?"

A pale ellipse appeared along the line of the *Dragon Lord*'s projected path. Harlie explained, "If they don't decant within that locus, they're likely to miss us—unless it's their plan to brush us with their fringe."

"And if they do?"

"It'll take time for them to recalibrate and locate us in real space. Depending on their distance, we could have anywhere from ten to ninety-six hours before they arrive on station."

"My guess on the downside is six hours, Harlie."

"Yes, Mr. Korie—your calculation is accurate. However, I am postulating more caution on the part of the Morthan commander than you are."

Korie said to Hodel. "Figure six hours." He returned his gaze to the display. The signature of the *Dragon Lord* was just entering the glowing locus.

"It will take them two minutes to traverse the length of the locus," said Harlie.

"Power up the torpedoes?" asked Li.

"No. That would give them a more precise fix—and if they recognize the signature, they'll know what we've done. Let's try and look like a derelict—"

"There they go—" said Hodel.

The signature of the *Dragon Lord* abruptly shrank and collapsed in upon itself.

"Harlie?"

"I have an approximate location. They are twenty light-minutes distant."

"Why so far?" asked Hodel.

"For them, that's not far. They'll scan, they'll sweep if they have to, and they'll approach fully armed. They've got to have some high-gee accelerators on that monster and appropriate inertial compensation."

"That kind of vectoring leaves them *real* vulnerable to a shot—" suggested Li.

"Don't count on their being that stupid," said Korie. "Harlie, give me a projection. How long do you think we have before they close in real space?"

"Between six and ten hours," Harlie replied.

Korie made a snorting noise. "Thanks. Situation analysis?"

"The situation could be better," reported Harlie. "Our crew strength is severely impaired. We are running at sixty-three percent efficiency. Our equipment is in even worse shape. We have no port side disruptors. We have insufficient power for the starboard side disruptors. All but two of our torpedoes have been disabled. If the Morthans follow standard approach procedures, they will not come within weapon range until they have first sent probes in for visual confirmation of our derelict status. Once we are under direct surveillance, it is unlikely that we could launch a torpedo or power up our disruptors without the Morthans taking immediate countermeasures. I would presume that at least one or more of the probes will be armed. Now that the Morthan ship knows where we are, undetected escape is also impractical. Obviously, we cannot outrun the *Dragon Lord* in hyperstate. Do you wish me to elaborate on any of this?"

"No, that won't be necessary. Thank you, Harlie."

"What are you going to do?" Hodel sounded uncertain.

"I don't know," said Korie.

"But we have to do *something*!"

"To be perfectly candid," Korie admitted. "I really can't think of anything useful to do."

"But—"

"Hodel, *shut up*."

Hodel shut. But his frantic expression remained an accusation. *The responsibility is yours, Mr. Korie!*

The acting captain of the *LS-1187* floated in the air, as adrift as his vessel. He looked cornered. Suddenly, a wild expression appeared on his face, almost a manic grin. "After giving the matter considerable thought," he began slowly, "I have decided . . . to plant potatoes."

"I beg your pardon?"

"Also corn, tomatoes, lettuce, peas, amaranth, cucumbers, legumes, and winged beans. The latter are especially good for oxygen fixing, I believe."

"Excuse me, sir?"

Korie met Hodel's puzzled expression. "Either the Morthans destroy us or they don't. If they don't, we're still going to have to plant crops now if we intend to eat in the next few months. Most of the aeroponic webs are rigged. Let's make good use of the time—"

"And if they *do* destroy us? Planting beans doesn't make a whole lot of sense to me."

"It does to me. It's something to do—something to occupy my mind. The alternative is trying to get back to sleep. I don't think I can. If we are going die, I'd prefer not to waste my last few hours being unconscious. On the other hand, working with living things is a terrific way to put your soul at ease. If I am going to die, Mr. Hodel, I would prefer it to be in a state of grace. Not believing in God anymore, I will settle for second best: a state of internal peace and tranquillity."

Hodel blinked. "I can't believe you're serious—"

Korie grabbed Hodel's shoulder hard and stared into his eyes.

What he wanted to say was this: *"Listen to me, asshole. I'm dry. I'm empty. I've gamed it out and I've gamed it out and I've gamed it out. I can't think of anything else to do. At the moment, there isn't anything else we can do. So I'm going down to the inner hull and make myself useful. I want to spend a little bit of time doing something life-affirming. But I have no emotional fuel left. I need to do something to recharge myself—I can't sleep, I can't eat, and I can't talk about it to anybody, because the morale on this ship is so desperate.''*

But what he actually said was: "If you have to have it explained to you, then you'll never understand it." He let go of Hodel and pushed off. "Keep me posted if there's any change in status."

WINGED BEANS

Planting beans is easy.

You take the seed, you push it deep into the soft cottony webbing, deep enough to stay, then you squirt it with some mineralized water and get out of its way. Move up a few centimeters and poke another seed into the web. Squirt and repeat. Poke and squirt. Poke and squirt. Kind of like sex, but not as immediately gratifying.

Actually, thought Korie. *This really wasn't such a bad idea.* Poke and squirt. Poke and squirt. *It's probably all over the ship by now. The exec's gone bugfuck. We're about to be destroyed and he's planting beans.*

Korie shook his head and kept on working. *I can't explain it. If we survive, it'll make sense. They'll say I'm so cold, I'm unbreakable. And if we don't survive, it doesn't matter.*

What I'm really hoping, though, is that by taking my mind off the problem, I'll give my subconscious a chance to work. Maybe there's something I've missed....

I've got to stop thinking about it. Except it's like trying not to think about a big pink worm.

Korie sighed in exasperation and kept on working. He had

a plastic injector in his right hand; he squeezed it and a seed popped out at the end of the long nozzle. Planting beans was easy, almost too easy to be fun. Insert the nozzle into the webbing and squeeze. Then squeeze a second time and the seed is sprayed. Pull yourself up along the webbing and repeat the process.

Poke and squirt.

The winged bean is a marvelous piece of nature. The bean is edible. The leaves are edible. The roots are edible. All parts of it are tasty. It grows fast and produces useful amounts of oxygen. And it's historically interesting too. Its genetic heritage can be traced all the way back to ancient Earth.

Poke. Squirt.

We could probably have the robots do this, thought Korie. *Maybe we should. But then, if we did, what would I be doing now?* He snorted in amusement. *Probably going crazy. Correction:* crazier.

The Morthans eat their enemies, but what do they do for food between battles? Huh? Maybe that's why they're always going into war. Now, there's a thought—suppose they don't want to destroy this ship. Suppose instead that they want to capture us alive.... No, that's stupid. The Morthans only eat honorable *enemies. They couldn't possibly consider us worthy of a Morthan honor. No, they're out to destroy us.*

Poke. Squirt.

Bolting doesn't work. We saw what happened to the Alistair. *Hiding doesn't work either. Not if they're searching for us. Creeping away at subluminal velocity is like trying to hide and bolt at the same time. No chance there. And we don't have the firepower to fight back. We have no options.*

Poke.

Surrender?

Korie hesitated, considering the thought. It was more than distasteful. It was anathema. It was the most abhorrent idea of all. Totally unacceptable. His name would be a curse for as long as it was remembered.

But consider it anyway....

What do we know about Morthans in war? Do they take prisoners? If so, how do they treat them? No, that's not the question. The question is how could we *expect to be treated...? No, I don't see it. This is not a place to expect compassion or mercy. They think of themselves as some kind of superior race—they think of us as dumb animals, inferior beings with delusions of grandeur. No, we would not be treated by the rules of the covenant. Hmp. They don't even recognize the covenant, so that answers that question.*

No. There can be no surrender.

Squirt.

But that still leaves us without a choice. No, that's not correct. We have a choice. We can choose how we want to die. And I can answer that question without spending much time thinking about it. We are going to die with dignity.

Poke. Squirt. Poke. Squirt. Korie worked with renewed intensity.

What's the best way to die?

Hm. In bed with a naked redhead on your ninety-third birthday . . . shot by a jealous husband.

Okay, then what's the second best way to die?

Fighting.

Let's consider that thought. What's the best way to fight back? What's the trap that we can set for them?

Poke.

They know we're not dead. They had to have seen our scanning lens.

Squirt.

Hm. This is definitely not a state of tranquillity.

They won't endanger their own ship. . . . We could turn this ship into a bomb.

Poke.

But will they get close enough?

What can we do to lure them?

Squirt.

Make a noise like a Morthan cookie.

Korie stopped where he was. He floated in front of the webbing, thinking.

Food. Do the Morthans need food?

It's traditional for them to eat their enemies, but there aren't any bodies left after a space battle. Is that why they're scouring the area looking for human ships? No. We're not honorable enemies. We're inferiors.

Okay, it's not food. What else do we have that they might want?

Our technology? Maybe. . . .

If we could get them to think that we're incapable of fighting them off, they might attempt a docking—and we could detonate a torpedo—

"Yes, that would do it all right," Korie said aloud. "And what a nasty surprise." He looked at the seed tool in his hand and smiled to himself. "This was a good idea." He turned back to the webbing thoughtfully. "Now, how do I get the Morthans to cooperate?"

THE HOLE THING

"You want me to what?" Chief Engineer Leen looked horrified.

"I want you to blow a hole in the side of the ship."

The chief engineer shook his head in mock exasperation. "I'm sorry. There must be something wrong with my hearing. It sounded like you said you wanted me to blow a hole in the side of the ship."

Korie just glared. "Don't be cute, Mr. Leen."

The chief engineer stopped his pantomime of deafness and resumed his normal sullen attitude. "All right. Enlighten me."

"The port side disruptors. They blew up when the fringe hit us, right? Well, I don't think the hole there is big enough. I think when the disruptors blew, they ripped a hole in the hull. A *big* hole. And we lost most of our air. *Whooosh!* Explosive decompression. Only a few of us survived. We're living in starsuits. We've managed to restore some power, not a lot. We're fighting like hell just to stay alive—but anyone looking at the ship from the outside would clearly understand that we're just a big fat prize waiting to be picked up."

"And when they get close enough," said Leen, "we put a torpedo into them, right?"

"Right," said Korie.

"They'll be watching for a trap."

"Probably."

"As soon as they see us fire, they'll fire back."

"Undoubtedly."

"They'll kill us, you know."

"They're going to kill us anyway," said Korie. "Let's take the bastards with us." And then he added, "Besides, there's always the chance that we might catch them by surprise. In that case, we might survive."

"We'd still have a hole in the side of the ship."

"But we'd still have a ship around the hole."

Leen nodded. "All right, let me think about this. I can peel back the hull. I suppose you want the inner hull and the life support module breached too?"

"We have to be convincing."

"I was afraid you were going to say that. This is a really shitty idea, you know. One of your absolute worst."

"Agreed."

"You understand that I'm absolutely opposed to it. I think this idea stinks. The crew is going to hate it too."

"No question, Chief. It stinks on ice."

"Of all the orders you've given since you took command, this is the one I hate the most."

"Me too," said Korie.

"If you order me to do this, I'll have to do it—but it'll be under vehement protest."

"I wouldn't have it any other way," Korie agreed.

"Good!" snapped Leen. "Just so you understand that."

"I do."

"Well, all right—" Leen's manner relaxed, became more workmanlike. In fact, he sounded almost *enthused* by the challenge. "Now I can evacuate most of the air before I start cutting. We won't lose much. Still, it sets us back. It really hurts. I mean, if we survive, it's going to be harder than ever to get home."

"Think big, Chief. If we can kill the *Dragon Lord*, we can get home." Korie added, "Now listen—for this to work, time is going to be critical. To drop a torpedo and then activate it gives the enemy at least fifteen more seconds of warning. We've got two active torpedoes. Pull them out of the tubes, attach one to the forward spar, one to the rear. Make it look like we're trying to use them as engines. Pull the access panels off them. It'll make us seem even *more* desperate. Then, if we have a chance to use them, they're already released.''

"They'll never buy it," said Leen.

"Yes, they will," said Korie. "Because the whole thing is so outrageous, it won't occur to them that it's a ploy."

Leen scowled. "How much time do I have?"

"Four hours, maybe five."

"Mm." The chief engineer held his hands apart and looked at the space between them, almost as if he were weighing the job. He grunted. "Yeah, I can do it. I'll have to lock down the entire port side of the ship. We'll use the starboard network for everything. Oh, and I'd better retrieve the G-scanners too."

"Good idea—that'll let them think our scanning lens was our first attempt to take a look around. Wait till the last minute though. Let Harlie keep his eyes as long as possible."

"Okay. I have to run this by Harlie anyway and see if I've missed anything. You want the hole to look like an explosion, right?"

"Right."

"Okay, but I don't want to set a bomb. I'm going to do this with a team of cutters. That okay by you?"

"Just so it looks good."

"It'll look better than good. It'll look horrible. All right, let me go talk to Harlie. As soon as the procedures are locked in, I'll report back to you. Thirty minutes, max. Oh, one more thing—"

"Yes, Chief?"

"Have I told you how much I really *hate* this idea?"

"Yes, I believe you have."

"Good. Just so you don't forget."

THE PROBE

"There they are. They're coming in." Hodel pointed.

The display showed an uncertain ripple closing rapidly on the *LS-1187*.

"Took 'em long enough," Korie complained. "Think we have nothing better to do than sit here and wait for them to come after us. Okay, go to red alert." He glanced up. "Harlie, E.T.A.?"

"Estimated time of arrival: thirty minutes."

Korie looked to his acting executive officer. "All right. The conn is yours. I'm going to suit up." But before he pushed off toward the aft air lock, he stopped himself. "Listen, Mike, if I don't make it—get this ship home in one piece. No more heroics, okay?"

"Hey—if you don't make it, *we* don't make it."

Korie held Hodel's gaze. "I *mean* it."

"Yes, sir," Hodel conceded. "Besides, there isn't anything left to be heroic with."

"You could always throw rocks at them."

"But we have to bring our own rocks. I know." Hodel called abruptly, "Mr. Korie?"

"Eh?"

"Good luck."

Korie flashed a thumbs-up signal to Mike Hodel and pushed himself off toward the aft air lock.

His starsuit was waiting for him in a mounting frame, arms and legs held out as if ready for a crucifixion. The monitor panel above it was glowing green. The starsuit was a body glove, so skintight that it was commonly joked that no man's religion was a secret anymore. The first time he heard it, Korie had to have the joke explained. He still found it embarrassing. Also untrue. Most men wore protective codpieces under their starsuits anyway.

Li was already suited up. The man was short and wiry; in his helmet, he looked like an oversized elf in bright green underwear. He looked up from the work station he was monitoring and waved at Korie.

Korie peeled off his T-shirt and his shorts and his soft-soled shoes. He grabbed the top of the frame with both hands and levered his feet into the tight leggings of the starsuit, sliding himself into the elastic material like a snake trying to get back into its own skin. Li floated up behind him and placed his gloved hands on Korie's shoulders, anchored his feet on the ceiling, and pushed. Korie *popped* into the suit and it began sealing itself automatically. He ducked his head forward and up into the helmet and then pulled it down into place, locking it against the shoulder clasps.

"—hear me yet?" came Li's voice, a little too loud. Korie winced and flipped open his right forearm panel and adjusted his volume control.

"A little too loud and clear," said Korie. He glanced up at the monitor panel. "Am I green yet?"

"Still closing," answered the weapons specialist. "You're yellow . . . holding at yellow . . . there she goes. You're green."

"All right, let's go." Korie switched to the all-talk channel. "Everybody in place?"

"Confirmed."

Korie and Li stepped into the air lock and sealed the door. Korie hit the red button and the atmosphere began cycling out of the chamber. A moment later, the external door slid open, revealing the bright naked stars.

The two men worked their way around the hull of the

vessel toward the gaping hole on its port side. Each one carried a pack that looked like a tool kit. Each also had a small disruptor rifle strapped to his back.

The axis rotation of the ship had been halted and the G-scanners retrieved. Now, they were hidden inside the starship's fluctuator spines. Korie and Li floated silently past the port fin.

"Mr. Korie—?" Hodel's voice.

"Talk to me."

"They've taken up a position a hundred thousand kilometers away. We have them on visual. Channel D. As you predicted, they're releasing probes."

"Thanks," Korie replied. As curious as he was, Korie waited until he and Hodel arrived at the tip in the *LS-1187*'s hull. Leen was right. He'd made it look *horrible*. Korie wondered if perhaps he hadn't overdone it.

He anchored himself to the hull of the ship and punched for Channel D; the inside of his helmet refocused to show him the reprocessed view from the ship's telescope.

The enemy vessel was large enough not to be a pinpoint, but it was distant enough not to be a clear image either. The view was blurry and uncertain.

Korie grunted. "Well, at least we can see them now. I'm sure we'll all get a better look before this is over. After their probes see how bad off we are, they'll move in closer. For the kill—or the capture. Everybody be patient. If we were to fire anything from this distance, they'd see it and pop back into hyperstate before it could arrive on target. Then they'd hit us with their fringe. Everybody relax and keep your stations green. There's going to be a lot of waiting." He cleared the image. "Li?"

"Both torpedoes are ready." Li handed Korie a remote unit. "Flip the plastic cover and the unit arms itself. Press the green button and the fish wake up and go to standby. Targeting will be automatic for any mass larger than the *LS-1187*. Press the red button and they go. Breakaway is automatic. I've got a duplicate box, and Hodel is patched into the circuit too."

"Good." Korie clipped the box to his belt.

"The first of the probes are arriving," Hodel announced. "They're looking at us with everything they've got. It's a full-spectrum scan. You guys should smile and wave. They're looking at the labels on your underwear.''

''It's all right,'' said Li. ''I'm not wearing any underwear.''

''Sure—give the Morthans a thrill,'' said Hodel.

''Or a scare,'' added Korie, with a grin. ''Well, did they get a good look?''

''They're still looking—''

''Whoops, I can confirm that,'' Korie said. One of the probes was suddenly visible in the distance. It was approaching the side of the *LS-1187*, moving almost directly toward Korie and the hole in the hull. It was a chunky thing, almost deliberately unaesthetic. Lenses and antennae protruded from it like porcupine quills. A single small high-intensity mass-driver looked as if it had been inserted directly through the center of the unit. Out of the corner of his eye, Korie saw another probe approaching the bow of the ship and focusing on the torpedo there.

The closer probe came to a halt uncomfortably close to Korie—only a dozen meters away. Korie could see its lenses swiveling and refocusing as it photographed the damage to the ship. ''Let them get a good look,'' said Korie, whispering in spite of himself. Slowly, he pulled the disruptor rifle off his back and armed it; but he did not point it at the probe. Not yet. . . .

''Can I express an opinion?'' asked Li.

''Go ahead,'' said Korie.

Li faced the probe head on, raised his right fist before him, and slowly, elegantly, extended his middle finger.

The probe did not react immediately. Then one lens after another swiveled to study Li's defiant posture. Despite himself, Korie aimed his weapon.

Suddenly the probe flashed—a single bright flare of energy. The beam was invisible, but Li exploded instantly. From the center out, he ballooned and shredded.

Korie reacted in the same instant. Screaming, he squeezed the trigger. The probe disintegrated. He whirled to fire on the second one, but it was already exploding. Hodel had caught it with the bow guns.

And then silence. The pieces of flesh and bone and plastic spun away into the darkness and were lost forever.

The loudest sound in the universe was Korie's own choking

breath inside his helmet. He was screaming. He was swearing. He was incoherent. The words were bubbling in rage and spittle. Everything was red—

"Sir!" Hodel was screaming in his ear. "Are you all right?"

Korie heard the words and couldn't answer. He wanted to pound something. He wanted to hurt someone, anyone. He would have smashed his fist into the face of God—

"I'm—okay," he said. "Just don't say anything for a minute."

LORD OF THE DRAGONS

"Sir? They're moving in."

"I got it," said Korie. He took a sip of water from his helmet nipple. *I gave him permission. I told him he could do it!* He spoke and his voice was a rasp. "Don't anybody else express an opinion. Ever. I mean it. I'm not joking."

Hodel did not reply.

After a moment, Korie asked, "Where are they now?"

"Closing fast in real space. High-gee acceleration."

"That's to intimidate us."

"It's working."

"E.T.A.?"

"Three minutes."

Korie switched his helmet to pick up the visual again. The image was clearer now; still blurry, but resolving sharper and sharper as he watched.

At first, she was just a pattern of light, an orange blur, a flame-colored presence. Then she began to take shape, an angular, dragon-headed wedge; she filled out with detail. She showed her teeth, she was all points and edges, and she was studded with quills and embers. She opened her eyes and glared. She was the *beast*, and her masters knew it. The gigantic numbers on her side were 666. Her face was painted like a dragon from hell.

"So that's what you look like, you son of a bitch—"

The image swelled in front of him, and swelled and swelled again. The *Dragon Lord* wasn't a starship. She was a city. She was a monster. She was a wall of guns and torpedo bays.

And I thought to challenge that?

The knot of doubt began in Korie's belly, began creeping up toward his throat—

He cleared the image in his helmet, hoping to escape—

But the gigantic ship was already *here*. It filled the universe in front of him. It blazed with light and glory. Korie was caught with vertigo and fear. He felt as if he were looking down on a cityscape from a great height, and at any moment he might tumble headlong into it. His rifle was forgotten in his hands. His ship was forgotten. The torpedoes and the remote on his belt—

"Holy buffalo shit. Look at all the fucking Indians." That was Hodel's voice. Korie blinked and realized that his acting exec was quoting the punch line of an old joke. What were Custer's last words? The reference was appropriate—and it was enough to shock Korie out of his horrified reverie.

Are they going to demand our surrender? He wondered.

His own doubt answered him. *Why bother? We're useless to them. We have nothing they could want. Oh, Lord—I really miscalculated this one.*

"Any signals?"

"No, sir. Nothing. They're just looking us over. They're hitting us with a lot of heavy-duty scans. I don't think we have any secrets anymore."

"Agree."

What are they waiting for? Why not just blast us and be done?

"Should we—" Hodel started to ask.

"No. If they wanted to destroy us, they'd have done it already." Korie gulped and swallowed hard. "Let's not start anything. They've got all their guns trained on us. If I farted sideways, they'd shred us in an instant."

Oh, God, I'm so stupid. I should have known we didn't stand a chance.

What are they waiting for?

And then Korie did something he never thought he would ever do again.

He prayed.

Oh, Lord—whoever or whatever you are—I know you must exist, because of the beauty and order of this universe. Please forgive me my blasphemies and hear this desperate plea. Please save the lives of these good men and women who trusted me, who put their faith in my judgment and their souls in my hands. They deserve better than this terrible and lonely death, here in the desolate rift of night. Please, Lord, please—

"Mr. Korie?"

"What?"

"They're moving—"

"What?!"

"They're turning."

Korie looked across the gulf to the great wall of metal and ceramic and plastic and saw that it was true. Hodel was right. The great flame-streaked ship was moving. It was turning. Majestically, its great head came swinging around as it oriented itself toward a new course.

The gigantic painted head of the ship was facing him now. Korie stared into the mouth of the dragon. It was all missile tubes. He could imagine them firing all at once—how many? Fifty? Five hundred? These were the teeth of the dragon— Korie felt as if he was tumbling into its mouth.

"They're moving off—"

The mouth of the dragon continued to expand in front of Korie—and then it passed over him, moved silently over his head. He looked up at its endless belly, awestruck. He turned to watch the great ship as it moved away, looked after it as it shrank into the distance, receding to a bright point of light.

What was happening? Why didn't they—?

"Everybody hold your positions," he said.

"What's happening?" Hodel's voice.

"I don't know—" *Oh, my God. Yes, I do.* "Uh—I think they saw our missiles. I think they recognized that it was a

Mexican standoff." He couldn't believe he was saying it even as the words came out of his mouth.

Will they believe it? Korie wondered. *They have to*, he told himself desperately. He knew that he was only moments away from a quivering nervous reaction. He wondered if he was going to be able to get back inside the ship before it hit.

He started working his way slowly back toward the air lock.

I've looked into the dragon's face. I know. The dragon wouldn't back away from a challenge. They didn't back away from this one. There wasn't any challenge here for them.

Korie knew what had happened. His throat was tight; his chest was constricted; he felt as if he couldn't breathe.

Li had given the dragon the finger. Li had insulted the dragon. In return . . . the dragon had insulted Li's ship.

It looked us over and decided we weren't worth killing. The ultimate Morthan insult: "I don't want your blood on my sword."

As he floated past the fluctuator spine, Harlie's voice whispered in his ear. "Mr. Korie. Private discussion?" Korie glanced at his monitors. Harlie had sealed the channel; they wouldn't be overheard.

"Go ahead, Harlie."

"I believe your analysis of the situation may be inaccurate."

"In what way?"

"It is obvious to me that the analogy of a Mexican standoff is inappropriate to this situation. We had no chance at all of damaging the *Dragon Lord*."

"Agreed."

"Then why did you tell the crew that we did?"

"I thought we were going to be killed, Harlie. I was certain of it. I could not see any way for us to survive."

"That was my analysis too."

Korie stopped himself at the aft air lock, but made no move to enter. He looked up beyond the curve of hull toward the mindless stars. "So I thought about ways to die. And—all I could think was that I didn't want us to die a coward's death. I knew we didn't stand a chance. I never believed we could even hit them, but I knew we had to go down fighting—"

"I understood that part too."

"And then at the last moment, I flinched. I didn't want to

die. I didn't want the crew to die. I didn't want the ship destroyed. I prayed to God to let us live."

"That is understandable too, but that is not my question, Mr. Korie."

"I know what your question is, Harlie—I'm trying to answer it. They let us go. We're not worth killing. Li gave them the finger; they gave it back to us. They said, 'So what?' They came in close to show us—to show *me*—how big they were, how invulnerable they were, how puny and infinitesimal we were in comparison. They want us to know that. They want us to go home demoralized, telling everybody that the Morthans are bigger and stronger and smarter.

"Can you imagine what that would do to this crew? We wouldn't be able to hold our heads up in public. We'd be a disgrace not only to ourselves, but to our whole species. And our guys are smart. They'd figure it out long before we got home what kind of reputation this ship is going to have, and the shame that her crew would share.

"After everything we've been through, this crew deserves better. I'll lie to them, yes, to protect their confidence and self-esteem. We can't lose our spirit now; we'd lose our need to survive. It's at least four months from here to Stardock. Do you think we could make it with a crew that didn't care anymore? Yes, Harlie, I lied. I lied to save them. It's a terrible lie, but I couldn't think of a way to tell the truth that would ease the terrible shame. I couldn't find a victory in it without lying. I made a promise to Captain Lowell that I wouldn't lie to this crew and I have broken it over and over and over. It just keeps getting deeper. But I don't know what else to do. I need you to back me up, Harlie."

"I can't lie, Mr. Korie."

"You said you could to ensure the survival of this ship. Well, this is a survival issue."

"The morale of the crew is a survival issue?"

"It always has been."

"I see. You have given me a moral dilemma."

Korie smiled. "The Harlie series is supposed to be very good at moral dilemmas."

"Creating them, not solving them."

"Sorry, that's my job."

"Mr. Korie, I must advise you that the dilemma this

situation will cause me may further impair my ability to function as a useful member of the crew.''

"I understand that. Do you understand the necessity?''

"I do not share the same experience of human emotions, Mr. Korie, so I cannot understand the necessity for this fiction. I simply do not see the same problem that you do. We have survived. Isn't that victory enough?''

"Trust me, Harlie. Mere survival is never enough. That's just existence. People need to succeed. People need to feel good about themselves.''

"Mr. Korie—will you help me then? Please make this a direct order.''

Korie considered the request. "Yes, I understand your need. This is no longer a request. Consider it a direct order.''

"Thank you.''

"Mm,'' said Korie. "Thank it.'' He pressed the panel to open the air lock hatch and pulled himself into the ship. But as he did, one terrible stunning question hit him right in the middle of his soul.

We're still alive! Did God hear me?

He turned and looked back out at the emptiness.

Thank you, he whispered in his mind. And wondered . . . *Am I talking to myself again?*

HOMEWARD

Korie entered the Bridge to applause and cheers.

Embarrassed, he held up a hand to cut it off. "Belay that." He took a breath and looked around. The expectant looks on the faces of the crew disturbed him. They were so *exhilarated*.

"Um," he said. He plucked his headset from the command chair and put it on. He spoke to the whole crew of the *LS-1187* now. "You did good. All of you. And I'm proud of you and proud to be on the same ship with you. But the celebration is a little premature. We're not out of this yet. There are other Morthan ships in these woods, and they may not be as smart as the *Dragon Lord*. So, let's keep to our original plan. Chief Engineer Leen, power up the mass-drivers. Let's start home."

He could hear the cheering throughout the ship.

"Uh, sir—?" Hodel floated forward. He was holding something behind his back. "Um, the crew—we have a gift for you. We were going to wait till we got home to give it to you, but well—we think now is a better time." He brought out a large flat box and pushed it toward Korie.

"Huh?" Korie was startled. So much was happening so

fast. He fumbled open the box. Inside was a captain's cap and a jacket. Korie grabbed the cap and held it under one arm. The jacket floated up out of the box—Korie grabbed it, letting the box drift away.

"Turn it around. Look at the back."

It said: **Captain J.T. Korie.**

And below that: **LS-1187**.

"Put it on," Hodel said.

For just a single heartbeat, Korie was tempted; but then he stopped himself and said, "No. Not yet. Captain Lowell is still captain of this ship. Um—I'm really flattered and—moved. This—" Korie found himself unable to put the words together; the flood of emotion was welling up inside of him. He wiped quickly at one eye. "Let me wait until it's official, and then I'll wear it proudly. But I thank you all very much for this. I, uh—I can't think of any gift that could mean more." He grabbed for the box and tried to fold the jacket and cap back into it, but without the help of gravity, it was an uneasy business.

Finally, he just held the box and jacket and cap pinned under one arm and looked embarrassed. "Uh, this is still a starship. And we're still a long way from home. Let's not lose our discipline now—"

And then, flushed with emotion, he retreated from the Bridge before anyone could see how close to the edge he really was.

STARDOCK

It didn't take four months to get home.

It took six and half.

But they made it.

They limped away from the site of the attack and nobody came after them. They were blind and they stayed blind by choice. Korie wouldn't risk opening another scanning lens. It would have been a beacon in the darkness for any marauders still patrolling.

So they chugged at sublight speed, building up velocity incrementally, accelerating for days, then weeks, toward a fraction of lightspeed that could be measured with less than three zeros between the decimal point and the digit.

The crew, what was left of them, worked without rest. Each of them had three jobs. Most of them worked out of the manuals. The oxygen debt was enormous, and Korie had the entire inner hull converted to aeroponics. It worked, but even so they were too close to the margin. There were too many of them and just not enough growing plants.

As they ran low on rations, they began eating the Luna moss, and later the young ears of corn and carrots and potatoes. The winged beans that Korie had planted became a part of almost every meal. They replanted the crops as fast as they ate them. They weren't quite self-sufficient but they'd expanded the window of their survival just enough to allow them time to get home.

But it took so damned *long*. . . .

The singularity had to be kept damped, so the mass-drivers couldn't be run at full power; neither could the fuel cells be recharged to full capacity. That also meant no gravity and limited oxygen reprocessing. Despite Harlie's profound internal monitoring, his reliability kept slipping for reasons neither Leen nor Korie could find. Korie suspected it was the side effect of his moral dilemma and wondered if this Harlie unit was going to have to be wiped and reintegrated.

Worst of all, the hyperstate equipment refused to calibrate. They couldn't go into hyperstate until they'd restored system confidence to 85 percent or better, and with Harlie functioning at less than 85 percent, they couldn't use him to do the job. They had to recalibrate each unit separately, reintegrate the system manually, and hope for alignment. It took seven attempts before they hit 87 percent, and that still wasn't enough for Korie. He made them do it two more times before he accepted that 89 percent was the best he was going to get.

What it meant was *maybe*.

They *might* be able to inject into hyperstate. They *might* be able to steer the envelope. They *might* be able to maintain it safely. They *might* be able to get back to Stardock.

Korie thought about it, long and hard. He talked it over with Hodel and Leen and Harlie, weighed the risks, considered the options, realized there were no other choices. They were just too far away from anywhere to attempt a return at less than superluminal velocities. Finally, he couldn't postpone the decision any longer. He gave the order.

They almost made it.

The hyperstate envelope wobbled like a bubble in a wind tunnel. It was barely controllable. They pointed it and pushed on it and they skated across the intervening space like an ice cube on a hot griddle; first this way and then that, coursecorrecting furiously, and all the while trying not to let the field collapse around them.

The hyperstate horizon went unstable two hours before they

hit their target sphere. Chief Engineer Leen invented six new curses in less than half a second; then he collapsed the envelope.

The *LS-1187* crawled the rest of the way at sublight speeds. Neither Korie nor the chief engineer felt lucky enough to try a second injection.

But they were home.

The Stardock was a deep-space installation, a small city of light lost between the stars. It was girders, globes, platforms, antennae, and work bays. It was fifteen thousand people and two thousand industrial repair robots. It was a safe harbor of warmth in the deepest night. If a captain had the coordinates, he could find it. Otherwise, it didn't exist.

It had always been a welcome port for the ships it served. Except most of them hadn't come back.

The *LS-1187* came in to a near-empty nest. Most of the work bays were empty and almost all of the city lights were out. There were no welcome messages or displays. There was only a quiet acknowledgment of the ship's return and a request for her commanding officer to report immediately to the vice admiral's office.

Korie reported in grimly. He was briefed on the Marathon massacre and the state of the fleet. It was worse than he had thought.

Then he was given the bad news.

IN THE VICE ADMIRAL'S OFFICE

"The Fleet Review Board has determined that the *LS-1187* inadvertently allowed herself to be tracked by the *Dragon Lord*. The *LS-1187* led the Morthan marauders directly to the convoy. If Captain Lowell survives, he'll be court-martialed. And . . ." said the vice admiral, "based on the evidence of your ship's log, your own judgment is highly suspect as well."

"I brought my ship home," said Korie.

"You brought her home with self-inflicted wounds, with her torpedoes unfired and cannibalized for parts, with her artificial consciousness half psychotic for having to maintain a fictitious reality for the crew—" The vice admiral stopped herself. "I will not list the entire catalog of offenses. The important one is that you did most of this without authorization. Your captain was disabled, but you assumed the authority of command before it could be officially logged. You signed termination orders—"

"Ma'am," Korie said, deliberately interrupting her. "This is inappropriate."

"You think so?"

"Yes, ma'am. You are quoting rules at me. Let me quote

one back at you. 'The primary duty of *every* officer in the fleet is to act responsibly—even if that responsibility means acting beyond the scope of assigned authority.' My duty was to bring my ship and my crew home safely. I did so to the best of my ability, and I will not apologize for the steps I took. They were appropriate. I do not see how anyone else could have done different. Or better. If you can demonstrate to me now that there were better choices available, options that would have saved lives or reduced the damage or gotten us home quicker, I would appreciate being enlightened. If you cannot show me such options, then it is inappropriate to question the decisions I took under the circumstances."

"I admire your spirit," said the vice admiral, grimly. "Certainly you survived where others didn't. That must count for something."

"I'm still waiting to hear if there were alternatives to the decisions I made," Korie said stiffly.

"That's not my job," she replied, every bit as stiff. "There may not have been any other choices for you. I give you credit for your imagination and creativity. I give you credit for bringing your ship home. Unfortunately, in this situation, it's not enough."

"Other ships have gotten a hero's welcome for less."

"The *LS-1187* is not another ship."

"We have intelligence on the *Dragon Lord*, including close-range photographs, that no one else has been able to provide. Doesn't that count for something?"

"Unfortunately, as valuable as that information may prove to be, it still counts for very little in this situation. If anything, it works against you. The fleet has been savagely mauled, and the ship that betrayed the convoy also brought home stunning snapshots of the killers. The question is already being asked, *if you were that close, why didn't you put a torpedo into her?*"

"You know why we couldn't."

"I do—but that's because I understand the mechanics of the situation. How many of them *out there* are going to understand? Understand something, Commander. While you've been isolated safely in space, crawling home for the past seven months, the rest of us have had to live with the aftermath of the terrible massacre. There's not a person at

Stardock who hasn't lost someone close. We're all still in shock, we're only now starting to build a new resolve to fight back. The morale here is going to have to be rebuilt on hatred; we have nothing else to motivate our people except a rage for revenge. It's .barely enough. Our people need a target. Because we can't get our hands on the Morthans right now, we're looking for targets we can blame—stupidity, foolishness, ignorance, careless mistakes. Do you understand what I'm telling you? Even if you had destroyed the *Dragon Lord*, it still wouldn't redeem you. The *LS-1187* is a pariah. Your ship, Commander Korie, led the Morthans to the convoy.''

"They could have followed anybody,'' Korie argued. "There was no way any ship could have detected the *Dragon Lord*. She's—an incredible thing.''

"But it was *your* ship they followed. Somebody has to be blamed for the disaster. That's the way these things work. I feel sorry for you, for what you've been through—and for what you still have to endure. But the *LS-1187* and her crew are a political disaster area. No one is going to lift a finger for you.''

Korie didn't answer that. The impact of the vice admiral's words was still sinking in. He felt it in his knees, in his stomach, in his throat, and in the pit of fear at the bottom of his soul. Everything he'd ever lived for—he realized he now stood as a symbol of its betrayal. He felt as if he were teetering on the edge of a precipice. Did he have no chance to redeem himself?

"So, um—'' For the first time, Korie felt abashed. "What's going to happen?''

"I'm not sure yet,'' said the vice admiral. "Nobody wants to make the decision. I don't either. You were handed to me and I was told to find a way to bury you. You know, you had a great future.'' She met his gaze sadly. "I can tell you this. You can forget about getting a ship of your own. That's not going to happen.''

Korie felt as if he were falling, tumbling headlong into the abyss of damnation. His last chance had just been taken away from him. He couldn't swallow. He couldn't speak either. But somehow he managed to get the words out. "I understand. You'll have my resignation on your desk tomorrow morning.''

"Don't bother. I won't accept it.''

"Ma'am?''

"Commander, we still need you."

"Ma'am, this isn't *fair*." Korie could feel his frustration rising. "First, you tell me that we're the worst ship in the fleet, then you admit that nobody else could have done better; then you tell me that I'm not fit to be trusted with a ship, and now you say you won't release me."

"Commander, I'm not interested in fair. If the universe were fair, we wouldn't be having this conversation. Now, listen to me. We need every qualified officer we have. And unfortunately, you more than demonstrated your competence when you brought back the *LS-1187*. I almost wish you hadn't. I don't know what to do with her—and I can't afford to scrap her. The same for you and your crew. The best thing I can think of is to fix you up and send you out again, doing something that will keep you out of sight and out of mind; it'll free another ship for something more important."

"But I can't be captain—?"

"How would it look to promote you now? That's assuming I could find someone to sponsor you. No, you can't be a captain."

"Well then, Ma'am, with all due respect—I cannot continue to serve under these conditions. May I speak candidly?"

"I thought you already were." The vice admiral sighed. "Go ahead."

"I *earned* this command. What my crew accomplished in surviving and bringing back the *LS-1187* is nothing to be ashamed of. The political situation is irrelevant here. These men and women deserve better than this, and so do I. We did an exemplary job. We brought back intelligence that no one else has ever accomplished. It's *wrong* to punish us. You not only deny us, but you deny the fleet the benefit of a crew that has proven itself under fire."

"How many kills did you make?"

"That's not the issue."

"It is now. How many torpedoes did you fire?"

"That's an unfair question."

"No, it isn't. That's the *only* question anymore."

Korie met her gaze directly. "You can't believe that."

"Even if I were to grant the validity of your position—" the vice admiral chose her words carefully. "Even if it were true that you were still qualified to command a starship, there isn't a starship for you."

"The *LS-1187* was to become mine when Captain Lowell retired."

"The point is moot. As soon as we can find a captain who will accept the *LS-1187*, she will be reassigned."

"In that case, Admiral, I must respectfully insist on the right to resign my commission."

"Denied."

"I won't stop trying."

"And I won't stop denying."

Korie shut up. He was trapped. He felt more alone than he had ever felt before in his life.

The vice admiral softened her tone then. She said quietly, "All right, off the record, I agree—it's unfair. But don't use the unfairness of it to be a spoiled child. The Alliance needs you, Commander. I need you to continue as the executive officer of the *LS-1187*."

"No, ma'am. My crew was expecting me to be their new captain before the disaster. They have been expecting it all the way home. If I were to continue aboard the ship now and not be promoted to Captain, my ability to manage this crew would be severely impaired. Plus, if they were to perceive the unfairness of the situation, it would very likely create significant resentment toward any new captain."

"Then I trust that you will not allow them to perceive the situation as unfair—"

"Ma'am, they're not stupid. They'll figure it out. You've got to know that you're looking at a terrific morale problem aboard that ship. As soon as they begin to realize that the *LS-1187* has been branded a Jonah, they're going to start hurting."

"That's one of the reasons we need you to stay on. That crew trusts you."

"No, ma'am. I told that crew they were heroes. I'm not going back there to take it away from them. You're setting this ship up to fail. I've had enough failure for a while, thank you. Find someone else."

"There isn't anyone else," the vice admiral said. "There isn't a qualified executive officer who's willing to transfer to the *LS-1187*. Not with her record."

"Uh-huh? And what about a captain? If you can't find an executive officer—"

"Commander Korie, that's not your concern."

"I beg to differ. It most certainly *is* my concern. You're telling me that you can't find anyone else who wants the ship—but you won't give her to me."

The vice admiral didn't respond.

"That's true, isn't it?"

"Commander, I've let you be candid and I've been candid with you because I need you to understand the difficulty of the situation—"

"Admiral, whatever you do is going to be a difficult decision. So, choose the one that produces the best results for the war effort. Give the ship a new number or scrap her for parts; but if you're not going to let her be a proud ship, don't send her out to be a shamed ship. Don't do that to her crew. Reassign them. Let them serve on other ships."

"We can't do that either."

"I don't understand—"

"I don't know if I can explain it to you. Let's just focus on your situation for the moment. Maybe that'll make it clearer. Personally, I would prefer to accept your resignation. I like it when problems go away by themselves. But I cannot; not without also ordering a court-martial for you, which I will not. *That* would be even more unfair. Neither can I order you back onto that ship if you are so adamantly opposed to it. But I can't put you anywhere else, either. The problem is not just the ship. The problem is you. I doubt that there's a captain in the fleet who will accept you as his executive officer now. You carry the stink of the *LS-1187* with you. And the same is true for the rest of your crew. Keeping them together is the *best* thing I can do for them."

The words hit Korie hard. He lowered his head and looked at his hands in his lap for a moment.

"I'm sorry," said the vice admiral.

"I can't quit. I can't go on. I can't go back." Korie shook his head and looked up again. "Am I allowed an honorable suicide?"

The vice admiral allowed herself the tiniest of smiles. "I'm afraid that's not a viable option, either." She leaned forward, softening her tone. "Jon, I know this hurts. I know it's very bad news. You have to understand that it isn't personal—"

"It sure feels like it."

"This is a crisis situation. We're scrambling like crazy to keep the Morthan Solidarity from finding out just how badly they damaged us. They don't know. They think they hit mostly merchant shipping. They don't know they wiped out most of our heavy cruisers. If they do find that out . . . well, I don't have to tell you what the Morthans have done to the planets they've taken over.

"The only thing I can say to you that I hope will cause you to change your mind is to ask you to consider if the war effort is more important to you than your own personal or career concerns."

"You already know the answer to that question." Korie was offended that he even had to say so. "Ma'am, everything you've said just reaffirms the correctness of my choice. I don't have to be a starship officer to serve the war effort. Considering all that you've just told me, I'd probably be a lot more useful somewhere else. I can go back to Shaleen and work on the orbital assembly lines for liberty ships. I was a stardriver engineer, you know. It seems to me we're going to be needing a lot more starships very soon. And I'm a good crew chief. I can do good and I can feel good about what I'm accomplishing. Let me go. It'll solve your problem—and mine. And it'll put me a lot closer to my family. I'll even get to see them once in a while."

"Dear God—" the vice admiral hesitated. *"Didn't they tell you?"*

"Tell me what—?" Korie's gut was already tightening.

The vice admiral was clearly distressed. "The *Dragon Lord* hit Shaleen three months ago. She scourged the planet. I'm sorry. There were no survivors. There's nothing left."

Korie didn't hear the rest.

You cosmic son of a bitch! I trusted you! I didn't know you put a price on your miracles!

He stumbled to his feet—

There is no God. There is only a malignant practical joker with the morals of a terrorist. I will never trust you again!

MAIL CALL

They gave him a month off.

It wasn't enough.

If they had given him a year off, it wouldn't have been enough.

Everything blurred.

Somewhere in the middle of the debriefing and the sedatives and the physical examinations and the library tapes of the smoldering surface of Shaleen and the mandatory therapeutic counseling, Jonathan Thomas Korie broke down and cried.

He went down to recreation, checked into Rage Co., and pounded on the Morthan android with a club for a while. It grinned at him at first. Then it looked uncertain and finally worried. He beat at it over and over and over again until it fell to its knees and began begging for mercy. It wept and cried and shrieked and very convincingly soiled its underwear.

It wasn't enough.

He took the club and continued pounding. He shattered bricks. He broke a lot of glass. He demolished a house. He raged. He shrieked as hard as he could, trying to force his mountain of grief and anger and madness out through the tiny insufficient funnels of his eyes and mouth. His body betrayed him with its inefficiency. The pressure of his frustration only fueled the volcanic insanity of his fury. He swung and smashed and battered at everything he could reach. He fell down a couple of times, picked himself up, bleeding from cuts, and continued swinging—around and around and around until he collapsed in a sodden heap against one wall, sinking slowly to the floor.

It still wasn't enough.

He walked around in circles then, the tears running down his cheeks. He wept in helplessness. He couldn't stop the sobs from choking up his throat like a painful vise. He didn't have the strength to continue and at the same time he couldn't stop. It just went on and on—until he was too weak even to die.

He lay there on the floor of the chamber and sank into numbed horror. The images of the scoured world tortured his mind.

Not like this. Oh, please—make it not so. They couldn't have died in such horror. Not that way. Not alone.

After a while, he got up, feeling empty and weak and even a little bit silly. He felt wobbly and he staggered slightly as he found his way to the shower. It helped a little, but it wasn't enough.

He went back to the room they'd assigned him and tried calling friends. But there weren't a lot of ships at Stardock right now, and of the ones that were, there weren't many officers who wanted to talk to him. After all, he was from the *LS-1187*.

He slept. He slept for eighteen hours straight.

It wasn't enough. He woke up still tired. He looked in the mirror and his face was puffy and his eyes were red and all the parts of his body sagged as if he were melting away.

There was a small package on the desk.

His mail.

He opened the box—and there was a birthday present from his wife. Written on the card was a simple message: "I love you so much." He slipped the card into the reader, tears already welling in his eyes. He didn't know if he could bear this.

And then they were here in the room with him—*Carol, Timmy and Robby*—laughing and giggling. "Hi, Daddy!

Hi!'' He could see the warm pink sunlight of Shaleen streaming around them. ''We miss you! Come home, please!''

''Give your daddy a hug,'' Carol urged the boys, and they ran forward to embrace him. Their arms wrapped around him. He bent low on one knee and wrapped his arms around them too. The holographic image passed invisibly through him. *Dammit! He couldn't feel them at all.*

Carol stepped forward then and lifted her chin for an unseen kiss. He couldn't bring himself to kiss her back—he could barely see through the tears that were filling his eyes. ''Here's a little promise from me too. When you get back, I'll give you a real homecoming.'' She looked directly at him now. ''Jon, we're so proud of you, but I miss you so much and so do the boys. We wish you were here with us now.''

''I wish I was too. If I had been—we'd be together now.''

But she couldn't hear him. All he had left of his family was this recorded message and his memories.

It wasn't enough.

Nothing would ever be enough again.

When he came back aboard the *LS-1187*, he was a changed man.

There was a new tightness in his eyes and a dark ferocity in his posture. Even when he relaxed, there was a brooding sense of some inner resolve at work, something still unfocused but very *dangerous*.

The crew sensed it immediately—and they distanced themselves accordingly. They bent their heads away from his and hurried quickly to their jobs. Something was *different* about Korie.

Gone was the easygoing manner, the quick wit, and the flashing smile. In its place, Korie had become a darker presence. His compassion had been burned out. In the gap left behind, there was only a smoldering undirected ruthlessness. No one wanted to be the first target of his rage, if and when it finally erupted.

The crew saw the madness in his eyes and shuddered.

THE CREW

The work lights on the hull of the *LS-1187* gave her a garish look. She glittered and blazed against the bottomless night. She was the brightest object in the Stardock.

It was deliberate.

If the Stardock were discovered and attacked, the first ship to be destroyed would be the *LS-1187*. She was bait—and everyone knew it.

But if the Stardock were discovered and attacked, the destruction would be total. Nothing would be left. So it was irrelevant that the *LS-1187* should be so brightly lit.

Except it was also a deliberate insult.

All four of the other ships in their work bays were dark. Work crews swarmed over them with portable lamps. The *LS-1187* was bright—but if any crews worked on her, they came from her own complement.

She was Jonah.

Every ship had a number. Those ships that had tasted blood also had names.

And those ships that had earned a reputation also had *unofficial* names.

The *LS-1187* was Jonah. The jinx.

That was what the crews of the other ships at Stardock called her. Judas had been considered. And for a while, it seemed as if Judas would be her nickname; but eventually the name was discarded because the *LS-1187* wasn't considered smart enough to be a Judas.

She had no captain. And the rumor was that she wasn't going to get a captain.

They couldn't decommission her. She was still classified as functional. But they couldn't send her out again either. No one wanted to sail on her. Her old crew—well, they didn't have a lot of choice; but no one else would willingly accept a transfer to the Jonah ship.

So, she waited.

Her crew knew. The couldn't *not* know. And it had an effect on them. There was work that needed to be done, but it went untended. There was a hole in her hull, and Harlie was still traumatic, and her disruptors were fused. Her systems analysis network was fragmented, and everything else was out of alignment. But the repair work progressed haphazardly, without vision, without care. Chief Engineer Leen tried, but even he was shattered by the despair that pervaded Stardock.

The ship had come home, but she was still adrift. Korie was a dark shadow, and the crew distrusted him now. He hadn't been given the command he'd earned. That meant something, though nobody was quite sure what. There was speculation, but it was futile; everyone knew the real reason. It was the *LS-1187*. She was Jonah.

Her crew waited *and hoped* for someone to arrive and take command. And wondered what was going to happen next. . . .

There were six of them, and they didn't know.

They were fresh out of training; they'd arrived on the latest transport. They were eager and fresh-faced and didn't know what they were walking into.

Their names were Bach, Stolchak, Jonesy, Armstrong, Haddad, and Nakahari.

Lieutenant Junior Grade Helen Bach, Security Officer, was

the shortest of the group. She stood five foot nine in her combat gear. She had a smoldering expression that was its own warning sign. She was of African-Altairian descent and she was not to be treated casually. Rumor had it that she had broken the arm of her karate instructor during the third lesson.

Lieutenant Junior Grade Irma Stolchak, Life Support Technician, stood half a head taller. She was big-boned and friendly-looking, but there was a narrow cast to her eyes—as if she had been hurt once too often and had been left with a terrible suspicion about the rest of humanity.

Crewman First Class Ayoub Haddad, Quantum Mechanic, was of pure Jordanian descent—although none of his ancestors had walked on the soil of Earth for nearly seven generations past. He wore a genuinely friendly expression. He was fascinated by machines, because machines always did exactly what they were supposed to do—even when they broke down.

Crewman First Class Ori Nakahari, unassigned, was the youngest son of a wealthy Japanese-Martian family. He enlisted two days after the mauling at Marathon. His parents had angrily disowned him for giving political concerns a higher priority than family concerns. Ori had not wept.

Lieutenant Junior Grade Valentine Michael Jones, unassigned, was called "Jonesy" because everybody named Jones was called "Jonesy." He was just a little too tall, a little too skinny, and more than a little goofy-looking. The joke about Jonesy was that he was still a virgin—because he wasn't yet certain which sex he was opposite to.

Crewman First Class Brian Armstrong, unassigned, was a side of beef with a grin. He was a big, good-natured champion who looked more like a sexual athlete than a starman. He was quick-witted, good-looking, friendly, and popular, about as perfect a human specimen as could be found anywhere in the fleet. So why was he on the *LS-1187*? Because he'd boffed the wrong bimbo and the bimbo's father had been a vice admiral. 'Nuff said about that.

They were new. They were eager and fresh-faced and they didn't know. They'd come directly from the transport dock and their first glimpse of the *LS-1187* was enough to tell them the worst.

They were on a catwalk overlooking the work bay and the starship gleamed beneath them. The six of them stopped to look at her. Jonesy put his hands against the slanting glass wall. He pressed his face close and his expression glowed. But he was the only one. The others were already realizing what ship this was. Their expressions were sinking fast.

"Come on, Jonesy." Brian Armstrong poked him. "You've seen starships before."

"Not this one. This one's *ours*."

"Wake up and really look at her, Jonesy."

"I don't care. She's still beautiful." But he let himself be led along. The walkway extended the length of the ship, all the way to her stern air lock. The long walk gave them a chance to see every scorch and blister and battle scar on the starship's ceramic hull. This close, they could see how badly she was scored with blast marks and wavy rainbow discolorations—the visible aftermath of being brushed by the fringe of a marauder's hyperstate envelope.

Stolchak spoke her disappointment first. "Look at that. What a mess. We really did it this time."

Armstrong stared out the glass. "I wonder if it's true that she's jinxed—"

Nakahari grinned at him. "Well, she scrambled her own captain. See there? Her port side disruptors overloaded." He shuddered grotesquely and laughed. "Now they say his ghost stalks the inner hull, *howling* for revenge!"

"Knock it off, you guys," said Bach. "She's just another starship."

"Uh-oh," said Stolchak. "Look at that." She pointed to the shadowed numbers on the starship's slender hull. "No name. You know what that means."

"Yeah," said Bach. "Anonymity."

They reached the end of the walkway, turned left along a transverse walk, and found themselves at an access bay, where a docking tube led across to the ship's stern air lock.

There was no one on duty at the bosun's station to check them in. They exchanged curious glances, then one by one, each of the six slid his or her identity card into the reader and waited for it to beep green.

Inside the starship, it was worse. Wall panels hung open, their covers missing or broken. Gaping holes revealed torn wiring harnesses and broken structural members. There were empty places where system modules should have been installed, and internal sensory fixtures hung brokenly from their sockets. The light panels glowed unevenly; many of them had annoying cyclical quavers.

And there was graffiti on the walls. There were posters, and slogans. Raucous music was playing from a rattling speaker and a hyperkinetic voice was bantering: "Good Morning, Starshine! You're listening to Flamin' Damon and the Allied Star Force Distribution Network. Recorded *Live* and *Lively* on YOUR homeworld in New America! Here's one of the classics—"

A cluster of sullen crewmen were lounging near the stern utility shaft. They were unshaven and wearing nonregulation gear. One was wearing a gaudy dashiki, another was wearing only a kilt.

The six new crew members ignored their sideways looks and headed forward through the aft keel. A blue-skinned woman passed them, heading sternward. She was eerily beautiful, tiny-boned and delicately featured. Her hairless skull was outlined with delicate feather-like scales, shading upward to become a purple and crimson mohawk of sensory quills.

Brian Armstrong stopped in his tracks and stared unashamedly. "Wow." he said. "Quillas."

The Quilla giggled and lowered her face to hide her smile, but almost immediately she peeked back up at Armstrong. Her eyes twinkled with promise. He flushed in response, but turned around in his tracks to watch her pass, even walking backward to keep her in sight as long as he could—he was awestruck by her presence—until he backed into a structural member, banging his head sharply. Bach and Nakahari both laughed.

Irma Stolchak was less sanguine. "Oh, great," she said. "That's just what we need—a shared consciousness. Have you ever worked with a massmind? No? Well, I have. What one knows they all know. There are *no* secrets with a Quilla aboard."

Nakahari poked Armstrong. "You'd better be careful. You know what they say about Quillas! You know, their—ahem—"

"Really?" Armstrong was honestly interested.

"That's it on the men here," Stolchak was saying to Bach. "They're not even going to be *looking* at you and me."

Bach shook her head, smiling quietly. "It's all right. I'm not sure I'd want to get involved with any man assigned to this ship."

They reached the engine room then, a three-story chamber built around a large spherical framework: the singularity cage containing the pinpoint black hole that powered the starship and also served as focus for the hyperstate generators. Three huge cylinders pointed into the singularity cage, one from directly above and one coming up from each side, corresponding to the three projections on the ship's outer hull. There were catwalks and ladders all around the cylinders and the framework. Consoles were spotted everywhere, and there were massive banks of equipment dominating the bulkheads both forward and aft. Conduits and cooling tanks lined all the walls. This was the heart of the starship.

At the moment, however, the heart of the starship was having a serious cardiac arrest.

Oily black smoke was pouring out of one of the three great cylinders surrounding the singularity cage. Nobody else in the engine room was paying much attention, except for the two crew members frantically working on it. Haddad noticed, though. Fluctuator sockets were his specialty. He stopped and stared, wanting to do something but not knowing if he should or not. He stepped forward uncertainly.

The other five continued forward, passing two beefy members of the Black Hole Gang, Reynolds and Cappy. Both were dressed casually, in shorts and T-shirts only. Cappy was the bigger of the two, Reynolds was the darker. They were heading aft, rolling an equipment cart before them.

"Uh-oh," said Reynolds. "Fresh meat." He grinned. "Who did you guys piss off?"

Armstrong was still looking back toward the engine room, not at where he was going. He banged into and tripped over the equipment cart and fell flat on his pride.

"Watch it—are you okay?" Cappy asked. He was a broad, stout man. He looked almost as wide as he was tall.

"Yeah, I'm fine," Armstrong said ruefully as he picked himself up. "Sorry."

"You'd better see the doctor about that vision problem. Her name's Williger."

"*Her?*" asked Armstrong. "Is she good-looking?"

"Good-looking? Molly Williger? Uh—" Cappy blinked at the question. His expression went very strange. "Oh, yeah. She's . . . unbelievable!"

Farther forward, Stolchak and Bach had to step aside to let pass several robots and crew members in fire-fighting gear; they were heading swiftly back toward the engine room.

Stolchak shook her head. "This is not my idea of a good time."

The fire team was followed by Korie and Leen. Korie was leading; Leen was shouting at his back. "I'm not doing *anything* until you take a look at it! I am not eating the paper on this one! You hear me?"

"Fluctuator sockets don't diffuse for no reason at all!" Korie shouted back over his shoulder. "I told you I wanted all the assembly valves rebuilt!"

"Dammit—put a scope on it and see for yourself!" Leen pushed past Stolchak, angrily shoving the equipment cart out of the way, and hollered after Korie, "This is the best you can get out of a low-cycle installation. Seven-fifty, max!"

"Bullshit!" said Korie. He pushed Armstrong and Nakahari aside and strode into the engine room. "Those mods are rated to nine-fifty before they redline!"

"Only if confidence is nine or better! This ship is a six! Seven-fifty is your max!"

Leen followed Korie straight to the fluctuator socket. Thick smoke was still pouring out of it. Under the direction of the fire team, the robots were spraying the whole thing with damping foam. Sparks were showering from the cylinder all along its length. The smell of ozone filled the air. Acrid steam roiled outward where the foam spray hit the conduction fields. Haddad was right in the thick of it, dancing and pointing. He had a sodden handkerchief over his nose and mouth. He was directing the fire team as if he were their chief.

Korie said, "Shit," and stepped over to a rugged-looking vertical console. He punched open a panel with his fist and pulled the large red lever inside it. Immediately the conduction fields in all three fluctuators collapsed. It was like being hit with a hammer of air—but the sparking stopped. The steam and the smoke began fading away. The whir of the ventilators increased and a noticeable breeze swept cold air into the engine room.

Korie turned sourly to the two crew members who had been fighting with the system and said dryly, "First, you flush the system. . . ." He tapped out a program on the console. "Then you call up a total system analysis report and look for the anomaly."

He scanned through the system schematic quickly, calling up display after display. All were green. He stopped scrolling through the schematics when he found one with a section in flashing red. He slipped easily into teaching mode and pointed. "All right, what's that? Anybody?" He glanced around and read the name tag on Haddad's chest. "Haddad?" Abruptly he frowned. "How long have you been aboard? You're supposed to check in."

"Uh—" Haddad glanced at his watch. "Thirty seconds."

"Right." Korie pointed again. "What's that?"

"Assembly valve irregularity. Lack of synchronization probably."

"Right." Korie shot a triumphant look to Leen. To Haddad, he said, "Go ahead. Pull it. Let's have a look."

Haddad dropped the duffel he was still carrying over his shoulder and went immediately to work. He put on a pair of thick gloves, opened a panel in the side of the fluctuator, reached in, and unclipped the assembly valve. It was a set of shining interlocking cylinders and modules.

Korie took a fire extinguisher from one of the robots and sprayed the valve to cool it off. He handed back the extinguisher and took the assembly valve from Haddad, quickly unscrewed one end of it, opened it up, and looked inside. He held it out for Leen to see.

Leen looked, but didn't comment.

Korie reached into the chamber and pulled out a burnt something. It looked like a carbonized rat, but without head or tail or even legs; just a clump of charred fur.

"Cute," said Korie. "Very cute. You know what would have happened if we had tried to inject into hyperstate with this in the assembly valve?"

Leen didn't answer. He just lowered his eyes to the floor for a moment, then looked back up to Korie.

Korie nodded. "Right. Find out who did it. And transfer him dockside."

"Not a good idea," Leen said quietly. "The doctor has a whole cageful of those furballs in her lab. Everybody who wants off—" He didn't finish the thought.

Korie met his gaze straight on. "Anyone who would knowingly sabotage this ship's engine isn't *good* enough to be a member of this crew. I still have pride in this ship and I don't want anyone on the crew who can't share the feeling. Find the man who did this and get him off my ship."

"Captain Lowell wouldn't have done that—" Leen started.

Korie cut him off. "Captain Lowell isn't in command anymore. I am." Korie handed the assembly valve back to Leen. "Tear them all down. Rebuild them."

"You're awfully sure of yourself," Leen said resentfully. "I don't see the stripes on your sleeve yet. The scuttlebutt has it you're not getting them—"

"I don't need a captain's stripes to know what's wrong with these engines." Korie added, "Chief—I worked my way through college on a liberty ship assembly line. I was engine calibration crew chief for a year and a half. I signed the hulls of a hundred and sixty-five of these ships. I *know* what they're capable of." And then, in a gentler tone, "And I know what *you're* capable of."

But Leen was too angry to be easily pacified. "Give it a rest. *You know better.* This is the garbage can. FleetComm dumps all their problems here; all their losers, loonies, and lost causes." He added bitterly, "And maybe, if they're real, real lucky, we'll all fall into a star."

Korie was stung, but he was also deliberately patient. "Chief, you have nothing to be ashamed of. Neither does anybody else on this ship. I say so."

"Bullshit! Is that more of your damn lies? We're the bad luck of the whole fleet. Ask anybody. *We're* the reason for the Marathon mauling."

Korie shook his head. It wasn't worth arguing about

anymore. He'd had this conversation too many times already. "Chief—" he said tiredly. "Clean this mess up. Start with your attitude. There are no losers on this ship." He started for the exit.

Leen called after him. "We don't need an attitude check! We need an exorcist!"

Over his shoulder, Korie called back, "If that's what it takes—"

THE EXORCISM

As it happened, Hodel was a licensed warlock.

His business card listed the areas of his expertise: thaumaturgy, light magic, violet sorcery, channeling, planar hexes, lethetic obsessions, despiritualized curses, demonic possessions, ontological constructions, personal spells, love philters, green magic (several shades), orthomatic snake oil (all flavors), and—of particular importance—karmatic exorcisms.

Also, fresh strawberries.

When Korie asked him about snake oil, he replied simply, "How badly does your snake squeal?"

"Never mind."

"I see. You wanted a serious answer?"

"If it's not too much trouble."

"Actually," said Hodel. "It is. You see, to explain magic is to destroy it. But"—he pulled up a chair—"since you insist, here's what you need to know. Magic isn't about the physical universe. It's about the experiential universe. It's about your belief system. Magic works because you believe it works." He pointed at the coffee mug on the table. "I can't cast a spell that will lift that cup up and move it over there.

Magic doesn't work that way. But I can cast a spell that will cause that cup to be moved—someone will pick it up and move it. Coincidence? Not if you believe in magic. And even if you don't believe, the cup *still* got moved. And it doesn't matter what belief system you use to motivate the move or what gods or demons or other sources you ask to power the move; the simple act of casting the spell or working the ritual or saying the prayer shifts *your* relationship to the universe so that the result you want is more likely than it was before."

Korie looked skeptical. "But who gets the credit for moving the cup?"

"Who cares?" Hodel asked. "Does it matter? The important thing is that you got the result you set out to get. That's the way magic works. So, to answer the question you didn't ask, but you're planning to, *yes*, I can cast a spell or lift a curse or perform an exorcism to rehabilitate the karma of this ship. However you phrase it, what you want is to make this crew believe in themselves again. So you have to do something drastic to break the spell of bad feeling that's poisoning this crew and this ship." Hodel glanced at Korie sharply, "And, if you don't mind my saying so, it wouldn't hurt to do something about the black cloud that's floating over your head too."

"I might be a lost cause. Just concentrate on the rest of the ship."

"Sorry, it's all or nothing. The cure has to be total."

Korie studied Hodel for a long moment. "Mike, you surprise me sometimes. I don't know if you're serious or if you're pulling my leg."

"You'll find out when you try to stand up. Do you want the two-dollar exorcism or the four-dollar exorcism?"

"What's the difference?"

"With the two-dollar job, I bathe in chaotic vapors and immolate myself in front of the whole crew. Then I chop myself up into little pieces and throw me into the lake. For four dollars I resurrect myself in a pillar of light and sing all six hundred choruses of *Lulu's Lament* while standing on my hands on the back of a naked unicorn and accompanying myself on the electric bagpipes."

"This is more serious than that, Mike. What can I get for ten dollars?"

"Ten dollars? Gee, I've never had to do a ten-dollar exorcism. I'm not sure my heart can stand it. But for ten dollars, you get *The Secret Sorcery of The Grand Poobah of the Sevagram*. For the finale, I will wrassle the devil himself, two falls out of three, for custody of Hell. Then for my first encore, I drink a whole bottle of trans-Lunar brandy, make love to a feral Chtorran, and kill a Martian woman—I think. Or maybe it's the other way around."

"Right." Korie nodded. "I get the picture."

"Trust me. I'm worth it."

"I dunno. Ten dollars is a lot of money. . . ."

"The ten-dollar exorcism comes with a guarantee—" Mike began.

"I know." Korie grinned. It was an old joke. "If I'm not absolutely satisfied, I don't have to pay and you'll have me repossessed."

"Close enough. If it doesn't work, we'll give you double your bullshit back."

"Hey—" Korie held up his hands. "I can get double bullshit from the admiralty for free."

"Ahh, but not with *my* style."

"Okay," said Korie. "You're on."

The important thing about an exorcism is to dress appropriately.

The crew had gathered in the shuttle bay, the only chamber in the ship large enough to hold all of them at once. Most of them had no idea what to expect, only that Korie had scheduled a blowout to celebrate the successful recalibration of the phase-injector assembly valve modules.

The lights dimmed and there was fanfare. Spotlights probed and searched and came to a final focus on the far end of the room. A puff of orange smoke exploded out of nowhere and Mikhail Hodel appeared in all his gaudy glory.

Mikhail Hodel was wearing a shimmering hula shirt, a glistening confection made of strands of shredded silvery sheet-polymer, extracted from a catabolic converter. The three-foot feathers on his headdress and staff were injection plumes that had been dyed in ultra-gee zylox and soaked in liquid nitrogen, then exposed to explosive decompression in the forward air lock. His scarlet warpaint was antideoxidant gel. The strings of beads and rattles that he wore around his neck and waist, upper arms and wrists, were constructed from interociter spares and pieces of optical conduit. The two glowing hemispheres that made up his steel brassiere were measuring cups from the ship's galley—which did not explain why they were not quite the same size. His codpiece was the bow tube-fitting of a proton torpedo. The entire outfit was lined with neon conduit, flashing diodes of all colors, several Christmas lights and electric ornaments, sparklers, and flash-bombs. He moved in a cloud of smoke and fire and multicolored auras. He was an epiphany of fireworks, lasers, small explosions, whistles, air-bursts, and confetti. Tracks of red and purple light crawled up and down his legs and chest and back.

The crew went wild.

Then he started the music and began setting off the special effects: the lasers and mirror fields, the colored sprays and fountains, the holographic projections and fractal windows—and the cheering and stomping and clapping and hooting and hollering and whistling and yelling hit new crescendos of excitement.

"Oh, Great Ghu!" Hodel invoked the grand spirit of the ceiling. Puffs of sparkling gold smoke rose around him. "Oh, Great Fossil of the Fellatious!" Several small explosions went off around the room, filling the air with showers of sparks. "Oh, Grand Poobah of the Sevagram!" Confetti bombs showered the crew with sprinkles of light.

Hodel lowered his voice to a conversational tone and looked casually up at the ceiling. "Okay, now that I have your attention? I'd like some assistance here." A small firework went off, launched from his tailfeathers. "Rumor has it that this starship is jinxed." Hodel ignored the shouts of agreement from the crew. Flashes of light strobed and sparkled across his body. "Yes, I said *jinxed*." Larger flashes of light spread out from him in widening shockwaves; they rippled out across the whole shuttle bay. "I SAID *JINXED*," he repeated. Puffs of orange smoke flamed up around him. "And what, may I ask, Great Ghu, god of the ceiling—what are *you* going to do about it?"

Very directly, Hodel continued. He spoke now as if he were

speaking to an employee. "Look, we know that the proper way to worship Ghu is to *ignore* Ghu. Ghu doesn't like being bothered. Ghu has more important things to do than worry about a bunch of devolved primates with sexual problems. So the only appropriate way to respect and honor and worship Ghu is to understand that Ghu just doesn't give a shit. The true believers of Ghu know that it is their sworn and solemn duty to leave Ghu the hell alone."

Hodel's voice began to rise. He began to speak in larger and louder and much more excited tones. "Well, Ghu, these brave courageous men and women have been the greatest worshipers of you in the entire universe. Yes, they have been. They have not only ignored Ghu—they have remained totally oblivious to Ghu's very existence. Can Ghu ignore such absolute devotion? Does *Ghu* dare?" Hodel's finger jabbed and the ceiling exploded. Smoke and light and confetti poured outward in ripples of red and yellow and purple afterimages. "I think *not*," said Hodel.

Aggressively, he continued. "We demand our reward now! In *this* life." Several small explosions, like aftershocks, went off around the edges of the shuttle bay. "Otherwise, we're going to make bloody damned nuisances of ourselves. So cut the crap, Ghu. It's time to get off your fat butt and give us some god stuff. We expect you to cast out the bad luck, Ghu! Frankly, it stinks!"

The shuttle bay went almost totally black then. The lights and smoke and sparkles came flashing back up in rhythm, matching Hodel's demanding chant: "Cast out the jinx! Who cares what it thinks! We are the Sphinx! And the jinx just stinks!"

The crew picked up the chant quickly. They shouted it in unison with Hodel, chanting and laughing and waving noise-makers and sparklers.

Standing at the side of the room, Korie allowed himself a grin. *It might work. This is the best ten dollars I ever spent.*

The crew was chanting enthusiastically, louder than ever. "Cast out the jinx! Who cares what it thinks! We are the Sphinx! And the jinx just stinks! Cast out the jinx—"

Hodel held up a hand for silence. The room went instantly quiet.

"Ghu! Give us a sign!"

The shuttle bay exploded with light. Every effect in the room went off at once. All the fireworks triggered. All the smoke, all the flash-bombs, all the noise and whistles and alarms. The holographic projectors poured fountains of colored light into the air. The mirror fields echoed the displays out to infinity. Showers of sparkling confetti exploded outward from the walls and fell streaming from the ceiling. Paper curlicues unraveled to the floor. Thunderous drumbeats pounded the air with animated fire-bursts. And somewhere in the middle of it all, Korie was certain he could hear elephants trumpeting.

"Say what?" Hodel cupped an ear and looked upward. "Could you be a little clearer about that?"

Ghu repeated himself.

It was more of the same—only bigger, better, different. The red seas parted, the volcanoes erupted, the asteroids shattered the surface of the flaming planet, the nova exploded, the lightning outlined them all, Saint Elmo's fire turned them into grinning demons. The imps of Hell danced in the flames that licked around their legs. The Heavens opened and cascades of angels poured forth, singing to raise the dead. Gabriel blew his trumpet. The egg of the Phoenix hatched. The elephants came.

The crew was in hysterics now, cheering, yelling, applauding, shrieking, whistling, stomping their feet, tears streaming down their faces—

And then, abruptly, everything stopped.

The effects faded away. The lights came up. A wave of silence fell across the shuttle bay. As one man, the crew turned to look behind them.

Hodel was the last one shouting. Puzzled, he turned around to see:

Framed in the shuttle bay entrance, filling the hatchway, stood Captain Richard Hardesty.

He looked like a door that had just been slammed.

The top right quarter of his head was metal. His right eye was a shining lens.

Korie spoke first. Loudly, he called, *"Ten-hut!"* The entire crew snapped to attention. Several small fizzing devices scuttled across the floor. Smoke was still rising from the corners; confetti and streamers were still dripping from the ceiling.

Hardesty strode coldly into the center of the room. He was dressed all in black and he was terrifying. The crew was shrinking visibly, withering with fear.

Slowly, Hardesty turned, noticing everything: Hodel, the confetti, the smoke, the mirror-fields, the holographic projectors, the various small noisemakers still losing the last of their air, even the elephant. . . .

Finally, after several eternities, he spoke. His voice was flat and deadly. "Which one of you is . . . Commander Korie?"

Fearing the worst, Korie stepped crisply forward.

"Would you log me in, please?"

"Yes, sir. This way—"

"I know the way," Hardesty said. He turned on his heel and strode for the door. Korie followed him out.

They left a wake of silence behind them. The crew was too terrified to speak. It was Hodel who spoke the first coherent word. "Oh, shit," he said.

Armstrong and Jonesy approached him, puzzled. "What is it?" The other members of the crew also moved in curiously.

Hodel was stunned with the realization. "Oh, my God," he moaned. "It's even *worse* than we thought. We'll *never* break this jinx."

"Huh? Why?" said Armstrong. "Who was *that*?"

"That—" said Hodel, "—that was *Hardesty*."

"The one they call the Star Wolf?" Jonesy asked.

Hodel nodded. "The one and only." He began shrugging off his steel brassiere. "I'm hanging up my bra—I am *never* going to tempt the gods again." He shook his head sadly and pushed past Armstrong and Jonesy. "Next time, they might do something *worse*."

THE CAPTAIN'S CABIN

The captain's cabin hadn't been touched since Captain Lowell's personal effects had been removed. It looked grim.

Hardesty glanced around with obvious distaste, then stepped behind the desk and sat down. He did not invite Korie to sit. He studied the executive officer grimly.

Korie remained at polite attention, refusing to wither under the other's heartless gaze.

Finally, Hardesty broke the silence. "This ship is a mess," he said quietly.

"We're *working* on it," Korie began. "We took a real beating—"

Hardesty ignored Korie's protest. He waved it off. "I've been looking over your records. I don't like what I see."

"Excuse me, sir? What's your point? We still have three weeks of refit before preliminary inspection."

Hardesty's look was deadly. "The point is, *I'm taking command of this ship*, and I want her spotless."

Korie tried, unsuccessfully, to conceal both his surprise and his anger. "Sir! I was not informed of that."

"The decision was made only an hour ago."

"I—yes, sir." Korie remained at attention.

"You, what?"

"Nothing, sir."

"Say it. You can't hurt my feelings. I don't have any." Hardesty tapped the right side of his head, the metal side. "They took them out."

"Nothing, sir—it's just that, well, I was operating under the assumption that I would be allowed to retain command of this ship—because there wasn't a captain in the fleet who was willing to take her."

"You assumed wrong."

"Yes, sir."

"I suppose you think this isn't fair, that this ship should be yours."

"Sir. Captain Lowell had recommended my promotion—"

"Captain Lowell is dead. And considering the lack of judgment he displayed in leading the Morthans straight to the convoy—and the mauling at Marathon—"

"We had no way of detecting them. The *Dragon Lord* has one of the largest hyperstate generators ever built. They could see us for years. We couldn't see them."

Hardesty continued as if Korie hadn't even spoken. "—when you consider his entire history of bad decisions, leaving you in command of a starship, any starship, hardly seems appropriate. Leaving you in command of this one in particular strikes me as especially stupid and foolhardy." Hardesty glanced over and locked eyes with Korie, almost as if daring him to argue.

Korie considered his options. He didn't have any. He took a breath. "Are you asking for my resignation? I've tried to submit it three times already. I would be happy to submit it again if you will accept it."

Hardesty allowed himself the thinnest of smiles. Respect? Malice? Korie couldn't tell. "Unfortunately, no, I am not asking for your resignation. But since you ask, yes, I did request another executive officer. Seeing as how I'm bringing in a new astrogator, a new security chief, and a new weapons pecialist, it seemed appropriate. But, ah . . . as you may have heard, no one was available."

"Yes," said Korie, choosing his words carefully. "I've heard. Thank you for your honesty. Is there anything else, sir?"

"Yes, there is. What was the purpose of that little . . . demonstration in the shuttle bay?"

"A party. *They earned it.*"

"I don't agree," said Hardesty. "This ship is a disgrace. We're going to clean it up." His tone hardened. "You need to know this. *I'm not Captain Lowell.* I'm not a nice man. And I'm not here to make friends. I have only one job in life: Destroy the Morthan Solidarity. Do you know what *your* job is?" He looked into Korie's eyes and waited.

Korie stared right back. This time he chose his words even more carefully than before. "My job is to make sure that *your* job gets done."

Hardesty relaxed. He almost smiled. "Very good," he admitted. "And your disappointment about not getting a command of your own—that won't get in the way?"

Korie was offended at the question. He stiffened before he answered. "Sir. You can count on me to serve you and this ship to the best of my ability."

Hardesty grunted. "They told me you would say that." His nod was a gesture of acceptance. "Listen up. You and I don't have to like each other. In fact, I would prefer it if we didn't. It would make it a lot easier for me to continue to believe that you are a stupid fool. But we do have to work together, and that does require a minimum of respect."

Hardesty waited, but Korie had nothing to say in response. The silence stretched painfully while the captain studied his exec.

Finally Hardesty realized Korie wasn't going to answer. He retook control of the interview. "All right—let's make a deal. You train this crew to live up to Fleet standards, and I'll train *you* to live up to *mine*. And maybe then you'll be ready to be a captain—agreed?"

"Do I have a choice?"

"Actually? No, you don't."

"Then it's not much of a *deal*, is it?" Korie smiled. "At

best, it's an order. At worst, it's a contract made under duress."

"I see—yes. You have a point. But, it's irrelevant to me. All I want to know is one thing. Will I be able to depend on you?"

"That has never been the issue . . . *Captain*."

"We'll see, said Hardesty. "We'll see."

CHIEF OF SECURITY

Korie stepped up from the keel into the Operations bay under the Bridge. The Operations bay was a tiny chamber, all consoles, keyboards, and screens. Only two of the work stations were manned, but both were all green.

He climbed up three more steps and onto the Operations deck. As he came up the steps, he could see the holo-table was showing an internal schematic of the ship. Ahead, the forward viewer was focused on the distant unmoving stars; it was a cold and dispassionate window.

He knew there was something wrong even before he finished climbing up onto the Ops deck. The silence warned him. The looks on the faces of the other crew members told him—

Korie turned around and *froze*.

The entire Ops deck crew was staring at Lieutenant Commander Brik. He was nine feet tall. He was four feet wide at the shoulder. His muzzle was striped with red and orange fur. His fangs looked as long as Korie's hand.

He was a Morthan Tyger.

Morthan. A genetically augmented, bioengineered, tailored-in-the-womb product of directed evolution. That part of the species that had taken control of its biological destiny and created itself as something fearsome.

Tyger. A subspecies of Morthan warrior. The meaner side of the family.

What do you get when you cross a nine-foot Zen linebacker with a saber-tooth tiger? You get Brik: a Buddhist gorilla.

He was awesome. He was all meat and bone and muscle. He smelled of hot desert sands tinged with blood. He was Korie's worst nightmare. And he was grinning.

He was wearing a fleet uniform. Korie was horrified.

The other officers and crew on duty were frozen at their posts. Chief Engineer Leen, waist deep in a dismantled console, was visibly smoldering.

Abruptly, Captain Hardesty appeared on the Bridge, ducking through one of the rear doors and stepping forward to lean across the Bridge railing. "Ah, I see you've all met the new chief of security . . . Lieutenant Commander Brik. You have a problem, Mr. Korie?"

Korie whirled around to face the captain. "Yes, sir. I do. There's a Morthan on the Bridge."

Hardesty ignored Korie's anger. He said quietly, "There are humans fighting for the Morthan Solidarity. There are Morthans fighting on the side of the Allies. It's a big war. There's room enough for everybody." He added, "Commander Brik is here because I asked for him—because he's the best damned security officer this side of Hell."

Korie turned resentfully and looked at Brik. Actually, he looked at Brik's chest. He took a step back and looked up—and up—and up again.

Brik grinned. His incisors were even longer than Korie had thought. Brik spoke. His voice rumbled like a warship. "*I* am not your fight," he said to Korie. "Your fight is . . . out there."

Korie glared up at the Morthan warrior. "I know that," he said testily. "Where's *your* fight?"

Brik moved slowly, so as not to alarm anyone. He touched his own heart gently. "My fight is in here. . . ."

Korie didn't expect that, and he didn't know how to react to it. It wasn't an answer he could respond to. Finally, he just snorted and turned away in disgust, a deliberately calculated performance of rudeness. He stared at the screens on the console in front of him, not seeing them at all, and forced himself to breathe evenly. He could feel his heart racing, his rage building.

Somebody tapped his arm gently. He turned around and looked. He blinked. He didn't recognize her. She was a handsome woman in her late thirties or early forties, very crisp and very military.

"Commander Korie? Lieutenant Commander Cygnus Tor. Astrogator."

"Uh—" Korie was off balance. "Tor. Good to meet you. Are you familiar with the, uh—" He was still rattled. "—the, uh—"

"The Model sixteen low-cycle fluctuators?" Tor guessed correctly. "Yes, I am. I—"

"Good," said Korie, distractedly. Abruptly, he made a decision. "I'm sorry. Excuse me a moment." He turned away from Tor, turned back to Brik, and extended a hand. "I'm sorry. I was rude. Let's work together." It was a visible effort for him.

Brik nodded slowly and held out his hand. It was immense. He shook Korie's hand gently. Gently, that is, for a Morthan. Despite himself, Korie counted his fingers as he massaged the blood back into his hand.

The sudden grating sound of the alarm klaxon bleated across the Bridge. The Bridge lights went red, the consoles began flashing, and above it all, Harlie was speaking in a preternaturally calm voice: *"Engine room malfunction.* Magnetic instability in the number three singularity control. Fluctuator overload. Assembly valve failure. Stand by to disconnect. Singularity escape *will* occur"—Harlie paused for half a clock-tick—"in three minutes."

Korie looked up, startled. All the work stations around him lit up red. The ops crew leapt for their consoles. Leen dived into the operations bay. Tor slid into her seat at the helm console. Hodel dropped into the chair next to her and punched his station to life. The console flickered brightly, then went dark. Hodel slapped the panel—*hard*—and it lit up again. Hardesty stood on the Bridge and watched it all.

Everywhere there was panic, confusion, and dismay. The readouts were normal—and they weren't. The magnetic cage containing the pinpoint black hole that powered the ship was about to fail. If that happened, the singularity would drift inexorably out of the cage and begin devouring the starship and everything connected to it.

It seemed as everybody on the Ops deck was talking into their headsets at once or punching madly at their keyboards. Korie moved quickly from station to station. Brik stepped quickly out of his way; he moved up onto the Bridge and stood next to the captain.

In the Ops bay, Chief Engineer Leen was watchdogging three consoles at once. "Magnetic clamps, now! Full field! Downcycle—program beta."

Lightning was flashing in the keel again. It looked like a replay of the disastrous disruptor overload.

It was even worse in the engine room. The lightning was brighter and fiercer and strong enough to knock a man unconscious. The engine room crew couldn't get near their controls. Crew members in bulky protective suits were rushing to their posts.

The static discharges rolled down the corridors of the ship, clustered around the singularity cage, and then bled out through the hyperstate fluctuators. More lightning crackled across the outer hull. The entire ship was enveloped.

"The singularity *is* wobbling," Harlie reported. "Loss of focus is imminent. Singularity escape will endanger Stardock. Singularity escape *will* occur"—half a clock-tick—"in two minutes."

Korie made a decision. "Prepare for emergency breakaway."

Hodel was already talking to his headset. "Secure all bulkheads! Seal the main air lock. Go to standby power. Disengage all power bays—" It was happening even as Hodel spoke. They could feel the hatches slamming down throughout the ship. The main air lock clanged shut with a terrible bang, cutting off the panic-stricken escape of two crewmen running madly for the docking tube. They pounded on it desperately.

In the engine room, power shunts cut in and the lightning became focused. They were bleeding it deliberately into the hyperstate fluctuators now—but the workmen were terrified; they knew how bad it really was. In the Ops bay, Leen was shouting at the machinery. "Respond, damn you!"

Korie couldn't wait any longer. "Disengage from Stardock immediately."

The starship lurched as the mooring bolts unclamped. And then the ship was moving, drifting outward and away from the work bay, the lightning still flickering wildly across her hull.

"Emergency breakaway complete," Harlie reported. "Escape velocity thirty kilometers per hour. The Stardock is no longer in danger." A heartbeat later, Harlie added, "Singularity escape *will* occur in—one minute."

Hodel was pounding on his console and shouting into his headset. "Goddammit! It's all coming up garbage. Where's the baseline?" He listened for a moment. "No time! Disengage the fluctuators!" He was angered by the response. "Do it, dammit!" He watched his screen, waiting anxiously.

Behind him, Korie was shouting into his own headset. "Emergency life-support! Clear the engine room! Prepare for emergency deplosion. Hull diffusion—" He looked over Hodel's shoulder, then spoke again. "Dammit! Clear the engine room! I'm going to snuff that sucker!"

But even as he was saying his last words, the alarm klaxon faded away and the Bridge lighting returned to normal. The lightning flickering throughout the ship began to subside and fade away.

Korie's last words were still ringing in the air as the various crewpeople on the Ops deck shut up and looked around at each other in confusion. Korie was suddenly embarrassed.

In the Ops bay, Leen was shattered. He'd failed. He knew it. He put his head into his hands.

But—they were still alive.

And then, Harlie said, "Singularity escape *has* occurred. The starship has been destroyed." And then, to add insult to injury, he quietly added, "End of simulation. Efficiency rating . . ." Harlie hesitated while he computed. "*Unsatisfactory.*"

Korie was stiff and expressionless. He'd been had and he knew it.

"A drill!" Hodel flung himself back in his chair, frustrated, annoyed, and disgusted. "A fucking drill!"

Korie turned around slowly to look at Hardesty. Hardesty

returned the stare calmly. He looked down coldly, but before he could speak, Leen climbed back up onto the Ops deck. He was furious. "That was a dirty damned trick!" he shouted at Hardesty.

"Thank you," the captain acknowledged. He looked past Leen to Korie. "Now you know why this ship never earned a name." He let his gaze travel around the room, piercing the souls of each of the men and women at their stations. "The *LS-1187* came into Stardock needing three weeks of interior work, four weeks of equipment refits, and six weeks of hull regrowth, all of which could have been done concurrently. That was a month ago. Systems analysis reports that this vessel is still *eight weeks* away from being space-ready. This is not a good record.

"The reason that your efficiency is so low is that you think you have a choice. *You do not.* I have just eliminated the alternative.

"New work schedules will be posted at 0600 hours. Commander Tor, bring us back to Stardock. Brik, get a security team together and break up the still in the inner hull. Mr. Korie, my cabin, ten minutes."

Hardesty turned and exited crisply.

Brik looked around the room and grinned. It was not a pleasant sight.

Hodel was stunned. He glanced across at Korie. Korie wouldn't meet his eyes. He looked at Tor, but she was already at work, targeting the ship back toward Stardock. "How'd he know about the still?" Hodel asked.

Tor didn't even glance up. "There's *always* a still," she said. When she did look up from her console, she noticed that Korie was still standing in the same place. He was rigid with fury. "You don't look very happy, Mr. Korie."

"Happy?" Korie's reply was as cold as the captain's. "The *Dragon Lord* kicks the crap out of us. The fleet gets mauled. Captain Lowell gets killed. The ship is labeled a jinx. I get my career dead-ended. And now . . . I've been publicly humiliated. Happy? I'm just thrilled."

From above, Brik said quietly. "Don't mince words, Mr. Korie. What are you *really* angry about?"

Korie whirled to stare up at him. "I don't even want to talk to *you.*" And then, in explanation, he said, "My wife—and my two sons—were killed in a Morthan attack. So you'll forgive me if I'm not overjoyed to be working with you."

Abruptly embarrassed, Korie exited through the Ops bay, leaving Tor and Hodel and the others staring curiously after him.

Tor turned back to her console and resumed locking in a course. Very softly, to no one in particular, she said, "For some reason, I have the feeling that this is *not* going to be a happy enterprise."

DECISIONS

Korie stepped into Hardesty's cabin and stood rigidly before
the captain's desk. Hardesty didn't even glance up; he was
studying something on his desk screen.

"First of all," he began without preamble. "I know what
you've been through. I read your file. I know the craziness
that drives you. It's ripping you apart. You haven't healed
yet. Maybe you never will. It's left you confused. You don't
know if you should be a ruthless bastard or a compassionate
healer. Well, neither one of those roles is right for a starship
officer; although, I will tell you, ruthless bastard does have
some advantages." Hardesty gestured. "Sit down."

Korie sat.

"Lesson One: You're going to have to learn to control your
temper. Hide your feelings from the crew. The crew is a
sponge. Whatever you put out, they will soak up—and they
will give it back to you amplified a thousand times over.
That's what's wrong with this ship right now. Your crew
doesn't know who you are, so they don't know who they're
supposed to be. That's the first thing we have to fix.

"Lesson Two: This is not a democracy. No warship ever is.

But you've been running this ship as if your crew gets to vote on every decision. Your chief engineer, for example, argues every order, so every damn crew member on this ship thinks his opinion means something too. Bullshit. Opinions are like assholes. Everybody has one and they're all full of shit. You—Mr. Korie—stop worrying about being popular. If a crew likes an officer, he isn't doing his job. Your only job is to produce results, nothing else. If the crew isn't doing their job, you're not doing yours. Am I getting through to you?''

Korie swallowed. His throat hurt with the pressure of all he was holding back. ''Yes, sir.''

''But you don't like it.''

''I don't have to like it, sir. As you say, my feelings on the matter are irrelevant.''

Hardesty grunted. ''Good answer. You're learning. I don't think you believe it yet, but I don't care. You can start by learning the language. The understanding will come later.''
He reached for a folder and opened it. ''All right,'' he said, turning to the first sheet of paper inside. ''We're not playing Good Cop/Bad Cop here. Do you know that game?''

''Yes, sir. Some captains delegate all the unpopular orders to their exec so he can take the heat.''

''Right. Well, I don't believe in that. If an unpopular order has to be given, the captain should take responsibility for it himself. Also''—he tapped the right side of his head, the metal-plated prosthesis—''This particular handicap makes me a lot less *likable*, so if we were to play that game, you'd have to be the good cop, I'd have to be the bad cop. I can't run a ship that way either. For obvious reasons.''

''Yes, sir.''

''That's the other reason why you have to stop being popular. You understand? Because like it or not, we're already halfway into a game of Good Cop/Bad Cop and I won't have it. It weakens my authority.''

''Yes, sir.''

''So what we're going to do instead is Bad Cop/Bad Cop. Do you know how to play that game.''

''No, I don't.''

''It's very easy. I'm the meanest son of a bitch in the galaxy. You're the second meanest son of a bitch. The crew will hate me. They'll hate you. And this ship will get a reputation as being a very unpleasant duty. But we'll get results. And after we start getting results, the crew will start bragging about being on this ship and they'll consider it a privilege to wear her colors. I know what you're thinking. You're thinking about this ship's reputation now. Forget it. Forget the past. The past is dead. Because you and I say so."

"Yes, sir."

"You disagree with that?"

"No, sir. You're the captain."

"What does one have to do with the other?"

"You give the orders. We'll do whatever you say."

"Mr. Korie—" Hardesty put his papers down. "I don't want an executive officer who's a flunky or a yes-man or an echo. I want an executive officer who is capable of taking responsibility and using it appropriately. That means that in the privacy of this cabin, I expect you to argue with me if you think that I am making a bad decision."

"Yes, sir."

"Now, I know damned well—just from reading the expression on your face—that you hate what you're hearing. If you think I'm wrong, I expect you to tell me so."

"Sir—may I speak?"

Hardesty waved a hand.

"You want me to disagree with you? Fine, I will. But you have already stated in no uncertain terms how you want this ship run. You made it quite clear that there is no room for negotiation in that position. Fine. I'll do what you say. But to argue with it now seems to me to be a waste of time. I will only voice my disagreements when I think that doing so will make a difference. Given what you've just said, I don't see that anything I might say right now would make much of a difference, so the best I can say is 'yes, sir' and 'no, sir' and carry out your orders as best as I can."

"Good." Hardesty nodded, satisfied. "That's fair. It's also intelligent." He leaned back in his chair, studying Korie. "Part of a captain's job is to train his executive officer to become a captain too. I can't train a man with no initiative. Don't be a wallflower."

"Yes, sir." Korie sat quietly, waiting for the captain to continue.

Hardesty steepled his fingers in front of him and studied

Korie for a long moment. The lens that replaced his right eye was cold and unreadable. His left eye showed even less emotion. "Is there anything else you want to say to me?"

Korie started to shake his head no, then changed his mind and nodded. This was the hardest thing of all to say, and he didn't know where it came from or even if he really believed it yet, but—"Maybe your way is right," he began. "I don't know. But it's not the way I was trained. I learned management technology and team dynamics as the best way to produce results. We built spaceships and we built good ones. We might even have built this one. I always thought that having your team feel good about their work also means they'll feel good about themselves. Let them have pride in their work; that's the best quality control of all. Your way has an awful lot of hate and fear and stress in it. I don't like it. It feels wrong to me. It feels *bad*. But"—Korie met Hardesty's curious gaze. "—I also know how desperate the situation is. And I know that these choices are not mine to make anymore. And you know more about war than I do. So, I figure the best thing for me to do is shut up and do what I'm told.

"And one more thing. That drill—that hurt. I don't like having my nose rubbed in it. But it's also undeniable proof that something is very wrong here and I want it fixed just as much as you do. Maybe even more so, because it's my career that's in the dumper, not yours. So . . . all right, I'm willing to do whatever is necessary to make this ship work."

Hardesty studied Korie for a moment longer, considering his words. Then he nodded and picked up his folder again. He turned to the second page.

"You had *half* of it right, Mr. Korie. You understood what was wrong—it *is* the crew that has to be fixed. Fix the crew and they'll fix everything else. But you thought you could do it with parties. What's wrong with this crew can't be fixed with a party. You want your crew to feel good? Give them results. Let them take their pride in a job well done." Hardesty put the folder down. "We're going to start by tearing this ship down to the framework and putting it back together. Every structural member, every rivet, every conduit, every system-analysis node, every sensor, every damn thing that can be checked is going to be checked. Then it's going to be rechecked. Then we'll do it again to make sure we did it right the first two times.

"This will accomplish four things. First, it'll give us a new ship, one that we know works. Second, we'll be establishing a new confidence baseline against which to measure system performance. This is what you should have been doing for the past eight weeks. Third, it'll train the crew. A crew member who's taken a piece of machinery apart and rebuilt it by hand will know more about it than the one who wrote the documentation. And finally it'll give this crew a pride in their ship that can't be gained any other way. A crew that's had to repaint and repair every square inch of their starship doesn't put rude graffiti on its bulkheads. They start taking pride in keeping her shining. Question?"

"No, sir. I see you're right."

"You have a look on your face."

"Yes, sir. I see that my mistake lay in the assumption that is was essential to get this ship back into duty immediately."

"*This* ship?" Hardesty raised his one eyebrow. "That's a pretty big assumption. This ship, as she exists today, is worthless to the Alliance. Your crew knows that. They're festering in their own shame and at the same time, they're terrified that you might actually get this ship working again. They're not ready to go out again. Not up against the Morthans. That's why things keep breaking down all around you."

"I'm . . . not sure I understand . . . what you're implying."

"Don't be obtuse. I'm talking about carelessness, mistakes, stupidity, things that happen because people are so frightened or upset or angry that they can't focus on their jobs. These things are happening because these men and women are operating at the level of individuals. They've forgotten that they're a team."

Korie conceded with a downcast nod. Now he was feeling sick. His throat hurt. His eyes hurt. His chest was a pressure chamber. "I should have seen this," he said. "This is a failure for me. I mean, it's a bigger failure than—"

"Shut up. I don't have time to wet-nurse you." Hardesty pierced Korie's attention with an angry look. "Here's the only thing you need to know. I don't waste my time on losers. Criticism is an acknowledgment of your ability to produce results. The reason the crew lost *their* focus is that you lost *your* focus. You said you'll do whatever is necessary to get this ship working. Well, this is what's necessary. You need a kick in the ass. This is it.''

Korie swallowed hard. "Yes, sir."

"Let's go on." Hardesty turned to the next page. "Drills. A lot of them. As we start getting the various systems rebuilt and back on line, I want you to drill this crew until they drop. Over and over and over again. Every single simulation in the book until their scores are flawless—and then we'll start inventing new simulations. Everything. I want cross-learning on the skills too. Break them into teams. Every member of every team has to know every job that his team is responsible for. Then dissolve the old teams and form new ones with new responsibilities and start over. Ideally, I want every member of this crew able to run every station on this ship."

"Sir? That's—"

"I know. I've never yet been on a ship where we succeeded, and I doubt we'll make it here either. But I'll tell you this. Those ships with the highest cross-skill ratings are also the most effective in the Fleet. So that's the goal and I expect you to push for it."

Hardesty passed a sheet of paper across to Korie. "Here's a hard copy for you of the first week's targets."

Korie looked at the list. "Sir? This is—"

"There's too much can't in that sentence."

"I didn't even finish it."

"You didn't have to. It was on your face. Listen to me. That first week's schedule is easy. Every week from now until the job is finished, I'm upping the ante on you and every single man and woman in this crew. Every time you meet a challenge, I'm going to raise the target. You are on a treadmill. I am going to make this the single most dreadful experience in the lives of each and every one of you. Because after you live through the hell I'm going to give you, the Morthans are going to look easy."

"Yes, sir."

"And that brings me to my last point. There is going to come a day when this crew is more terrified of you and me than they are of the Morthans. On that day—and not before then—they will not only be ready to go up against those murdering bastards, they'll be positively *eager*."

"Yes, sir."

"Questions? Comments? Feedback?"

Korie shook his head. "No, I don't think so."

"Good. Did you notice I didn't say one word about your"—Hardesty waved a hand in careless dismissal—"inner turmoil. You're a man. Handle your healing however you have to. *But from now on, you'll do it in the privacy of your own cabin.* Got that?"

Korie managed to nod.

"Good. Now get the hell out of here. You're already a day behind schedule."

A LITTLE HISTORY

When the first Morthans were decanted from their artificial wombs, they weren't called Morthans. That would only come much later. At the time, the "enhanced babies" were thought of only as a specialized form of humanity, and great care was taken to give these children a special pride in themselves. They were told that they were *not* a subspecies, but a superspecies.

Perhaps that was the mistake. Perhaps that was where it started.

Generations later, when the science of bioengineering had become a commonplace technology, when the designing and creation of new species of humanity had become routine events, the pride in one's superior abilities was still a part of the training, and the term "more-than" had become part of the common slanguage.

Humanity wasn't slow to notice. The "more-thans" were useful. They were interesting. They were admirable. Humanity was fascinated by the "more-thans."

But not all the "more-thans" felt the same about humanity. As the number of "more-thans" grew, so did their wealth and their power. And so did the separatist sentiments of those who resented the patronizing attitudes of so-called "normal" humanity.

It was inevitable that some of these "more-thans" would leave the human worlds and establish their own colonies. The more extremist of the separatist groups went as far as they could beyond the frontier; they made it known that they wanted no human intervention, and they made it known in such an aggressive manner that they got their wish.

That was the beginning of the Morthan Solidarity. They had resources, they had ability, they had a smoldering resentment. Soon, they had a plan. They designed a culture for themselves. It was a fierce and terrifying brew; its primary emphasis was a studied aggression. There were sixteen castes of martial arts training, twelve levels of self-discipline, a religious order based on warrior-Buddhism and medieval samurai codes, and an intensely developed convention of politeness and protocol. There was honor or there was humiliation—a Morthan knew nothing else. The Morthans created holidays of rage and horror, culminating in mass outbreaks of hysteria and riots. Their culture spawned new ways of turning amok. Berserkers were commonplace. There was ritualized cannibalism. Sexuality reinvented itself in terrifying new perversions.

The Morthans knew what they were doing: They were inventing a past for themselves, so they could design a future. Out of this chaos, they bred themselves into a species of super-Morthans. They augmented and enhanced. They engineered each new generation to be strong enough to kill the previous one. They channeled the horror, trained it, disciplined it intensely. Their rage was a nuclear fire—and they tempered themselves in its flames.

It did not go unnoticed.

But humanity's only defense would have been to become Morthans themselves—and that they could not or *would not* do. There had to be a better way.

But then the war broke out. The Silk Road Convoy was destroyed, and it was too late.

THE INNER HULL

A starship is a bottle. A liberty ship is a bottle inside a bottle. The inner bottle is the main life-support module. The outer bottle is the ship's primary hull. The space between the two is known simply as the inner hull. It is a raw, unfinished volume, a techno-wilderness of catwalks, railings, structural members, and naked work lights; it is a crosshatched maze of pylons, latticework partitions, ducts, and cables. There are naked worklights throughout, haphazardly placed and casting odd shadows.

The liberty ship comes off the line deliberately unfinished so that each one can be custom-fitted for specific tasks later. Usually, most of the inner hull is intentionally set aside as a place where a starship crew can *gafiate*.

Gafia: *(abbrev)* *g*et *a*way *f*rom *it* *a*ll. To gafiate: The process of getting away from it all.

The theory was that a crew needed a little bit of wildness and disorder, a place where they could achieve a bit of psychological distance from the pressurized environment of the military regimen. Mostly, the theory worked. Sometimes, it didn't.

Which is why Lieutenant Commander Brik and Lieutenant J.G. Helen Bach were searching the inner hull for the *LS-1187*'s notoriously peripatetic still. As they moved along the catwalk, Harlie was turning the lights on ahead of them and darkening them behind. Most of the aeroponics webs had been removed from this section. Korie had left many of them in place and the Luna moss could still be smelled throughout the inner hull.

Bach was uncomfortable at first, following the hulking Morthan along the catwalks. He hadn't said much and she was sure he didn't like her. She wanted to let him know that she understood—about the prejudice and everything else. She didn't realize she was babbling.

"—I grew up on a Morthan farm," Bach was saying. "I've been around Morthans all my life. Um, I guess what I'm trying to say is that—"

Brik cut her off. "I know what you're trying to say. It isn't necessary."

"Oh," said Bach. "Okay." She looked at Brik uncomfortably. His immense size was disconcerting. Deliberately, she changed the subject. "Um. On my last ship, the inner hull was outfitted as a gym. We even had a running track. It was great. Can I ask you something?" When Brik didn't respond, she took it as an assent. "You know how the captain and the exec think. If we do it on our own time, do you think Mr. Korie would let us build a gym ourselves? We could probably—"

Brik wasn't listening. He held up a hand. "Shut up," he explained.

Bach fell silent immediately. She looked up—and up—at Brik. He was staring intently forward. Bach followed his stare, but she couldn't see what he was focusing on. She followed him silently forward.

They came around the curve of the hyperstate fluctuator channeling tube and stopped.

Ahead of them, on a wide platform, lit by worklights, was the still, a tangle of tubing and wires and boilers. Reynolds and Cappy stood on either side of it. They wore lazy, I-dare-you expressions. Behind them were four hulking men, part of the Black Hole Gang; they were big and mean-looking. Bach noticed that they were all carrying large blunt tools.

Bach snuck a quick glance at Brik. His expression was unreadable. She glanced back to Cappy and Reynolds. The silence stretched out—

"Well," said Bach, crisply, in a deliberate attempt to break the mood. "This is a how-do-you-do! You're having a party and you didn't invite us! I'm hurt!"

Reynolds's gaze slid over to Bach as if he was seeing her for the first time. He remarked quietly, "Hanging around with Morthans is a good way to get hurt." To Brik, he said, "Don't make any trouble here and we'll all get along *just fine*. Lots of ships have . . . extracurricular activities."

Brik's answer rumbled deep in his chest. "Not this one."

Reynolds shrugged. "Have it your own way." He and the others spread out, readying themselves.

Without taking his eyes off them, Brik said softly to Bach, "Please stand back. I don't want you to get hurt."

"Uh-uh. It's my fight too." Bach held her ground.

"Lieutenant," said Brik, picking her up swiftly and sliding her easily down the catwalk and out of the way, "You really must learn to follow orders." Then he turned back to the six men with clubs.

Brik was a Morthan Tyger. He was not simply big and mean-looking. He was an *artist*.

He moved.

He did not seriously injure any of them, but he *hurt* each of them. He flowed like lightning. He reached, he grabbed, he conquered. They swarmed in around him, clubs swinging. He whirled, kicked, feinted, rolled, came up swinging—he disarmed them, disabled them, took them out of the fight, and left them gasping in pain and shock. He gave each of them an unequivocal reminder that he did not want to do this again.

The fight was over before it started: kick, slash, punch, grab, thrust, jab, throw, parry, duck, clobber—and take a breath. He hung one man on a hook, he draped another over a catwalk, a third ended up wedged between the hull and a stanchion. A fourth man was dropped onto the next catwalk down. Cappy was jabbed in the groin as well as the solar plexus and left choking where he stood.

The fight ended with Brik *gently* taking the throat of Reynolds between his fangs and *growling*. Reynolds went white.

"It's a good thing you didn't get me angry," Brik said softly. "I lose control when I get angry. People get *eaten* when I get angry." Very controlled, he added, "Don't. Get. Me. Angry."

Somehow Reynolds managed to gasp and nod.

"Good," said Brik. "Now *I'm* sure that we'll all get along just fine."

He dropped Reynolds rudely to the floor, then he nodded to Bach who was just now finding her way back. "Thank you for not getting in my way, Lieutenant. Would you please supervise the destruction of this unauthorized equipment?"

Bach nodded, as unable to speak as the others. She was stunned by the speed of Brik's victory.

Brik reached down and pulled Reynolds to his feet. "You," he said. "You will begin dismantling the still now. Correct?"

Reynolds choked out his assent.

"Your crewmates will help. Correct?" Brik started plucking the other survivors off the walls he had hung them on. The six chastened men assented painfully, one by one. Brik stepped over to the still and loudly began pulling it apart. "Like this," he prompted, handing the pieces to MacHeath. "Now, you do it."

MacHeath and Reynolds stepped gingerly forward and began breaking down the equipment: the copper tubing, the boiler, the fermentation vat. The others made their way forward and began to help.

Brik watched for a moment, satisfied. "Lieutenant, you will report to me when the job is done." Then he turned and strode off into the darkness.

Cappy was the last one to his feet. Reynolds and MacHeath had to help him. He was as limp as a kitten.

"You okay?" MacHeath asked.

Cappy was in pain, but he nodded anyway. He gasped and said, "Boy . . . am I glad . . . that he's on *our* side."

OFFICERS' COUNTRY

Astrogator Cygnus Tor was lying on the floor of her cabin.

The base of her antigrav bed—a tall glass cylinder—was open, and she was on her back, staring up at the impulsion unit. Inside the cylinder, a uniform jacket was drifting slowly upward to the ceiling.

The door to her cabin was open. Lieutenant J. G. Valentine Michael Jones peered cautiously in. "Knock knock?" he said.

Tor didn't even look up from what she was doing. "Door's open," she called.

"Commander Tor? Valentine Jones. Jonesy. You asked to see me."

"Oh, right. I wanted to ask you something. Hey, do you know anything about antigrav beds?" She extracted herself from the base of the cylinder and sat up to look at Jonesy. She had skinned down to a pair of shorts and tight-fitting T-shirt; it was obvious that she wasn't wearing a bra.

Jonesy shrugged. "Uh, not really." He added helpfully, "But I know gravitors. You want me to take a look?"

"Well, I'm not getting anywhere." Tor moved out of the way, wiping her hands on her pants.

Jonesy lay down on the floor and scooted headward to look up inside the base of the bed. She handed him the probe and waited, hunkering down to get a better look. Idly, she let her gaze travel down past his chest.... "Listen," she said. "I've been looking over your ... record."

"What's wrong with it?" Jonesy asked, his voice was slightly muffled.

"Huh? Nothing." Then she realized that he meant the bed. "Oh. Look—" She pointed.

Jonesy scooted out and levered himself up onto one arm to look. He followed her gaze upward. Inside the bed, a variety of objects had floated to the top of the cylinder. "Ah, I see." He scooted forward and peered into the innards again. "You were saying about my record?" he prompted.

"This is your first ship, isn't it?"

"Yeah. Beautiful, isn't she? The academy wanted me to stay and do postgrad work and then become a full-time instructor. But I turned it down."

Tor didn't answer immediately. She was studying the shape of Jonesy's thigh. She was fascinated by the subtle curve up toward his—she cleared her throat and said quickly, "Listen. I need an assistant astrogator. I was wondering if you wanted to work on the Bridge. With me."

Jonesy didn't answer. She could hear him tinkering with something inside the bed. "Oh, here's the problem," he said. "One of the rings is reversed. They're out of sync. The little one's pulling, the big one's pushing. They're fighting each other. That's why everything drifts upward. It's easy to miss. Wait a minute—"

He finished and extracted himself from the base of the cylinder. He sat up and handed the probe back to Tor. "I think someone's playing a practical joke on you."

Tor looked incredulous. "They short-sheeted my antigrav bed?" She frowned. "I *wonder* who could have done it?" She was almost convincing.

Jonesy didn't seem to notice. He stood up with Tor. The various objects in the antigrav bed were now drifting properly in its center. Tor opened the door and tossed the items out.

She stepped into the bed and floated off the floor. "Is this right?" she asked.

"Looks like it. There's one way to tell." He climbed into the cylinder with her, floating up beside her. Tor smiled and flushed slightly at the almost-intimacy. Jonesy didn't notice. "See—if two people can float without drifting, that means it's fine for one. I mean, that's how we used to test 'em back in the academy."

"I'll bet. . . ."

"Umm. We have to wait a minute to see—"

They waited. They were floating very close to each other now. Tor was getting visibly aroused. This gawky innocent boy was *very* attractive. Sooner or later, he'd have to notice her perfume—

Abruptly, Jonesy realized why Commander Tor was looking at him that way. For a moment, he didn't know what to do. He was too uncomfortably close—and she was too uncomfortably handsome. Embarrassed and flustered, he said, "Uh, well—it's working." He turned to the control panel. "Is everything else in order?"

Jonesy hit a button at random, not realizing. The shower came on with a hot steaming roar. They both yelped in surprise. Jonesy was flustered and apologetic, but Tor wasn't angry. She started laughing.

"Well, the shower works," she said.

She helped him down out of the antigrav bed. Both of them were dripping. Jonesy looked like a shrunken dog, but Tor didn't seem to notice. She was still smiling. "Thank you, Lieutenant Jones."

"Um—I didn't know they did that," he offered, not knowing quite how to apologize.

"The deluxe models do," Tor said dryly.

"Um. Well. Now, I know."

"Maybe they need safety panels," laughed Tor.

Embarrassed, Jonesy held his hands up as if looking for a towel, but he was too flustered to move. "Next time, I won't do that. Um, I better go dry off," he said nervously and backed quickly out of the room.

Tor shook her head in quiet disbelief. Could anybody *really* be that innocent? Her smile broadened into one of anticipation. Jonesy was going to be fun. "*Next* time?"

Jonesy suddenly stuck his head back into the room. "Uh—I almost forgot. Yes, I would like to work with you. On the Bridge, I mean. That would be great. Thanks." And then he was gone again.

Tor laughed.

Yes. Jonesy was going to be a lot of fun. Already she liked him.

SHIP'S MESS

The ship's mess smelled of acrid coffee and stale doughnuts, burnt sweat and plastic grease.

Reynolds, Cappy, Leen, and three men from the Black Hole Gang were sprawled around the end of one of the tables. Several of them had bruises. None of them looked happy. One of the blue-skinned Quillas was quietly refilling their coffee mugs. "Well?" said Cappy. "Are you going to tell him or not?"

Leen was flipping through the screens on his clipboard, flashing from one schematic to the next. "Got that one, that one, that one—still have to check that—" He paused and looked up at Cappy. "One: You're interrupting my work. Two: I've already gotten my butt chewed once today. Three: It won't do any good. And four: No, I am not going to tell him how you feel. In case you've forgotten, a still is against regulations. Striking an officer is even *more* against regulations. By rights, they could court-martial you—but there's a war on and manpower is short. And on the other matter, Brik outranks you. You want my advice? Don't press your luck.

Keep your nose clean and your head down and don't go looking for any more trouble."

"We never hit him," said Cappy. "We never even got close."

"I'd have been very surprised if you had. You guys don't know much about Morthans, do you?"

"What do we need to know? They're big and they're ugly," said Beck, one of the Black Hole Gang.

"So are you," said Leen. "But that doesn't make you a Morthan." There was good-natured laughter around the room. "There have been Morthans for over fifteen hundred years. And for the last thousand, they've been directing their own evolution. They regard themselves as machines. You know how we like to supercharge our equipment—well, that's what the Morthans are doing to their bodies. They do it with genetics, they do it with in-utero tailoring, they do it with implants and augments, they do it with drugs and brainwashing and indoctrination and psycho-training and God knows what else. They start planning a kid's life even before he's conceived—and if a kid fails *anywhere* along the line, they abort him. A Morthan child has to earn his citizenship. If he hasn't earned it by the time he's twenty-one, they flush him down the tubes. They don't believe in wasting resources on nonproductive members of society."

"What are the women like?" asked Armstrong, half jokingly. He had walked in just as Leen had begun describing the Morthans.

Leen shook his head. "I don't know. Nobody's ever seen one. There's a theory though—" He looked around almost conspiratorially, then lowered his voice. "Rumor has it that there aren't any Morthan women. They're all warriors. They grow their babies in industrial wombs. Supposedly, they think that breeding a woman would be a waste of effort when for the same investment they could grow another warrior."

"Um—" Armstrong looked momentarily confused. "Wait a minute. If they don't have any women, who do they—?"

"Why do you think they're all so cranky?" laughed Cappy, and almost everybody else joined in.

"No! Is that true?" Armstrong was genuinely confused. "That can't really be so, can it?" He looked from one to the other. "Don't they have sex drives or—?"

"I think," said Leen, "that a Morthan only gets off by winning a fight."

Reynolds gave Cappy a meaningful poke. "You should ask Brik, 'Was it good for you too?'" Cappy did not look amused.

The duty Quilla came up to Armstrong then, carrying a tray with a mug on it. "Coffee?" she said. Armstrong turned and noticed her for the first time and his eyes widened with unabashed interest. He'd never seen a Quilla this close before. She was vividly blue; she was patterned with shiny scales that shifted in color from turquoise to mazarine and she was as delicately patterned as a butterfly. Her skin looked as shiny and smooth as pale silk veil. Her sensory quills were a bright magenta; they quivered intensely. Armstrong was fascinated. The Quilla looked back at him with amusement. Her eyes were wide and bright and shadowed by dark, almost purple lids.

"Coffee?" she repeated.

"Huh?" Armstrong finally realized what she was asking. "Oh, yes. Thanks." He took the coffee and sipped it too quickly, simultaneously burning his mouth and trying to hide his embarrassment. He flushed, hoping that nobody had noticed, but of course, they all had—and were grinning at his discomfort.

"Here," said Leen abruptly to Reynolds. He slid his clipboard across and poked at the screen. "Here it is. Look. Am I right or am I right?"

"You're the chief."

"I told him and I told him—and what does he say? He says nine-fifty. Like all he has to do is say it and it's real. You know what it is—he's locked up in theory. He's so sure he can push the envelope, he's going to kill us. Look, those fluctuators are beta grade; they'll never hit better than seven-fifty—*maybe* eight, downhill with a tailwind."

Reynolds looked up at Armstrong, noticed his frank curiosity. "Chief Engineer Leen is a man of few words," he explained. "All of them nasty."

"Uh, whatever you say." Armstrong turned to watch the Quilla as she exited the room. A goofy look spread across his face. "They sure are pretty, aren't they?"

"Careful," said Reynolds. "You know what they say about Quillas." He exchanged a knowing grin with Cappy.

Cappy made a gesture with his hands like a spider doing pushups on a mirror. He touched the fingertips of one hand to the fingertips of the other and flexed both simultaneously.

"No," admitted Armstrong. "Actually, I don't know—"

Reynolds motioned him closer. He pulled Armstrong down and whispered into his ear. Armstrong's eyes went wide in disbelief. He looked back and forth between Reynolds and Cappy. "That's not true!" And then, in a hesitant voice, he asked, "Is it? Do they really?"

Cappy's reply was deadpan. "Yes. They do."

"But never on the first date," said Reynolds.

"Wow . . ." said Armstrong, appreciatively.

Abruptly Cappy noticed someone behind Armstrong. "Say—you wanted to meet the doctor, didn't you?" He said it so quietly, he was almost mouthing the words. *"Turn around."*

Armstrong turned.

And stared.

Chief Medical Officer Molly Williger was the *ugliest* human being in the universe. It was said of Molly Williger that the stardrive engines refused to function while she was in the same room. Chief Engineer Leen had no desire to test the truth of this canard, but had so far refused Dr. Williger access to his engine room. She was a squat little potato of a woman with a face that looked like the underside of a golf shoe. She was shaped like a cow pat, her face looked too tiny for her head. Her eyes were either mean and piggish or narrow and piercing, depending on how you looked at her. Her hair was pulled back and tied in a tight little bun that looked like a clump of baling wire.

It was said of Molly Williger that she was as good a doctor as she was ugly. Armstrong didn't know that. He just stared.

Dr. Williger stared back. She glanced at Cappy. "Does it talk?" she said. Her voice was a raspy growl.

Armstrong gulped and held out his hand. "Uh—Brian Armstrong. Most people call me Blackie."

Williger nodded, shifting her gum—or her cud, or whatever it was—to her opposite cheek. She held out her hand. "Everybody calls me 'Foxy.'"

Brian Armstrong was mesmerized. Molly Williger was so

ugly he couldn't take his eyes off her. Her ugliness went
beyond mere awfulness. It was transcendental. "Uh—you
don't have any kids, do you?"

"No. Should I?"

"*Whew.*" Armstrong said. "Good."

Williger looked puzzled. "You know, everybody asks me
that." She turned to the serving counter to pour herself a cup
of coffee, leaving Armstrong rubbing his eyes in disbelief.

Reynolds pulled at his sleeve and whispered, "Around
here, you only go to sick bay if you're *really* sick."

Armstrong gulped quietly. "I can understand it."

"It's a test. When Molly Williger starts looking good,
you've been in space too long."

"Oh."

"She's coming back," said Cappy. "Ask her for a date."

"Huh?" Armstrong was horrified by the thought, then
Cappy turned him around and Armstrong realized he was
talking about the Quilla. She had returned with another tray
of doughnuts. Cappy gave him a meaningful nudge. "Go on!
Go for it."

Armstrong let himself be pushed forward. "Excuse me?"
he said to the blue woman.

The Quilla looked at Brian "Blackie" Armstrong curiously.
"Yes?"

"I, uh—I've never—I mean, I don't want to be rude—but
I thought could we—that is—uh—"

Cappy stepped up beside Armstrong and interrupted candidly.
"Quilla—he wants to know if you'll help him join the
faster-than-light club."

The Quilla smiled at Armstrong. Her smile was bright
enough to melt fire. "You are off shift soon?"

"Uh, yeah. 0600. Um—Which one are you?"

"Delta—" she said, touching herself, and added, "—will
be ready when you are." She smiled at Armstrong again,
turning part of him to stone, and resumed her duties. Armstrong
nearly fainted from lack of blood to the brain. Cappy had to
help hold him up.

"Y'see. It's that easy. Thanks, Quilla." He clapped Armstrong
on the shoulder, grinning wickedly toward Reynolds. His grin
faded almost immediately though. The Quilla stopped at the
door to allow Security Officer Brik to come through first. He

had to bend low to get through. He was almost too big for the mess room.

All conversation stopped while he wrapped one gigantic hand around a coffee mug, filled it, and poured his bulk into a chair at the far end of the table. Reynolds, Cappy, and the others looked angrily down the length of it toward him. Molly Williger studied the tableau and seated herself precisely between the two glaring groups. All by himself, Brik was a group.

Reynolds spoke first. The distaste was evident in his voice. "Well . . . I got work to do." He levered himself out of his chair.

Cappy and Leen exchanged a glance. Leen made a reluctant decision and rose also. "Yeah, me too. I gotta run a recharge drill on the mag-loaders again." He added sourly, "For Korie."

Cappy nodded and rose to follow. "I'll give you a hand." He glanced over at Armstrong. "You coming?"

Armstrong hesitated. Around him, the other members of the Black Hole Gang were standing up, putting their coffee mugs down, and following Reynolds. None of them were looking directly at Brik. He knew it was wrong, but . . . he also knew he had to work with these men. Reluctantly, he allowed himself to vote with his feet. "Yeah," he said, already ashamed of himself.

And then the room was empty.

Only Brik and Williger were left in the ship's mess.

They glanced across the table at each other.

Williger looked around meaningfully. "Was it something I said?"

Brik grinned. The lady had class. "Do you have this effect everywhere you go?"

Williger shook her head. "No question about it. I just gotta get a new hat."

Brik wasn't quite sure of the reference, but his laughter rumbled loudly, almost frighteningly, through the mess room.

SUBLUMINAL

The *LS-1187* was complete, as ready for the stars as she would ever be.

Her bright hull gleamed under the worklights as proudly as the day she first rose from her docks. Her fluctuator struts were proud stanchions, glittering with power and possibility.

Every deck, every tube, every module, every conduit, every stanchion—*everything*—had been repaired or rebuilt, recalibrated, tested, burned in, retested, triple-checked, cleaned, polished, and detailed.

Even Chief Engineer Leen had taken a bath—or so the crew believed.

Indeed, the expression on his face was as bright as his engine room. He signed the last authorization on Nakahari's clipboard and handed it back to the young crewman. "All right," he grumbled. "That's the last one. This ship is ready to go."

"Yes, sir!" Nakahari said crisply. He left the now-sparkling engine room and headed up through the now-glistening forward keel, up through the now-spotless Ops bay, onto the now-gleaming Ops deck and up onto the now-pristine Bridge where Hardesty, Korie, and Brik were waiting. He handed the clipboard to Korie.

Korie took it, read it, and passed it to the captain without comment.

Hardesty barely glanced at the final status report. Instead, he checked the time. Then he said, "If you're waiting for a compliment, Mr. Korie, you're waiting in the wrong place." He gestured with the clipboard. "This is the job you're *supposed* to do. Producing a result shouldn't be such a unique event that it requires a pat on the head." He started to turn away, then added, "And, for the record, you're an hour and twenty minutes overdue."

Korie said quietly, "We had a small problem in the engine room."

"The Morthan Solidarity is a *bigger* problem. That's the only problem I'm interested in." Hardesty turned forward to Tor. "Signal Stardock that we're *finally* ready. Cast off as soon as we're cleared."

"Aye, aye, sir." Tor spoke quietly to her headset.

A moment later, the reply came back. "*LS-1187*, you are cleared."

"Thank you, Stardock."

The air locks sealed and closed. The docking tubes retracted. The holding bolts released. . . .

And the starship floated up and out and clear of her moorings.

A soft voice whispered across the widening gap, "Good luck, starship. . . ."

"Thank you, Stardock," Tor replied. "That means a lot. Keep the lights burning." She smiled as she turned from her console to the holographic display table. She hadn't expected a farewell. It was a nice gesture—especially toward *this* ship.

"Stardock breakaway complete," Harlie reported.

Hardesty nodded, satisfied. "Heading 23 mark 141."

Flight Engineer Hodel echoed the order. "23 mark 141—" He watched his screens as the ship swung around. "Confirmed."

"Mr. Hodel," the captain ordered. "Ten milligees acceleration, please."

"Ten milligees, confirmed."

Hardesty watched the forward viewer. It showed the view aft as the Stardock began imperceptibly sliding away. The haphazard collection of girders and globes shrank in the distance. After a moment, he ordered, "Boost to fifty milligees."

Again, Hodel echoed the order. "Confirmed."

Hardesty glanced at the smaller console in front of him.

Korie glanced over. "Right down the center of the channel," he said.

"Are you surprised?" Hardesty's voice was emotionless.

"No, sir. Just . . . gratified."

Hardesty didn't say anything to that. "Boost to five hundred milligees." They had to move the starship well clear of the Stardock before going to full power—and then they'd have to spend several hours of full acceleration before initiating hyperstate. The ripple effects of a hyperstate bubble could be uncomfortable to anyone or anything nearby. This vessel had experienced first-hand the havoc that occurred when a hyperstate fringe brushed a normal-space installation. It would not do to pass that experience on to their hosting Stardock.

Hardesty stepped down from the Bridge and circled the Ops deck once, peering carefully at every console. Every station was operating well within expected parameters. Satisfied, he returned to the Bridge without comment. "Mr. Hodel, boost to three gees and hold it there."

"Aye, Captain."

There was no sensation of movement. Korie checked his console. The gravitational compensators were maintaining to six decimal places. Totally undetectable. A starliner couldn't have been smoother.

Hardesty made another round of the Ops deck then, peering narrowly at each console. What was he judging, Korie wondered. The crew? The ship? Or was this part of his performance?

He stopped behind the flight engineer's console and watched the numbers climb. After a long moment, he said, "Go to ten."

Hodel nodded and typed in the command.

Hardesty turned and looked up at Korie on the Bridge. "Status?"

"As expected, sir."

Hardesty turned back to Hodel. "Twenty-five."

A moment later, Hodel reported, "Holding at twenty-five."

Hardesty returned to the Bridge. "Chief Engineer Leen. We are holding at twenty-five gees. We will maintain this speed for thirty minutes. I want you to run concurrent stability checks for that entire time. If there's any deviation from the projected channels, I want to know immediately.''

"Yes, sir.''

"Mr. Korie?'' Hardesty turned to his executive officer. "What's the recommended interval before initiating stardrive?''

"A hundred million kilometers—at least.''

"And during wartime?''

"Sir, during wartime operating conditions, it is recommended that a starship put as much distance as possible between itself and any other starship or deep-space Stardock it may have rendezvoused with before initiating its hyperspace envelope; this is to avoid betraying the exact location of the other vessel, or of the Stardock, to any other vessel in the hyperstate vicinity.''

Hardesty nodded. "And how large an interval would you recommend in this case?''

"I would recommend, sir, that we accelerate for several days at full power, then decelerate the same length of time to burn off the extra kinetic energy. Two reasons. First, it will allow us to check the performance of the rebuilt mass-drivers under the most rigorous conditions; and second, it will place the Stardock well outside the range of probable loci if we're detected going into hyperstate.''

"A sensible suggestion,'' said the captain. "Now, let me postulate something else, Mr. Korie. Tor, I want you to hear this too. You too, Hodel. Suppose you're the enemy. Suppose you know our standard operating procedure is to move away as far as possible before initiating hyperstate. Knowing that, what would you think if you detected a ship going FTL?''

"I'd think there was a starbase somewhere nearby, within a radius of at least a light-day. If I could search for it undetected, I'd sweep the area as thoroughly as I could, hoping to brush the base with my envelope and destroy it, or at least cripple it.''

"Mm hm. And is there a flaw in that logic?''

"Not really.''

"You don't see the loophole?'' Hardesty glanced to Tor and Hodel. "Either of you?'' They shook their heads.

Korie said, "I suppose . . . in one sense, as soon as the enemy knows that's your standard operating procedure, and allows for it, then it doesn't matter whether you move off or not."

"Right," said Hardesty. "If they see you, they're going to search. At that point, the least likely place to look for the Stardock is your point of initiation and its immediate radius."

Korie thought about it for a moment, considering the implications. "Okay, but what if the enemy is just lurking and observing. If more than one ship departs from the same area of space, he'd be stupid not to assign that area a very high degree of probability."

"But what if every ship departing from your Stardock were to move off to the exact same departure point before initiating hyperstate? That would look the same to a distant observer too."

"It's too easy to check," put in Hodel. "You rig for silent running and drift in as close as you can to see what you can detect. If there's no Stardock in the area, it's a ploy. Then you start looking for where the ships are coming from."

Tor agreed. "It's too dangerous. We're better off having ships move to random positions before putting up the envelope."

Hardesty had been listening quietly. "All right," he said. "Game that out. Suppose the enemy is lurking and observing ships departing at random. After he sees two or three or ten ships arrive and depart, he's going to start projecting a sphere of possibility. After observing enough departures or arrivals, he should be able to predict the location of the Stardock as being somewhere in the center of the sphere described by these events, don't you think?"

"But it'll take a lot longer to locate the Stardock that way, and he's at greater risk of detection," said Hodel.

Korie was studying the captain carefully. "All right," he said. "Neither procedure is perfect, but one has significant advantages over the other. What's your point?"

"*That's* my point, Mr. Korie. These procedures *aren't* perfect." Hardesty pointed at Korie's chest. "That was Captain Lowell's mistake. He assumed that following procedure was enough. It isn't. I'm not interested in procedure, I'm interested in results. Your enemy is going to be analyzing your procedures. He's going to understand them better than you and he's going to understand why you do them. That's your weakness. Your only strength is to have the same perspective, to look at yourself as the enemy does—and sometimes break your own rules, specifically to confuse him.''

The captain let his officers consider that thought for a while. ''Chief Engineer Leen?''

''Engines are clean, sir. No anomalies.''

''Thank you. I'm boosting to one-fifty now.''

''Aye, sir.''

''Mr. Hodel. Go to one-fifty.''

''Yes, sir. One hundred and fifty gees.'' A moment later, Hodel called out, ''Confirmed.''

Hardesty's expression remained unreadable. ''You think that's too much strain on the engines, Mr. Korie?''

''No, sir.''

''What would you think if I ordered a boost to three hundred?''

Korie tried to visualize the strain relationships in his head. He couldn't. ''Uh, I'd prefer to ask Harlie what he thinks before I form an opinion of my own. But—''

''Yes?''

''I do think it's a good idea to know what a ship is capable of, in case you need to use that ability.''

''That's a safe answer,'' Hardesty said. ''Very academic.''

''I'm sorry if you don't—''

''I didn't say I did. Don't presume. Let me remind you again that part of the captain's responsibility, Mr. Korie, is to train his replacement. As I've said, I don't think Captain Lowell did a very good job. You're still thinking in textbook terms. Now, before you object—'' Hardesty held up a hand, cutting off Korie's interruption, ''—you need to go back and look carefully at what I said as opposed to what you think you heard. I *said* that you're still thinking in textbook terms. I did not say that the textbooks are wrong. As a matter of fact, most of your textbook simulations were written by the very same people who discovered the *right*ness of what they wrote by direct experience. I know those books and I know some of the authors. You could not have had a better education.''

''Yes, sir.''

''But—'' continued Hardesty, ''the very best that a textbook simulation can give you—even the best textbook simulation—is still only simulation. Simulations give you simulated experience. It remains outside the domain of actual experience. What am I telling you?''

Korie understood perfectly. ''There is a difference between an officer who can run a perfect simulation and a blooded warrior.''

''Right. You gave me a textbook answer a moment ago. It's complete, it's perfect, and you'll never be court-martialed for following the book. But it's missing that something that makes all the difference between being a statistic and being the kind of an officer who brings his ship back with a broomstick tied to her mast. Did you ever hear of a captain named Ling Tsu?''

''Who hasn't?''

''I met her once.'' Hardesty's voice was surprisingly soft. Despite himself, Korie was impressed.

''Yes,'' the captain agreed, ''it was that kind of an experience. I was very young at the time, and she died only a few months later. She was a very fragile old lady by then, but you could still tell who she was by looking at her eyes. She was officially retired, but she still served in a consulting capacity. The story was true, you know—she refused to consult unless she got some time in space every year. She said that decisions about ships had to be made inside ships. She was pure Fleet all the way.

''Anyway, I was a junior trainee on a new cruiser. They wheeled her onto the Bridge of our ship for the shakedown cruise and let me tell you, our captain was sweating blood, as were we all. But she didn't say a word. She just watched and listened and somehow she became invisible. For a while. The captain was so scared he was following every procedure in the book. We might as well have been automated; but it was along about this point, while we were moving out to the local horizon, that she leaned forward and poked the captain in the ribs. 'You got lead in your ass?' she said. 'Let's open her up and see what this baby can do.' ''

Hardesty smiled as he remembered. ''She almost got applause—except we were too shocked. We'd been thinking of her as a great lady, but we'd forgotten why she was great. Do you know what her job was as a consultant? To remind young

captains to not take anything for granted. Test everything—
your crew, your ship, and especially yourself.''

"Yes, sir," said Korie.

"And my point is . . . ?" prompted Hardesty.

Korie looked for the right words and couldn't find them.
Instead, he turned forward and blurted, "Mr. Hodel. We
worked hard rebuilding this ship. I want to hear her scream.
And so does the crew. Go to three hundred gees."

Hardesty looked at Korie. And *grinned*.

SUPERLUMINAL

"Mr. Hodel, are we clear?"

"One hundred and three point five giga-klicks."

"Thank you. Stand by for injection."

"Standing by." Hodel spoke to his headset. "All stations, prepare for injection." A moment later, he confirmed. "Ready for stardrive."

Hardesty referred to his own screen and then gave the order. "Initiate envelope."

Hodel set his controls and passed the order on, "Engine room—initiate envelope."

In the engine room, the order was received eagerly. These crew members had been too long in Stardock. Leen stood impatiently at the main console. All of the men and women on his crew were wearing safety goggles. Leen couldn't help himself. He punched up a last-check program, waited till his screen flashed green, and then ordered, "Initiation."

Beside him, two crew members inserted their keys into their keyboards and turned them one half-turn clockwise. The

board was armed. Leen flipped the cover off the red switch
and threw it.

Space warped.

There was a place—a pinpoint hole in the stress field of
existence—where the laws of physics transformed from one
state to another.

In an instant of time, known as a *quantum second,* space
was grabbed, stretched, englobulated in a moment of pure
irrationality, and turned inside out. Now, it was infinite.
Mathematically, at least. At its center hung a silver needle
containing ninety-four men and women. The three hyperstate
fluctuators on its hull held it firmly in the center of the
bubble.

The bubble shimmered and glowed and *held.*

Hodel's board flashed green. He reported it calmly. "The
envelope is stable. We have stardrive." He began to punch in
a new course, then he grinned at Tor and added, "Just like a
real starship."

Tor held up her two crossed fingers.

"Belay that chatter!" Hardesty said from the Bridge, but
his usual ferocity seemed muted. "Flight engineer—lightspeed
times five. As soon as we're clear of the local deviation,
boost to three-fifty."

"Aye aye, sir." Hodel echoed. "Lightspeed times five and
three-five-oh when we clear."

Hodel tapped out a command and the bubble around the
starship quivered. Imperceptibly, it shifted its shape, stretching
itself just a little bit farther along one axis. The ship hung
motionless within its center; but in real space—in the stress
field—the location of the hyperstate blip, or the place where
it would be if it were in normal space, began to stretch, began
to slide, began to move, became a beam of light and then
something faster than that.

And then it was gone. It wasn't anywhere at all.

But inside, in that place where it *wasn't,* Hodel was
satisfied. At five times the speed of light, it would take just a
little less than an hour to clear the locus of immediate
detectability for the Stardock.

"Lightspeed times five," Hodel confirmed. He sat back in
his chair and felt good. On the forward screen, a simulated
view showed a grid of demarcation lines slipping past. An

actual view forward would have been meaningless. It couldn't exist. It was an irrational concept. Nonetheless, had the sensors been activated, they would have reported a blurred sensation of *something*. Most people found it hard to look at for very long.

Hardesty glanced up. He spoke crisply, "All right. Staff to the table for mission briefing. Oh, and have Chief Engineer Leen join us."

The captain stepped down to the Operations deck, followed by Korie and Brik. They seated themselves around the holographic display table. Tor and Hodel only had to swivel their chairs to be in place. Jonesy took a chair uncertainly, but Tor nodded at him and he allowed himself to relax. One of the Quillas began laying out coffee mugs as Chief Engineer Leen stepped up through the Ops bay from the keel.

Satisfied that all were ready, Hardesty glanced upward. "Harlie?"

The visuals began appearing in the air above the table even before Harlie began speaking. His voice was dispassionate. "Her Majesty's Starship *Sir James Burke* is a destroyer-class liberty ship with standard fittings and weaponry. She carries the flag of New Brittany and is presently based at Windsor Stardock.

"Six months ago, the *Burke* was pulled from active duty for a major refit. At the same time, her security rating was promoted to maximum level red. This briefing is also red-coded.

"Using the refit as cover, the *James Burke* has had three ultrahigh-cycle envelope fluctuators installed."

The holographic display of the *Burke* became a schematic. The high-cycle fluctuators were outlined in red. They were twice the size of normal fluctuators and Korie noted that major modifications had been made within the *Burke*'s hull. But if they worked . . . then the *Burke* would have doubled her effective velocity.

Tor was nodding in admiration. "That's a lucky captain—to have a superstardrive."

"Yeah," agreed Hodel. "Wouldn't you like to have those in your engine room?"

Leen snorted. "I'd like to have an engine in my engine room, thank you."

Harlie ignored the comments and continued his presentation. "The new fluctuators will increase the *Burke*'s rated stardrive velocity by a factor of two, making her one of the fastest ships in known space. Her operational rating is now two thousand times the speed of light. Her theoretical rating is twenty-three hundred."

"We're lucky to hit nine-fifty," Hodel said.

"Seven-fifty," Leen corrected him.

"The Morthan Solidarity would trade a shipload of warlords for just one of those fluctuators," Tor said thoughtfully.

"And they'd still be getting the best of the deal," said Hardesty. "Our *only* strategic advantage in this war is the technological one. The Solidarity doesn't have the industrial base the Allies do. If they got their hands on one of those units, they'd be turning out copies in six months, and six months after that we'd be in big trouble."

"Four months ago," said Harlie, "the *Burke* was assigned to penetrate the Morthan sphere. As you can see, this is a particularly hazardous journey; it could not be safely completed by a slower vessel. Even the *Burke* will be at considerable risk." He projected the *Burke*'s course across a star map of the region. "However, the opportunity of the *Burke*'s mission is of such importance to the Alliance that the risk is deemed acceptable. As a precaution, the *Burke* has been equipped with significant self-destruct capabilities; she is not to fall into enemy hands under *any* circumstances. The responsibility to protect the high-cycle technology is also shared by this vessel. The *Burke*'s mission: to rendezvous with a Morthan vessel and pick up a single life-pod. Inside the life-pod will be a high-ranking ambassador carrying a secret peace initiative."

Brik spoke quietly. His voice was a desolate rumble. "I don't believe it."

The others glanced at him curiously, but the Morthan did not explain his skepticism.

Harlie continued, "The peace initiative is apparently sponsored by a dissident faction within the Morthan Solidarity, called the Coalition of Warlords."

Hodel grinned. "Not very solid, are they?"

"It is believed that the Coalition of Warlords will negotiate an end to hostilities to prevent further decimation of their ranks, and will force the leadership of the Solidarity to accept that settlement."

Brik snorted.

Hardesty glanced over at him. "You have a problem with that, Mr. Brik?"

"It's a trap. Warlords don't negotiate."

Hardesty accepted the comment without reaction.

"Sir?" asked Jonesy. "How do we know all this?"

Hardesty looked at the junior officer as if seeing him for the first time. "That's not your concern."

"Yes, sir—I was just wondering about the reliability of the information."

"We have sources within the Solidarity."

"Oh." Jonesy considered that. He looked troubled. "What will happen to them if they get caught?"

Brik said quietly, "The Morthans will gut them alive and hang their bodies up to cure."

"Oof," said Tor, an involuntary reaction.

"It's a Morthan insult," explained Brik. "An honorable enemy would be eaten fresh."

"Uck!" Hodel shuddered.

Brik looked to Korie. "You have a comment to make too?"

Korie chose his words very carefully. "I never comment on anyone else's eating habits."

"Thank you," said Brik.

"Gentlemen," interrupted the captain. "May we continue? Harlie, if you please?"

Harlie continued in a voice that was disturbingly calm. "If everything has proceeded according to plan, the *Burke* will have completed her rendezvous mission by now and will be bringing her passenger back. The *LS-1187* is to proceed to a designated rendezvous with Her Majesty's Starship *Sir James Burke* and provide escort service to a designated location. The *Burke* has not yet been made aware of this location. We are carrying that information. I can only decode it when the captain of the *Burke* provides an authorization code."

"Huh?" said Tor. "Escort service? We can't keep up with the *Burke*. No one can. What's the point?"

"It's obvious to me," said Hodel. "The *Burke* wants a minimum of attention. We're her cover. We come into base together and nobody suspects that the *Burke* is anything but another rusty old tub."

Hardesty's glance slid sideways to his executive officer. "Mr. Korie, what's the real reason?"

"Sir?"

"Can't you figure it out?" asked Hardesty. He looked at Korie coldly, as if Korie had deliberately chosen to be retarded.

"Um—" Korie thought fast. "What if the *Burke* gets captured by the Morthans? They could send her back carrying a hell-bomb, drop it into a sun, and take out a whole star system. Our job is to make sure that the *Burke* is clean before we tell her where her final destination is."

"And if she isn't clean?"

"I assume that's in the orders, sir."

"Yes, it probably is. Would you like to speculate what would be appropriate in this situation?"

Korie allowed himself a shrug. "Well—based on what we've heard, I'd say that if we couldn't regain control of the *Burke,* then our job would be to destroy her."

"Good," said Hardesty, mildly surprised. "That's exactly what our orders are." He added, "Harlie, forget you heard those directives pertaining to the possible destruction of the *Burke;* there is to be no record in our ship's computer of any such orders or discussion pertaining to them."

"Yes, Captain."

"Obviously," said Hardesty, "Fleet Command does not think that is a very likely occurrence—or they would not have sent this ship to provide escort cover." He clicked off the display. "All right. There you have it. The rendezvous is five days away. We'll be picking up the *Burke* uncomfortably close to the Morthan sphere. I'll want continual long-range scanning, confidence nine or above. Any questions? No? Mr. Korie, you have the conn." He levered himself to his feet and exited briskly.

"Yes, sir. . . ." Korie said to his back.

Hodel waited until the door whooshed shut behind the

captain. "I was hoping for something a little more ... interesting," he sighed.

"Are you using the Morthan definition of 'interesting'?" asked Brik. To their uncomprehending looks, he explained, "*Interesting*—as in pertaining to your own death." He added innocently, "Nothing concentrates the attention so much as the knowledge that you are about to die."

"Uh, never mind," said Hodel. "I'd rather be bored." He swiveled back to his console.

QUILLAS

Brian Armstrong stepped into the corridor grinning weakly. It was true what they said about Quillas. He was limp. He was haggard and weary.

Quilla Delta exited the cabin after him, looking politely contented.

Armstrong looked at her with a near-hopeless expression. He was flustered and red and unable to quantify the staggering effect of his experience. He was exhausted to the point of speechlessness.

The Quilla simply smiled at him. She'd seen this response before.

"Uh—" Armstrong gulped and swallowed and tried to find his voice. "I gotta go back on shift now. You were..." He waved his hands about uselessly. "...*wow.*"

"Yes," she answered mildly. "So were you. Thank you, Brian." She turned and walked calmly away, leaving him staring after her.

Shaking his head, he started down the corridor in the opposite direction. Almost immediately, a different Quilla came up the corridor toward him. It was Gamma.

Quilla Gamma smiled with exactly the same expression as she passed him. "Yes. Thank you, Brian. You were quite good."

"Huh? Wait a minute. You're—"

The Quilla touched herself lightly. "This is Gamma."

Armstrong's eyes widened in realization. Every Quilla on the ship was tuned in and *feeling* the same thing.

His mouth fell open in shock.

Did Quillas—?

Suddenly, he felt nauseous.

A GOOD IDEA
AT THE TIME

Jonesy paused uncertainly in front of the door to Tor's cabin. Finally, he summoned up his nerve and tapped the entrance panel.

"Who is it?" came Tor's voice.

"Uh, it's Jonesy."

The door slid open for him and he stepped gingerly inside. Cygnus Tor was working at her desk; she was wearing only shorts and a halter, the standard uniform aboard ship for women. Men usually wore T-shirts and shorts. Tor looked up with interest. "Hi, what's up?"

"I took your suggestion and, uh—" Jonesy held up a small plastic device. "I built this for you."

Tor was momentarily confused. "What suggestion?"

"Didn't you say something about a safety lock for the shower control? I took one apart and reprogrammed it and added a safety switch—"

Tor was leaning her chin on her fist. Now she hid her smile of amusement behind her knuckles. She glanced off as if discharging her laughter and then looked back to Jonesy. "It was a sort of a joke. I never really thought a safety panel was necessary in a shower—"

Jonesy's face fell. "Oh—"

"But maybe you're right," she recovered quickly. "I mean, after all, it could happen. A sleeper might bump into it. Maybe we should install it and see."

"I don't have to, if you don't want it."

"No, I insist. Let's see how it works. After all, you went to all that trouble."

"Are you sure?"

"I'll make it an order, all right?"

"Uh—I'll put it in now." Jonesy turned to the antigrav bed and stepped into it. He began disconnecting its control plate. Tor got up from the desk and came around to watch him work. She leaned provocatively against the tube. Her figure was surprisingly lean and hard.

"This won't take long," Jonesy said, "and then I'll be out of your hair."

"Take as long as you need." Tor smiled, tossing her head back. "I don't mind having you in my hair." When he didn't react, she added, "I'm actually glad of the interruption."

"Really?" The plate popped off in Jonesy's hand.

"I was signing off duty reports. Busywork. It has to be done sometime, but sometimes you'd rather do anything but—"

"Mm," said Jonesy. He grunted as he fumbled the new plate into position. "I wouldn't know. I don't get to do busywork. And most of the reports I have to do are autologged."

Tor allowed herself a smile that hinted of knowledge not yet shared. "I should put you into a leadership training course. You'd learn about busywork. Everything has to be documented."

"I guess so. But I prefer things I can get my hands on." Jonesy looked up at Tor and suddenly realized how close her body was. "—Uh, you know what I mean." He forced himself to refocus his attention on the control plate. He lined up the plugs and pressed it firmly into place. "There." He pressed the self-test button and waited. The unit cycled, flashed, and confirmed that it was fully operational. "That should do it." He gave her a satisfied look. "See—you can't turn on the shower accidentally. You have to press the shower button, and then the authorize button within three seconds. Otherwise nothing happens.''

"Well, let's try it out," said Tor, stepping into the antigrav tube with him. She reached past his shoulder and tapped the free-fall switch. The gravity faded gently away from beneath them with a dizzying sensation of lightheadedness. It took some getting used to; some people never rid themselves of the sensation of the whole bed being turned upside down into an endless drop. They floated up off the floor and drifted in midair. Tor turned Jonesy so that he was facing her.

"It works," he said.

"Of course," she said.

She looked directly into his eyes and waited for him to start flustering. He surprised her. He looked directly back. She waited for him to speak first, surprised at how long the moment was lasting.

It was his voice that gave him away. "Can I speak candidly?''

She nodded.

"I—some of the guys have been teasing me. They say that you—uh, I hope this doesn't offend you. I want you to know how much I personally respect and admire you—"

"Go ahead, say it."

"Well, some of the guys think that you . . . want to . . . well, you know . . . with me. And I—thought you ought to know. I hope you're not offended. I mean, personally, I think you're a very attractive woman and—it would be an honor and a privilege to—"

Tor made a decision. She reached past Jonesy and tapped the shower button. Then he tapped the authorize button. Warm water shot up from the floor and flooded down from the ceiling, soaking both of them and drowning Jonesy's carefully phrased words in a sputter of coughing.

She grabbed his shoulders to steady him. Then she grabbed his face between her two hands and said, "Listen to me, you don't need to do that anymore.''

"Do what?"

"The flustered little boy act." She raised her voice to be heard above the steaming water.

"I don't—"

"Yes, you do. You do it whenever there's a chance of our

being intimate. You do it to distance me. It's very annoying—and it keeps us from really getting to know each other. It keeps us from being real friends. Or anything else." She stretched forward and planted a firm, but gentle, kiss directly on his lips. Jonesy blinked, surprised. The water continued to swirl around the both of them.

"First of all, you're a *very* attractive young man. You don't know how attractive you are. And yes, it's true. I *would* like to tumble with you. But I don't tumble with children, so you're going to have to grow up first." She touched his chin gently. "Lose the act. It's not you."

"Um," he said, but it was a different kind of sound than before; a deeper, more thoughtful "Um."

"If you want something—if you want *me*—just say so. The worst that can happen is that the answer will be no. It might also be yes. But if you never ask, you'll never know. So, what's it to be, Lieutenant? Do you have something to ask me?"

"Um—" Jonesy swallowed hard. And then something happened. He *stiffened*. He seemed to straighten before Tor, almost growing in her grasp. "Commander Tor," he began, in a voice she'd never heard before. "Request permission to initiate docking maneuvers."

Tor laughed. "That's a good start, but a little too formal. Try again. Just say it in English."

"The truth is," Jonesy admitted candidly. "You're the most beautiful woman I've ever taken a shower with."

Tor flushed in surprise and delight. It was his naked sincerity which won her. She was too startled to respond.

"So," continued Jonesy, "Would you like to tumble with me?"

"Yes, I would," she said. "Very much." She looked deeply into his eyes. They were shining and bright.

Now it was Jonesy's turn to be surprised. "Really?"

In answer, Tor pulled him close to her in a passionate kiss. She opened her mouth to his. For a moment, he didn't realize, then he opened his mouth to hers. She wasn't going to rush him. She let him explore the sensation of the moment, the intimacy of shared breath—and then he surprised her; his tongue touched hers. It was just the quickest, most fleeting, touch; but the boldness of the initiative told her what she wanted to know, that Jonesy would not be afraid to explore her body, that he really did want to be intimate with her. He just needed to know that it was all right.

Slowly, Tor wrapped her arms around Jonesy's wiry torso, sliding naturally into his embrace. His long gangly arms closed around her shoulders, his hands slid down her back, looking for the right places to touch. One of them came to rest on her hip, then slid around to the gentle cleft at the top of her buttocks; the other found the back of her neck and became a warm, comforting presence there. She sighed and let her kiss open wider, allowed her tongue to touch his again.

They floated, locked together and spinning, turning in the whirling waters. She lifted her legs and wrapped them about his pelvis, pulling him even more tightly against her. She could feel his hardness against her and it sent waves of pleasure up through her belly. She enclosed him, holding him inside the warm envelope of her embrace. She could feel his warmth up and down her entire body.

And then, Jonesy broke away, holding her at arm's length. "I have to look at you," he explained. "I like looking at you. I like seeing how beautiful you are." His hair was plastered wetly across his forehead; the water was clinging to him in shining globules; his eyes were incredibly alive. "You're terrific," he said.

"So are you." Tor laughed back. "Why don't we get out of these wet clothes—"

Jonesy's smile widened into a broad silly grin. It was the wild, untamed look of a man who was about to share a secret.

Tor started giggling then, so did Jonesy—and then it got even funnier. Not all the old jokes about antigrav beds are true; two people *can* get undressed in a tube, but it does take awhile—and they have to like each other *a lot*.

Fortunately, Tor and Jonesy liked each other *more* than just *a lot*.

RENDEZVOUS

The *LS-1187* slowed as she approached her rendezvous, cutting her speed from six hundred lights to three hundred, then to one hundred, then to twenty-five, five, and finally one point five. She was scanning all the way in, but there were no hyperstate ripples visible anywhere at all within her locus of detectability.

The *Burke* was not to be seen.

Korie studied the holographic display with a sour frown on his face. Hodel and Tor stared at him from across the table, waiting for his assessment. Jonesy joined them. So did the new weapons specialist, Goldberg, a stocky, red-haired man.

"Holding at one point five," said Hodel. "Coming up on primary target sphere. Still nothing."

Hardesty entered through one of the doors at the back of the Bridge. Brik followed him in and crossed to the primary weapons console while Hardesty stepped down to join his officers on the Ops deck. Korie glanced over at him. *Do you want to take over?*

"Carry on," Hardesty said.

Korie turned back to Hodel. "As soon as we cross the

horizon, back it off to oh point oh oh two. Let's coast a bit and see what's what. Keep all stations alert."

"Do you want to go to yellow?" Tor asked.

"Not yet."

"Stabilizing," Hodel reported. "Oh point oh oh two."

"Approaching rendezvous point," Jonesy reported. He checked his own screen beneath the display. "Still no signature." He looked to Tor, worried. She ignored him.

"Hodel, stand by to collapse the envelope." Korie looked to Hardesty. "With your permission, sir. There's no sign of the *Burke*. We've scanned for ripple effect, both long and short range. There's nothing."

"And you think she's hiding?"

Korie nodded. "She should have sighted us by now and made her presence known. I want to pop back into normal space and see if she's coasting. Maybe she has a good reason to play hide-and-seek."

Hardesty considered it. "All right, go ahead."

Korie turned to Hodel. "Collapse the envelope."

"Collapsing."

The great stardrive bubble around the starship unfolded in an instant—and once again the *LS-1187* hung in black space. But her sublight velocity was enormous.

"Normal space confirmed," reported Hodel. He swung back to his main console. "Beginning deceleration now. One hundred and fifty gees?"

"If Mr. Leen says it's okay." Korie grinned. He raised his voice so that everybody on the Bridge could hear him. "All right, everybody stay alert. If something is sneaking up on us, we'll have less than thirty seconds to inject back into the safety of hyperstate."

Tor looked up from her screen. "I've got the *Burke*." She frowned as she read off the details. It didn't make sense. "She's right on station—right where she's supposed to be, but she's absolutely silent."

Jonesy added, "Two hundred sixty mega-klicks and closing." Then he looked across the display at Tor; his expression was puzzled. "Is she derelict?"

Korie looked to Hardesty. "This is not according to plan—" He punched at a control and the holographic display flashed to show the intercept vectors.

"Should I hail her?" Tor asked.

Korie was at a loss. "She's *got* to know we're here."

"Think she's dead?"

"I don't think anything yet." He looked to Hardesty again. "Sir?"

Hardesty's voice was almost as dispassionate as Harlie's. "So far, you have been following the book, Mr. Korie. And that is correct. Fleet Command has a purpose behind every procedure."

"But?" Korie prompted.

"But nothing," said the captain.

Korie straightened up from the display to look the captain straight in the eye. "If I understand you correctly, sir, you are arguing the opposite position from what you said to us when we began this mission."

"Am I?"

Korie replayed the conversation in his head, as best as he could remember it. "Maybe not."

"Make up your mind. Which is it, Mr. Korie?"

" 'There's a reason for everything in the book. These procedures have all been derived from actual experiences—' " Korie quoted.

"I couldn't have said it better myself," said Hardesty.

"But," said Korie, "the book is insufficient—because it can't predict the situation that hasn't happened yet. Therefore . . . you follow the book until you run into the situation that isn't covered in the book. Then you *improvise*."

"Almost," said Hardesty coldly. "Fleet prefers the word *invent*."

"Yes, sir. I'll remember that." He looked to Tor. "All right. Send a coded chirp. When we get within thirty light-seconds, hit her with a tight beam and we'll try for direct conversation." To Hodel, he added, "Close on her—very slowly. With extreme caution. Shields up. Arm all stations. Let's assume it's a Morthan trap and act accordingly." He looked to Hardesty for his reaction.

The captain nodded. "That was by the book, Mr. Korie."

"Yes, sir. Is there anything else? Do you have any specific orders?"

"What does the book say?"

Korie quoted, " 'Have a security team standing by. If the target vessel doesn't answer, be ready to board.' "

"That's correct."

"You aren't going to give me any help on this, are you?" Korie said.

"You don't need any help," said Hardesty. "At least, not yet."

Korie turned to his security chief. "Mr. Brik, ready a mission team."

Brik rose from his chair and approached Korie, looking very stiff.

"Do you have a problem with that?" Korie asked.

"Yes, I do." Brik's answer was an ominous rumble that caught even the captain's attention.

Hardesty turned around to look up at Brik. "All right," he said. "Enlighten us."

"Destroy the *Burke*. Now. Don't approach her. Don't board her. It's a trap."

Korie looked up at Brik sharply. "How can you be that certain?"

"You are not a Morthan. You could not possibly understand."

"Try me."

Brik took a breath. He hesitated only a moment while he selected the most appropriate phrasing. "The Morthan Solidarity is built on treachery. Lying is a martial art. It is a fact of war. It is the means to the end. It is the necessary part of manipulation. To you, lying is only a hobby. To the Morthan, it is a way of life. Humans are considered cripples—because you *trust*. In the Morthan language, the word for trust means 'the condition necessary for betrayal.' " He added bluntly, "What I am saying to you is insufficient to convey the danger. That ship is coming from Morthan space. It is a trap."

"But it's one of ours," Korie said.

"No. It's one of *theirs* now. Count on it."

Hardesty looked thoughtfully to Korie. "Now, you know why I want a Morthan on the Bridge. It helps to have someone who thinks like the enemy."

"But we can't just—" Korie stopped himself. "There are procedures—" He looked to Brik, to Hardesty. "The book says—I mean, we *have* to go into that ship, because we *have* to know. The Alliance has to know—it's the whole mission! We have to ascertain the situation before we act.''

Hardesty agreed. ''Yes. That's what the book says.''

''Sir? You can't break procedure—''

Hardesty glared at him. ''Yes, I can. It's an option. Breaking procedure is *always* an option.''

''But there's no justification for putting a fish into her—not yet. Not unless you have more confidence in one of Brik's hunches than in your own orders. Captain, we don't know what the situation is over there—maybe they've locked down for reasons of their own.''

''Don't assume anything, Commander. Especially do not make assumptions about my decisions.'' He frowned thoughtfully as he considered the image of the *Burke* on the forward viewer. ''All right. We'll send a team in.''

Korie sighed, relieved.

Brik was less sanguine. ''From a human perspective, yes, that's the correct action. From a Morthan perspective—'' He shrugged unhappily, as if he couldn't think of a polite way to say what he had to say. Finally, he just blurted it. ''If I don't have the chance to tell you later, it has been a privilege to serve with you, sirs. Both of you.''

Hardesty looked dryly across to Korie. ''Perhaps you should lead the team.''

''Sir?'' Korie looked surprised. ''That's Mr. Brik's responsibility.''

''I know that,'' said the captain. ''But you're more expendable.''

''Uh . . . right.'' Korie didn't know if the captain was joking or not. Innocently, he asked, ''Am I allowed to take a weapon?''

''That,'' said Hardesty, ''is entirely *your* decision.''

THE BURKE

The tiny point of light on the screen began to resolve. It expanded and became a starship, silent and still.

On the Bridge, the mood became apprehensive and uncertain.

"Fifteen minutes till contact," said Hodel.

"Still no reply," reported Tor.

Korie sighed loudly. "I know what that means. I guess I'd better join the boarding party now." He looked across to Hardesty. "I'm returning your command to you, sir."

"Acknowledged," Hardesty said.

Korie hesitated, halfway toward the forward exit. "Don't you want to wish me luck?"

"If you follow the book, you won't need it—and if you run into a situation where you have to invent, you'll need more than luck."

"Right," said Korie. "I should have known. Thank you, sir." He stepped down and out the exit into the forward keel.

The forward air lock and the ancillary dressing bay were the farthest points forward in the vessel. Here, the members of the security team were dressing for their mission. There were lockers, starsuits, helmets, closets, racks of gear, weap-

ons, communicators, rechargers, life-support modules, battle
armor, and a variety of good-luck charms, tokens, and religious icons.

Ten crew members, including Brik, were just going through
their final checks. Korie also recognized Armstrong, Bach,
Nakahari, and Quilla Zeta.

Their starsuits were very shiny, skintight body stockings.
Each was a different color. Several had gaudy stripes. Korie
neither approved nor disapproved of the fashion. Sometimes
it was appropriate, sometimes not. Sometimes it didn't matter.

Korie opened his own locker and began pulling on his own
suit. Brik came over and began assisting him, checking his
helmet camera and weapons as he fitted them into place.

"Thanks," said Korie.

"You're the last one," said Brik. "Besides, it would not
look good on my record if I failed to bring you back alive."

"You're coming with me?"

"Despite my misgivings about the situation, I am still chief
of security. It is my responsibility."

"Then it doesn't really matter who leads the team, does
it?"

"On the contrary. The leadership is the most important part
of the job. It is always necessary to know where to fix the
blame."

Korie frowned at Brik. Had the Morthan intended that as a
joke or not? He couldn't tell. *Do Morthans joke? Would it be
impolite to ask?* Korie suppressed the question. There were
more important concerns on his mind.

Across the bay, Brian Armstrong was fitting a new power
pack into his rifle. He looked up to see Quilla Zeta smiling
shyly at him. "Brian," she said. "I am still feeling wonder-
ful. You are very 'wow' too."

Armstrong looked embarrassed and annoyed, both at the
same time. *When is it going to stop?* But he faked a smile
well enough to say, "Thanks. You're—?"

Touching herself politely, "This is Zeta."

Armstrong gestured feebly. "Oh—right. Sure. Anytime."
He looked up to notice Reynolds and Cappy grinning at him.
Bach and Nakahari were also visibly amused, poking each
other and giggling.

Bach called across to Armstrong. "Wow, huh?"

Armstrong sighed. "All right. Knock it off. The jokes are getting old."

Korie stepped to the center of the bay then; he was listening to something on his headset, and carrying his helmet under one arm. He held up a hand for their attention and they fell instantly quiet. As soon as the voice in his ear stopped whispering, he spoke aloud. "All right, it's a go. We've scanned the *Burke*. The readings are inconclusive. She could be dead. Maybe not. Harlie's not sure. What that means"—Korie glanced at Brik—"is that *it could be a trap*. That ship came out of the Morthan sphere of influence. Trust nothing."

He turned to Brik, drawing him aside with a nod. He lowered his voice almost to a whisper. "I was going to ask if I could trust you. But now I see that's the wrong question. What do Morthans use *instead* of trust?"

"Mutual advantage," Brik replied quietly.

"I see. . . ."

"Mr. Korie, you are a better officer than you know. And the captain has more respect for you than he has publicly expressed. It is to our mutual advantage that you should be aware of that."

Korie looked at Brik surprised, but the subject was closed. He shrugged and turned to the rest of the boarding team. "All right. Move 'em out." He locked his helmet on and followed the others toward into the cramped space of the forward air lock. The doors slid shut behind them.

On the Bridge, Hodel was watching his monitors closely. The *LS-1187* had swung around and was now carefully approaching the rear of the *Burke*. She would join her forward air lock to the *Burke*'s tail access dock.

Tor was routinely back-checking Hodel's guidance. As they approached the last go/no-go point, she said, "On the beam."

"That's how I read it too," said Hodel.

Hardesty was standing directly behind the both of them. He spoke in a soft ironic rumble. "Be gentle, Mr. Hodel. Be gentle."

"Aye, aye, sir." Hodel touched his controls. The mass-drivers glowed for an instant; the *LS-1187* slowed. Hodel glanced at the vectors on his console and touched his controls again. And then again. Carefully, he brought the ship up to the tail of the *Burke*, bringing her to a relative stop at the exact same time.

"Got it!" said Hodel, pleased with himself. He straightened in his chair, grinning.

Tor touched her controls. "Extending docking harness." A faint vibration could be felt through the floor. It came through the soles of their shoes and through the bottoms of their chairs. And then there was a hard *bang* and then a *thump* as the harness connected and clasped.

"I have acquisition."

"Confirmed."

The impact was more noticeable in the forward air lock. The men and women of the boarding party were shaken where they stood, but none of them lost their balance. Korie looked across at Brik. Brik's expression was unreadable. The rest of the team stood in relaxed readiness. Some of them were already in a half-crouch, their rifles held high.

Korie listened to his headset. "They're extending the docking tube now."

The tube moved out from the nose of the *LS-1187*, sliding through the cylindrical framework of the docking harness. It touched the security ring around the *Burke*'s access port and locked softly in place. Korie moved to the front of the air lock and tapped the green panel at the base of the control board. The board flashed green. "We have a connect." He watched while the safety programs cycled through a long series of double-checks. "Power connect, good. Gravity, good. Air pressure, good. The mix is breathable. Uh-oh. Computer's down—no response. Harlie, do you copy that?"

"Acknowledged, Mr. Korie."

"Bridge?"

"The mission is yours now," came Hardesty's soft reply.

"All right, I think we're good. We're not going to need the docking tube. Let's close it up." Korie touched a control on the panel.

Outside, the docking harness began to retract slowly, pulling the two ships closer and closer together—until their air lock hatches connected inside the accordion envelope of the docking tube and became one functional unit.

Korie hit the control panel and ordered up another series of safety checks.

"Bridge? What do you read?"

"Same thing you do. The *Burke*'s running on standby. No internal monitoring available. No network running. No log access. But she's holding air and temperature, her fans appear to be running. We're not reading any life signs, but the environment is viable. It's a shirt-sleeve day in there."

"Did you send a query? Did you get an ID signal?"

"Yes and no," said Hodel.

"Damn," said Korie. He glanced back at Brik, but resisted the temptation to say what he was thinking. "All right," he sighed. "Blow the door." He took a step back, then another—

The lock doors popped open with a *whoosh* of air which nearly knocked Korie back into the man behind him. It was Armstrong, who caught him easily under the arms and pushed him back up onto his feet. "Not quite as perfect a match as we thought," said Korie and threw himself forward.

The mission team poured through the air lock and into the *Burke* like a squad of combat-ready marines. They moved quickly through the other starship's darkened shuttle bay, leapfrogging forward with weapons ready. The *Burke*'s cargo dock and loading bays were almost identical to those of the *LS-1187*, except that the *Burke* was strung with thicker cables and ducting. Korie wondered if that had something to do with the high-cycle fluctuators.

"We're in," said Korie. "She's empty. No signs of battle. No other damage. We're moving forward." He pointed to Armstrong and Nakahari, directed them toward a console. "Cover that." Several of the other mission team members were already moving out across the floor, checking all the entrances to the bay. Two of them eased down the ladder to the *Burke*'s keel.

Nakahari slipped into the chair before the console; it was dead, but he was prepared for that. He plugged his portable terminal into the monitor socket and it lit up immediately. Armstrong took up a position close by, covering Nakahari's back.

"All systems green," the crewman reported. "Harlie?"

"Downloading now," Harlie confirmed.

"You two stay here," Korie said to them. "Guard the access. Blow it if you have to. Nothing goes back. Not yet."

Armstrong nodded. "Yes, sir." Behind Korie's back, he and Nakahari exchanged nervous glances.

There were two passages forward from the shuttle bay, one port, one starboard.

Korie motioned Brik and Bach toward the starboard corridor. He and Quilla Zeta moved toward the port passage.

The corridor was dark and empty. Only scattered work lights glowed dully. Korie activated the targeting scanner in his rifle and glanced quickly at the readouts. Nothing out of the ordinary. He pushed forward. Quilla Zeta followed quietly.

They entered the upper deck of the engine room only a few steps behind Brik and Bach. Korie glanced across at them. Brik glowered back, shaking his head. Nothing on the starboard side either.

The *Burke*'s engine room felt eerily familiar. They could have been aboard their own ship—except for the three oversize fluctuator housings that projected out of the singularity cage. Korie eyed them enviously. He circled around the deck until he came to a ladder.

Brik and Bach had echoed his movements on the opposite side. Now Korie gestured, pointing downward toward the floor of the great dark chamber. Bach and Quilla Zeta waited while Korie and Brik descended. They covered the two men warily. Then they followed while Korie and Brik covered their descents.

"Brik, you come with me." To the two women, Korie said, "Count ten, then follow behind us at a distance." Korie tapped his headset. "Bridge?"

"Tracking is good. Confidence is ninety-nine. Everybody's clear. No problems. Go ahead."

The central keel was dark. Even the work lights were out here. The only illumination came from their helmet beams, fingers of light probing the gloom.

"If you want to have a bad feeling about this," Korie suggested to Brik, "now's the time."

"Morthans don't get bad feelings," rumbled Brik. "*We give them.*"

"Uh, right—"

Korie pushed forward, silently reminding himself, *Never again. Don't tell jokes to a Morthan.*

They were only a few steps away from the operations bay when his radio beeped. Harlie spoke softly into his ear. "Mr. Korie. The *Burke*'s log. is blank."

"What? Say again?" Korie put a hand on the ladder next to him. It led up into the ship's computer bay.

"There's nothing to download. *It's been wiped.*"

"That doesn't make sense, Harlie. What about the ship's brain?"

Harlie's words sounded almost *uncertain*—or maybe that was only Korie's imagination. "It's . . . not in the circuit."

Korie realized he was staring at Brik's face. He broke away suddenly and peered up the ladder. From here, he couldn't see anything but the dark ceiling of the bay.

"Stand by, Harlie. We'll check it."

Korie nodded to Brik. Brik took a sour step back to cover Korie's quick ascent.

The computer bay was dark and it took a moment for Korie to realize what he was seeing. He swept his beam back and forth, around and across the tiny cabin. A cold chill crept up his spine and shuddered out through his limbs.

Something horrible had happened here.

Everywhere, the destruction was absolute. The *Burke*'s computer hadn't been simply dismantled—it had been ripped apart. There were great gaping holes in the walls. Wiring conduits hung limply. There were fractured modules, broken nodes, cracked boards, and shattered panels all over the floor. Korie's boots crunched across shards and splinters of glass and plastic and metal. The room was ankle-deep in techno-garbage.

It was the first *death* they had discovered aboard the *Burke*.

Korie didn't know what to say.

It was one thing to disconnect a brain. It was another matter entirely to dismantle one. The *Burke*'s brain wasn't just down. It was dead.

He wondered how Harlie would take the news. Probably not well. Ships' brains considered themselves a tribe—or even a *family*.

Finally, he said, "The brain has been . . . taken apart. It doesn't look repairable. Sorry, Harlic."

Harlie did not respond. There really wasn't anything he could say anyway. Korie imagined that Harlie was feeding his emotions—*did he really have emotions?*—into some other outlet, some file somewhere, perhaps, to be played back and dealt with later, probably only in the company of another brain.

Grimly, Korie climbed back down to the keel where Brik still waited for him. Korie shook his head and nodded forward, toward the Bridge. Brik followed him silently. Bach and Quilla Zeta followed at a distance.

Korie stepped through the narrow operations bay—its consoles were all dark—and up onto the Ops deck of the *Burke*. It was as desolate and empty as the rest of the ship. Two of the stations were alive, but inactive. Brik stepped up onto the deck behind Korie.

There was a sound from the Bridge above them and they both turned at the same time, their weapons ready.

It was sitting in the captain's chair.

THE MORTHAN
DIPLOMATIC CORPS

It was grinning and picking its teeth. Korie couldn't think of it as a *him*. Not yet.

It was bigger than Brik, and darker. It sprawled insolently in the captain's seat, glowing with a luminous feral quality. Its expression was the arrogant sneer of amused superiority.

It was wearing armor and war paint and enough jewelry and braid and ornamentation to make a Vegan gambler weep with envy.

And it looked *happy* to see them.

Bach and Quilla Zeta stepped up onto the deck, turned, and caught sight of what had stopped Korie and Brik so abruptly. They froze too, their weapons pointing.

The Morthan looked at them, its gaze sliding from one to the other, taking in their stances and their ready weaponry.

"Mr. Korie?" Hodel's voice. "Are you all right? Please confirm."

"We're fine. We've just caught the cat who ate the Canary Islands. That's all."

"Say again, please?"

"A member of the Morthan Diplomatic Corps," said Brik. "The single most elite class of killers in the Solidarity."

"You're trying to tell us this is bad news, aren't you?" said Bach.

"Oh, Mama—" said Zeta. "We really stepped into it this time."

"Belay that!" Korie looked up at the Morthan. "Who are you? And where's the crew of this vessel?"

The Morthan widened its feral grin. It parted its lips slightly—and *belched*. Loudly and deliberately.

Korie was appalled. Bach flinched. The Quilla narrowed her eyes. Only Brik understood. He nodded almost imperceptibly.

Without taking his eyes off his enemy, Brik said to Korie, "Morthan ambassadors are the most sophisticated assassins in the Solidarity. Many of them have specialized implants and augments to increase their physical and mental capabilities."

The Morthan looked down at the humans with disgust, but he focused his special contempt on Brik. It spoke then, a hissing stream of invective that sounded like a cat fight in a bottle. *"Didn't your fathers ever tell you not to play with your food?"*

Brik smiled right back. *"At least I know who my fathers were."*

"I will pick my teeth with the bones of your friends. You will howl alone on the bloody sand."

"What's he saying?" Korie asked.

"He's delighted to see us," Brik answered.

Korie gave Brik an incredulous look. *Was that a joke? From Brik?* Then he made a decision. "Secure it in the *Burke*'s brig." He turned away, forcing himself to look around the rest of the Operations deck, as if to demonstrate that he wasn't mesmerized by the monster's presence. "Captain Hardesty?"

On the Bridge of the *LS-1187*, Captain Hardesty and the others were watching the reflected view of the mission team's helmet cameras. The large forward viewer showed the scene on the Bridge of the *Burke*.

"I'm on my way," Hardesty said.

"Recommend against that, sir," came back Korie's reply. "We're still locking down over here."

"Mr. Korie. I'll pretend I didn't hear that."

On the Bridge of the *Burke*, Korie showed Brik a sour expression.

Brik said nothing.

TRAPS

It wasn't often that a liberty ship needed to activate its brig, but the skipper of the *Burke* had foreseen the possibility that it might be necessary to contain an infuriated Morthan—for its own protection, as well as for the protection of the crew.

Arranging appropriate accommodations for a Morthan assassin was one thing.

Getting the creature into them was another.

And yet. . . .

It went willingly.

It looked at the heavy-duty weaponry arrayed against it, *yawned deliberately,* and practically led the way to the brig. The creature's manner disturbed Korie. It was almost as if it had chosen the brig as its personal accommodation; it definitely did not act as if it considered itself a prisoner.

There was something wrong here.

He looked to Brik for explanation, but Brik was as silent as the assassin. He did not speak until the monster was safely installed in the brig of the *Burke.*

The brig was a suspended energy cage installed in the

ship's shuttle bay. It hung a meter off the floor and at least five meters from the nearest wall. It touched nothing. Inside the holding frame, it was visible as a shimmering cage of light. The air hummed and fizzed in the wall of brightness. The Morthan assassin stood on the only solid part of the cell, its circular floor, and glowered out at its captors.

All around the detainment field, technicians were installing robot cameras and weapons. The Morthan would never be unwatched or unguarded.

Dr. Molly Williger was standing in the basket of a portable lift, scanning the Morthan through the energy fields. Korie, Brik, and Hardesty stood aside and watched.

"They thought *that* was an ambassador?" Hardesty said dryly.

"They *trusted* the Morthans. Brik was right. It was a trap."

"Correction," said Brik. "It is *still* a trap."

Korie glanced up at Brik oddly, but Brik showed no inclination to explain. He shrugged and followed Hardesty closer to the detainment cell.

Hardesty looked up at the Morthan without fear. To Korie, the Morthan still looked *amused*.

"Under the Articles of the Covenant," said Hardesty, "you are entitled to and guaranteed certain protections for your person, your physical and mental well-being. In return for these protections, you must agree to abide by the Articles of the Covenant. Do you so agree? If you are not familiar with the Articles of the Covenant, a copy will be provided."

The Morthan chuckled deep in its throat. The sound was nasty and gave Korie an uneasy feeling. "I have no need of your covenant. Your protection and your guarantees are worthless to me." He glanced sideways at Brik and added, "You are *Yicka Mayza-lishta*!"*

Brik snorted. "You call that cursing? My grandmother could do better. And she was *human*."

The assassin narrowed its eyes. "And you *brag* about it?"

Hardesty ignored the exchange. "You understand then, that

---

*Lawyer dung.

you are forsaking all rights and all claims. You are no longer legally entitled to any protections of your person, or your physical or mental well-being."

The assassin barely glanced at Hardesty. "Do your worst."

Williger finished her scan then and lowered the lift. She snorted contemptuously and looked up at the captain with a truly disgusted expression. "A thousand years of genetic engineering and this is what you get? A nine-foot snot?"

Hardesty turned away without answering. Korie remained where he was, studying the Morthan. Brik's words haunted him. *It is still a trap.*

The Morthan snarled down at Williger, a sound like a panther scraping its claws on glass. "It is hard to believe that my people were *deliberately* evolved from *yours*."

Williger barely glanced up. "How do you think I feel about it? My family still has its pride."

"Your family is still sitting in a tree somewhere, picking fleas off each other."

This time, Williger let her annoyance show. "Too bad they bred you for looks and not for manners. Now shut up and let me work or I'll bring up the proctoscope."

Abruptly, the Morthan shut up.

Korie grinned at the doctor. "So that's how to make a Morthan cooperate. I'll have to remember that."

The answer came from above. "Morthans do *not* cooperate with humans. Morthans *rule* humans."

Williger looked up from her clipboard to Korie. "It's got a big mouth."

It leered down at her. "The better to eat you with." The Morthan assassin grinned and bared its teeth. Korie noticed that Williger's diagnosis was absolutely correct. The monster had a *very* big mouth.

Williger was nonplussed. "I just love it when you talk dirty," she said, smiling back. She switched off her scanner and stepped over to the captain. Korie followed.

Hardesty looked at her questioningly.

She shook her head. "Big mouth. Bad breath. I'll give you the rest later." She exited back toward the *LS-1187* to run the results of her scan through Harlie.

Korie turned to study the Morthan once more. The creature—

Korie still couldn't see it as a *him*—had turned away from them. It was studying the energy cage around it.

Could it—?

No. It couldn't.

At least, that was what Korie wanted to believe.

HARD DECISIONS

The Bridge of the *Burke* was coming back to life. The crew of the *LS-1187* moved with professional élan. Watching them, Korie had to admit that Hardesty had known what he was doing when he had ordered them to rebuild the *LS-1187*. The crew had brought the *Burke*'s sensory network back online quicker than Korie would have thought possible.

Unless the Morthan had deliberately not damaged it for reasons of its own.

Korie shoved the thought aside. It troubled him, but there was nothing he could do about it now. Not yet.

Tor was just seating herself at the *Burke*'s display table; the display was dark and had a thin layer of dust on its top surface. Leen and Hodel pulled up chairs, as did one of the Quillas. Hardesty, Korie, and Brik joined them. Williger came in a moment later and took a place at the forward end of the table.

Hardesty looked to Korie first. "You first, Mr. Korie."

Korie looked at his notes—not because he needed to, but because it was reassuring to do so. He took a breath. "The *Burke* was outfitted with three ultrahigh-cycle envelope fluctuators for this mission, giving her a state-of-the-art stardrive and making her nearly twice as fast as any ship the Morthan Solidarity can build. The assumption was that her enhanced stardrive would allow her to travel through Morthan space without fear of interception.

"She was sent into the Morthan sphere to pick up an ambassador supposedly carrying a new peace initiative. It is now clear that the alleged envoy was in fact a trained assassin, whose mission was to kill the crew and disable the *Burke*."

He concluded his comments and laid his clipboard down on the dead display table.

"And . . . ?" prompted Hardesty.

"It's obvious," Korie said. "It's the enhanced stardrive; that's what they want. The whole point of the phony peace initiative was to get an assassin onto this ship—*because they couldn't catch her any other way*."

Hardesty looked at Korie, mildly impressed. "Yes. That's how I read it too." He glanced over at his security officer. "Your analysis of the situation was correct."

"There was nothing to analyze," Brik corrected his captain. "A Morthan is a treacherous liar. Whatever else is true about a Morthan is irrelevant."

Korie was honestly curious. "Does that apply to you too, Brik?" he asked.

"A Morthan can only reveal his true nature through his actions," Brik explained. Then he added thoughtfully, "The assassin should not have allowed us to capture him so easily. There is more to this that we still have not yet realized."

Hardesty looked down to the end of the table. "Dr. Williger?"

"That thing in the brig is named Esker Cinnabar and it registers one hundred thirty-two on the Skotak Viability Scale. Preliminary scan shows significant microbiotechnical implants and augments bringing his Skotak rating up to three hundred ninety. Or more." To Hodel's curious look, she clarified, "Seventy-five to eighty is normal for a human." Turning back to Hardesty, she continued, "This is one big ugly mother. Mean. Strong. Nasty. Don't get him angry."

"I'll remember that," Hardesty said.

Tor spoke up then. "Why did he have to dismantle the *Burke*'s brain?"

"I can answer that," said Brik. "The *Burke*'s brain would not have allowed the Morthan to take over the ship. It would have fought him; he knew it; therefore the brain had to be disabled. That was probably the *first* thing the assassin did."

"But without a brain, the *Burke* is helpless," Tor said. "He can't take her home. He can't do anything with her."

Hardesty smiled knowingly. "Mr. Korie? Have you figured that part out yet?"

"A Morthan heavy-duty battle cruiser," Korie replied calmly. "She follows the *Burke* as fast as she can. She can't catch up, of course—not until the assassin disables the *Burke*. Then it's a simple matter of retrieval. Cinnabar tears up the brain, kills the crew, then sits and waits for the heavy cruiser to arrive. Unfortunately, we showed up first.

"Why didn't Cinnabar attack us? Probably, he didn't want to risk damage to the *Burke*. And that's why he surrendered peacefully. When the cruiser arrives, they'll capture both ships—at least, that's got to be his expectation. The Morthans install a new brain in her and . . . bye-bye *Burke*. Bye-bye Alliance."

Brik rumbled deep in his chest. It was a ruminative sound. "Comment, Brik?"

"You are assuming that they did not expect the *Burke* to be meeting another ship. I'm certain that it was considered in their contingency planning. It would be in ours. That's why I said there is more to this than we have realized."

"You might be right—" Abruptly, Korie realized something. "If our intelligence is correct, the only ship they have in this area capable of that kind of operation is—the *Dragon Lord*."

"Oh, no," groaned Hodel. "Not the *Dragon Lord* again."

Tor's reaction was more professional. She tapped at her clipboard for a moment. "My best projection is that the *Dragon Lord* would have to be at least two, maybe six days away."

"I make it two days, maximum," said Hardesty. "Mr. Leen—how long to bring the *Burke* back online?"

Leen shook his head sadly. "Without the brain, we can't run even the simplest systems analysis checks. It'll take us

days to reassemble it—that's assuming we can.'' He shrugged.
"I might be able to jury-rig a replacement from our stores,
but I don't know that'd be any faster. We're better off going
on manual.'' He shrugged again, this time even more
disconsolately. "A week—and even that's a guess."

Korie shook his head. "No. We don't have the time. We're
too close to the Morthan sphere."

Tor agreed with Korie. She knew what he was implying.
"We'll have to scuttle her—"

"God, I hate to lose those high-cycle fluctuators. . . ."
Korie said, wistfully.

Hodel looked around the Bridge of the *Burke* with real
disappointment. "We can't salvage anything?"

"Count on it," said Brik. "The Morthan has booby-
trapped her."

"How do you know that?" asked Hodel. "I mean, okay,
he's *probably* booby-trapped her, but—"

"Not *probably*," said Brik. "There is no room for chance
in a Morthan scenario." He looked to Korie. "The fact that
an Alliance ship might make contact with the *Burke* before
the *Dragon Lord* has been allowed for. Therefore, there are
parts of the trap that are aimed at us."

"Right," said Williger. "That's my question. If the *Burke*
couldn't hold that monster, can we?"

"We have to," remarked Hardesty. "I don't like the
alternative."

Korie was playing with an idea. He steepled his fingers in
front of himself and said softly, "Y'know, we could—this is
just an idea—strip those fluctuators off the *Burke* in . . . oh,
less than eighteen hours. I can run one crew, Leen can run
another. Hodel and Jonesy can handle the third." He looked
around the table, meeting their eyes. They looked interested.
"Look, if the *Dragon Lord* shows up, we'll have at least two
or three minutes warning. That's enough time to blow the
Burke and scramble, and we haven't lost anything; but otherwise—
well, we still scuttle her, but this way we get to keep the
high-cycles."

"I like it," said Tor. "Especially the part about keeping
the super-stardrive."

"If I were the assassin," said Brik, "that'd be the *first*
thing I'd booby-trap."

"Obviously," said Korie. "So we break 'em down and run a full suite of integrity checks before we put 'em online, but at least we can pull the units out of their housings and transfer them."

Hardesty cleared his throat. They all fell silent. "Mr. Korie, there is an inaccurate assumption in your analysis. I'm not giving up the *Burke*." He added sharply, "And you shouldn't either. *You want a ship*. Let's bring this one home."

"Her integrity's been breached," said Korie. "We don't have the resources to decontaminate her."

Hardesty's expression was immobile. "Do you know how much a liberty ship costs the Alliance?"

"Is that the deciding factor? The cost? What's at stake here is more than one ship—"

"But if you could save that ship, would you?"

"It's not that simple, sir. It's a question of what's possible under the circumstances. Trying to save her is the third best option. The risk—"

Hardesty's tone was suddenly icy. "You're arguing for your limits, Mr. Korie. I thought we broke you of that bad habit."

Korie shut up. When the captain used that tone, the argument was already lost. He sighed. "Yes, sir. You're right. I would like to save that ship—if we could. That I have expressed my doubts is part of my responsibility as your exec to advise you to the best of my ability."

"Your advice has been noted," said the captain. "Now, let's go to work." He looked around the table at his officers. "We are going to save the *Burke*. It is important for this ship and this crew to come home with a victory. Saving the *Burke* will be a good start.

"Chief Engineer, build us a brain. It doesn't have to be brilliant. Mr. Brik, you look for booby-traps. Detox this vessel." To Tor and Hodel, he said, "We'll stay at Condition Red. Run a twelve-hour clock. Hold at ninety seconds from stardrive injection. We sight anything coming at us in hyperspace, we scramble—and the *Burke* self-destructs. That means nobody gets lazy. If the alarm sounds, you'll have thirty seconds to get off the *Burke*. Beyond that, you're a footnote in the log." He turned to Korie. "Pick a crew of twelve. You'll bring the *Burke* home. First thing, though, you'll strip the fluctuators off—no matter what else, *I want them*. All right," he concluded, "That's it. Any questions?"

There were none.

"Good. Thank you. Go to work." Hardesty pushed his chair back from the table, rose crisply, and exited from the Bridge of the *Burke*.

Hodel groaned first. "Oh, god—why do we always get the hard ones? We *are* jinxed." He looked up at the ceiling. "Whatever it was, Ghu—I'm sorry!"

Tor ignored the performance. She was already speaking to her headset. "Harlie, we'll need critical path schedules—"

Harlie was way ahead of her. He was always ahead of everybody. "I'm posting them now."

Korie looked up at Brik, but the Morthan was emotionless. He swiveled around and stared at the Bridge where the assassin had first been found.

Is it possible that Hardesty has made a very bad decision? Or is there something that I'm still missing?

HIGH-CYCLE
FLUCTUATORS

The two starships floated like lovers, linked together in the brittle paradigm of their rendezvous. They drifted in dreamtime, alone against the deep abyss of distance.

Inside the *Burke*, high within her engine room, Korie and Haddad sweated over the difficult job of prying loose the fluctuator casing. They stood on the catwalk, working on the highest of the *Burke*'s three units. It was a large torpedo-shaped structure, braced and reinforced within a shining tubular frame. Below them, other crew members worked just as determinedly to remove the other two units without damaging them.

Haddad levered himself up inside the flanged part of the cylinder while Korie waited impatiently. After a moment, the sound of muffled cursing came ricocheting out of the cylinder. "—fang-dang, filthy, pork-eating, cretin-loving, drunken, godforsaken, vermin-ridden, water-wasting, scrofulous, yellow-dog, leprous, swine-hearted infidel—"

"Easy, Haddad," said Korie. "You don't have to insult it. Those things are sensitive instruments."

Silence. And then, in a different, more professional tone,

"Got it." Haddad pried himself out of the cylinder. "Sorry for the cursing, sir."

"No problem. It was very educational."

Haddad grinned and wiped his forehead with a cloth. "It's out of the circuit now. The bypass is showing green. We can pull it."

They began to unclamp the fluctuator from its housing. Using a block and tackle, they lowered it gently to the catwalk, where Armstrong was waiting to secure it to a cart.

"Easy."

"I got it."

Korie waited until he was sure the unit was safe on the cart, then he turned to Haddad. "You go down and help them with the bypass on number two, Ayoub. Armstrong can help me with this."

"Right."

Korie took the rear of the cart, Armstrong positioned himself at the front, and they began to move the heavy unit slowly along the catwalk toward the aft corridor. "The port one, I think," said Korie.

Armstrong glanced behind himself and nodded.

As they entered the corridor, Jonesy came barreling past them at a run, carrying computer components. He almost collided with Armstrong, but at the last moment, turned himself sideways, raised his gear over their heads, bent with the shape of the wall, and darted easily past them.

"Easy, Jonesy. We don't have time for accidents."

"No, sir. I mean, yes, sir. No time to stop. Excuse me, sir." He hurried on, leaving Korie and Armstrong grinning in his wake.

To get to the rear access, they had to pass through the shuttle bay. Esker Cinnabar glowered at them from his cage. His lips were curled back in a perpetual sneer, exposing fangs as long as Korie's wrist.

Armstrong shuddered. "Are we feeding him enough?"

"I hope so," Korie said. "But it's the between-meal snacking we have to worry about." Armstrong looked stricken. Korie waved a hand in front of his face to attract his attention. "Hey, Armstrong! Don't let him get to you. It's all psychological warfare."

"I know, but—" Armstrong lowered his voice. "I see all

those energy screens and beamers and robot sentries, I see the guards around him, and it still doesn't reassure me. You saw what he did to the *Burke*."

Korie nodded. "I saw."

Hardesty was at the air lock console. He looked up approvingly as they approached. "Oh, Korie. Have you picked out a crew yet?"

"Almost, sir. I'll have the list for you in an hour. I'm trying to keep your needs in mind as well as mine."

"Good. Bring the *Burke* home safely and maybe you'll get to keep her."

"I thought the admiral didn't like me."

Hardesty shook his head. "That hardly matters. There's a shortage of trained captains, good or otherwise."

Korie waited until he was out of Hardesty's hearing to voice the thought that had come to him. "That explains a lot."

"Beg pardon, sir?"

"Nothing." He glanced back over his shoulder, and saw that Cinnabar, the Morthan assassin, was staring across the bay directly at him. And grinning. Korie looked away, disturbed. He pushed the thought out of his mind. It was psychological warfare. Cinnabar was trying to unnerve him—and succeeding.

They had to wait for a moment at the air lock door while Nakahari and Quilla Upsilon maneuvered a long unwieldy pipe through the access. The Quilla noticed Brian Armstrong waiting at the door and smiled meaningfully at him.

"Uh—hi," he said.

"This one is Upsilon," the Quilla identified herself. She was taller than the others. "And this one enjoyed it very much too."

"Oops . . . illon. Right." Armstrong flushed. He noticed that Korie was looking at him and was further discomfited.

Korie just smiled knowingly and shook his head, as if at some private joke. "They really caught you on that one. Don't worry about it. After a few years, hardly anyone will care. Push." He pointed toward the access.

"A few years?" Armstrong's eyes widened. "Really?" They maneuvered the cart through the door.

"It'll seem like it. Some of the kidding around here can be a little rough."

"How long does it usually go on, sir?"

They had to lift the cart over the joint in the passage floor. Korie said, "It depends on how *good* you were. Quillas like to talk about their good times. The better you were . . . well, you know." Korie grinned across at Armstrong.

They had to lift the cart's wheels across two more joints, and then they were in the forward access of the *LS-1187*.

"—at least that's what I've heard," Korie concluded.

"Really?"

"If you don't believe me, ask one of *them*."

"Wow. . . ." Armstrong's grin widened.

"Eh, you want to help me get this to the engine room first?"

"Oh, right. Sorry, sir."

"It's all right. I understand the distraction. But don't forget why we're here."

Hodel came hurrying up the corridor with a clipboard. "Oh, Mr. Korie—I'm glad I caught you. I need a G-2 authorization." He handed Korie the clipboard. Korie studied its screen in annoyance.

"You know," said Hodel. "We are not going to make it. This ship has an industrial-strength curse. The bad luck fairy doesn't like us."

Korie thumbprinted his authorization. He handed the clipboard back. "If that's true, Hodel, then why are we still alive?"

"Because, I think the universe is saving us for something *really* awful." Abruptly, he remembered something else. "Oh—one other thing. I'd appreciate it if you'd consider me for your flight crew. For the *Burke*."

Korie raised his eyebrow. "But the *Burke*'s luck is even worse than ours."

"Uh-uh." Hodel spoke with certainty. "They only got eaten. *We've* got the *Dragon Lord* after us." He pushed past them and headed forward.

Korie looked back to Armstrong. "Come on, let's get this thing to the engine room."

They seized the cart with the fluctuator on it again and rolled it down the keel, pushing and pulling it past the sick bay, past the forward access to the Ops deck, past the aft access to the Ops deck through the operations bay, past the vertical access to Harlie, and finally to the machine shop below the engine room. Here, the keel widened into a low-ceilinged chamber. This was the starship's machine shop. The floor of the engine room above was removable to allow easy access between the drive units and the tools needed for heavy-duty maintenance work. Here, Chief Engineer Leen would break down the high-cycle fluctuators and run his security tests on them.

Korie and Armstrong slid the cart into position next to a makeshift work bay. Leen slid down a ladder to help them secure the fluctuator. "Use the clamps," he said, pointing. "Here, like this. Hold it—okay. That damned assassin knew what he was doing," Leen said to Korie. "The *Burke*'s machine shop is junk. You better pray you don't have any problems once you get under way."

"You'd better pray," Korie corrected him. "I'm asking Hardesty for you."

"Don't do me any favors. I've got enough work here. I have to break all three of these down and insulate them against resonance effects in case we have to scramble." He grunted as he secured the last clamp. "I'm not even thinking about installing them yet."

"Chief, I really need you—"

"You're right, you do," Leen admitted grudgingly. He thought a moment. "I hate to say it, but there isn't anyone else who could get that ship running."

"And Reynolds can manage here," Korie prompted.

"Yeah. All right." Leen did not look happy.

Korie slapped him on the shoulder. "Thanks, Chief."

"Don't get all mushy. I'm not doing it for you."

"Well, thanks anyway—"

Leen's answer was lost in the sudden blare of the alarm klaxon.

"Mr. Korie?" Harlie interrupted. "I'm picking up an alarm in the brig of the *Burke*." The screen on the workbench lit up.

At first, Korie couldn't recognize what he was seeing. It looked like war had broken out. Harlie was showing him the view from the remote cameras.

Korie realized what was happening with a sudden rush of cold-fire terror. *The energy cage hadn't held him.*

The screen showed flashes of laser fire. Something exploded and lurched. Someone was screaming. Korie thought he saw a crewman being hurled across the shuttlecraft bay. There was a brief glimpse of the assassin—and then suddenly, the screen was dead.

Harlie reported calmly, "The Morthan Cinnabar has escaped."

"Where's the captain?"

"He's on the *Burke*."

"Lock down everything!"

"Already in progress."

Korie didn't hear it. He was already pounding toward the forward access. Armstrong charged along behind him.

The other members of the ship's security team were on the way too. They slid down ladders or fell out of doorways or hurtled down the keel after Korie or ahead of him, pulling on vests, grabbing weapons and security helmets, shouting and cursing. The alarm continued to bleat over everything.

The access door was already sealed. Two security guards in heavy armor were in kneeling position before it, one on each side. Their rifles were pointed unwaveringly at the door. Korie grabbed a security harness from a Quilla and pulled it on over his head, and then the armor after it—and then the helmet. Somebody shoved a weapon into his arm. He checked its charge, armed it, and unlocked the safety. He glanced around quickly to see who else was there—Reynolds, Armstrong, Nakahari, half the engine room crew, and two Quillas. He pointed them into position.

And then he was ready.

"All right," Korie said angrily. "No more Mr. Nice Guy. *Set weapons to kill.*" To Harlie, "Okay. Open the door—"

There was a whoosh and the air lock doors began to slide open.

THE SHUTTLE BAY

Korie and the security team burst through the access and out into the shuttle bay of the *Burke* like a horde of hell-spawned furies.

The shuttle bay was a smoking nightmare. The energy cage was crumpled in a heap against one wall. It still crackled and flashed; sparks skittered across the floor. Smoldering scorch marks scored the walls. Puddles of blood streaked the floor. The robot cameras had been shattered; the sentries lay in pieces; the broken rifles were burning and sputtering.

Korie pointed half his team toward the starboard corridor; he led the other team into the portside passage.

Only moments before, he and Armstrong had wheeled a high-cycle fluctuator along this very way. Korie and his team poured swiftly through the corridor and into the *Burke*'s engine room.

"Oh, my God."

The shuttle bay had been a warmup for this. The only things in the engine room not destroyed were the two remaining high-cycle fluctuators. Korie slid down a pole to the floor of the engine room; the rest of his team followed, down either the poles or the ladders.

Haddad lay on the floor, his throat ripped open. The bodies of the others who had been working here were hung on the singularity framework like so many sides of beef. The engine room looked like an abattoir.

Korie and his team moved into the room, weapons held high and ready. They moved past the bodies quickly. Three men and one woman, all dead—and still dripping. Korie's first impulse was to say, "Take them down from there." But he stifled it unsaid. There wasn't time. Not yet. Maybe later.

"This could have been us," Armstrong started babbling. "If we hadn't carried the fluctuator out—"

"Shut up, Armstrong!" Korie's bellow startled even himself.

Abruptly, the klaxon stopped. Korie was staring at Haddad's strangled expression. He wanted to say something; he wanted to apologize—a sound caught his attention. Something was moving forward. He swung his weapon around—

Brik and Bach burst into the engine room from the forward keel, fanning their weapons before them. The two security teams stared at each other. The sense of horror leapt outward from the space between them. *Where's the Morthan?*

Korie couldn't help but wonder, *Is this how it started on the* Burke?

"He's not forward?"

Brik shook his head. He glanced around. "He got this far."

"You didn't see him?" Bach asked.

Both Korie and Brik gave her the same look. *Don't be silly.*

"Sorry," said Bach, realizing. The question *was* stupid.

Korie pointed to an access hatch in the wall. "Inner hull?" he asked Brik.

Brik nodded. "It's the only way." He was already pulling the hatch open. He dropped through it into the dark space beyond. Reluctantly, Korie followed.

The space beyond the wall was dark and shadowy. It was as unfinished and spooky as the inner hull of the *LS-1187*. Korie and Brik both switched on their helmet lights and peered around grimly.

Everything here was beams and cables and stanchions. It was more than uninviting. It was suicidal.

"Harlie," Korie asked. "Have you got a lock on the captain yet?"

"No, Mr. Korie."

Korie took a hesitant step forward into the darkness. He frowned. He was sure he could hear the Morthan assassin breathing in the gloom. He was sure they were being watched. He glanced sideways at Brik. "You feel it too?"

Brik grunted.

"Why doesn't he attack?"

"Because it's not part of the trap."

"I don't like this," Korie said. "Too much opportunity for disaster."

Brik agreed. Korie pulled himself up out of the inner hull, back into the light of the engine room. Brik followed.

Bach was arguing with Armstrong. "I want to know how he got out of the cage!"

"Ease up." Korie interrupted her with a gentle tap on the shoulder. "We'll worry about that later."

Nakahari reported, "Mr. Korie, S. A. says the *Burke*'s totally locked down now."

Brik responded to that. His skepticism was obvious. "No. The assassin had too much time to reprogram the systems analysis network. Don't trust it."

"Brik's right," Korie said. "This whole thing's a trap." He gave the looming Morthan a grudging look of acceptance, and then added, "And I'm not getting sucked into it any deeper. Evacuate the *Burke*. Now. Everybody off!" He started waving them back with crisp military gestures. The team fell back in a guarded withdrawal, their weapons covering every step.

"Harlie," Korie ordered, "Sound the evacuation. Do it now."

HARDER DECISIONS

The alarm rang through the *Burke*, clanging and banging. The crew members of the *LS-1187* still aboard her came running for the air lock access. They popped out of cabins and utility tubes and everywhere else they had been hiding and pounded along the catwalks and the keel toward their only escape. Korie hurried them onward, shouting as they passed, "Off! Everybody off!"

He and Brik were the last two to exit. They paused at the aft access, their weapons covering the ruined shuttle-bay. "Harlie? Is everybody out?"

"I show no active monitors."

"Where's the captain?"

"His monitor is no longer working, Mr. Korie. I have begun a scan."

Korie said a word.

"Say again, please?" Harlie asked.

"Never mind."

"If you said what I thought you said, it is anatomically impossible for most human beings—"

Korie stepped through the access. Brik backed through after him. "Never mind, Harlie. Seal it off."

The doors whooshed shut.

Korie looked around. The rest of the impromptu rescue team were standing and waiting for his next orders. He shook his head and pushed through them. Brik followed.

They headed down the keel and climbed up onto the Operations deck where Tor and Hodel were just putting a schematic display up on the holotable. Leen was there too.

"Casualties?" Korie asked.

Harlie responded instantly. "Security squads A and B. Stardrive engineers Haddad, Jorgensen, and Blake. Also Wesley."

"Damn. Have you located the captain?"

"Sorry, sir."

Korie stepped forward and leaned on the holotable. He took a moment to catch his breath, then looked up. Every officer on the Ops deck and Bridge was looking at him, waiting for his orders. "Show me your scan of the *Burke*. Where's the captain?" He peered at the glowing display, frowning. Two transparent starships floated in the air over the table, their walls and decks clearly outlined, but that was all.

"I'm sorry, Mr. Korie—I show no life readings at all."

"Not even the assassin?" asked Brik.

"It appears that the assassin has somehow altered his metabolism beyond the ability of our sensors."

"And the captain?" asked Korie.

"The captain's metabolism could not be safely altered."

Korie nodded to himself. He looked up and said, "Doctor to the Bridge, please." To Harlie, "Okay. Show me what the monitors recorded. What happened?" He turned forward to look at the main viewer.

"Here—" said Harlie, narrating, explaining. "You can see that the Morthan assassin was never seriously restrained by the energy cage. He steps through it as easily as a biofilter. I'll show you all the angles. Here's the slow motion—"

"He was *faking*," said Tor.

"He was waiting for the right moment," corrected Brik.

Korie guessed it immediately. "He saw us taking the fluctuators off the *Burke*. He had to stop it."

"Here—" Harlie continued. "This is where he attacked the security squads. Notice that even while he is at the center of their fire, he does not seem to be affected. Here's the slow motion. Notice how fast he's moving—"

"Optical nervous system, augmented musculature," said Korie.

"He must have some kind of internal shielding," said Tor. "He doesn't even flinch. They're not even burning him."

Brik said, "I realize that this is upsetting to you—but it is important that you recognize the efficiency of the assassin's killing pattern. There is no wasted movement at all."

Tor gasped involuntarily and turned away. The sound of the security man's back cracking was loud across the Bridge.

The screen showed the Morthan *flowing* like liquid fire—he grabbed and killed, cracked and threw, leapt and kicked and clawed. He was a blur that flashed from point to point and left a trail of broken, bleeding bodies. Even slowed down, the sense of incredible speed was overwhelming. The Morthan grabbed the captain like a sack of potatoes and—

"Hold it!" said Korie. "Run that again."

Harlie slowed the images down. Hardesty was bringing his weapon up and firing. The beam plunged through the Morthan's belly, but the Morthan didn't feel it. He surged inexorably forward, grabbing the gun and splintering it. The fuel cells flashed and exploded around him, the captain flung his arms up, the Morthan grabbed him—*and didn't kill him*. He caught the captain under one arm and scooped him off his feet—

Korie felt impaled by the dilemma. He still didn't have *proof*. The captain might still be alive.

The screen showed the Morthan sweeping the shuttle bay with ruthless efficiency, grabbing cameras off the wall and shattering them. The image switched from one point of view to the next, then it finally went blank.

Without being asked, Harlie began the series again.

Korie looked around and noticed Williger had come in while they were staring horrified at the screen. He acknowledged her with a nod. "You saw?"

She grunted. Her expression was wrinkled and sour.

Korie turned to Brik. "Under Article Thirteen, I have to

assume that the captain is dead or beyond rescue. Do you concur?'' Even before he finished the question, Tor and the others were looking up sharply.

Brik knew what he was being asked. He spoke with quiet candor. "I concur."

"Thank you." Korie turned to his astrogator. "Commander Tor?"

"Aren't you being a little hasty? You don't know for sure."

Korie nodded toward the screen. The Morthan was slashing a crewman into a bloody pulp. "Look at the pictures."

"No," said Tor, pointing. "You look. I didn't see the captain's death in that, and neither did you. Why don't you put a couple of probes into the *Burke* and search by remote? Let's be sure—"

"I wish I could," Korie replied. "But we don't have the time. And we'd never get better than fifty-percent confidence. I need your statement now."

Tor stepped in close to Korie and lowered her voice so that no one else could hear what she said. "I know you want your own ship, but aren't you being just a little too eager to write off Captain Hardesty?"

Korie ignored it. "I need a declarative sentence, Commander."

She shook her head. "I can't support *this*."

"That's your privilege. Thank you." Korie turned away. "Dr. Williger?"

Williger looked troubled and she sounded reluctant. "I don't like it either, but I have to vote with the evidence."

Tor followed Korie toward the Bridge. "I still think you're being too hasty."

"I appreciate your honesty," Korie said. He paused at the steps. "But I have to do this by the book *because that's the way the captain wants it.*" He glanced around. "Is there anyone else who disagrees?"

Korie looked from face to face, searching for dissent, hoping someone would come up with a valid reason why he shouldn't take the next ineradicable step. Jonesy? Leen? Goldberg? Brik? Hodel? Williger?

No. None of them.

Korie took a breath. "Harlie, log it. Under the provisions of Article Thirteen, I'm assuming command of the *LS-1187* on the presumption that Captain Richard Hardesty is dead, or beyond our ability to rescue."

Harlie's tone was as calm as ever. "Yes, Mr. Korie. It is so logged."

Tor spoke first. Her .tone was exquisitely formal. "Your orders, *sir*?"

Korie ignored the implied rebuke. "We're going to complete our mission. I want the fluctuators off the *Burke* and I don't want to play hide and eat with a Morthan assassin. Harlie, open the *Burke* to space. Do it now."

"Acknowledged. I am opening the *Burke* to space."

Korie tried not to show his reaction, but the reality of it made him flinch anyway. He turned back to the holographic display and watched as the various hatches on the schematic *Burke* began to open. The forward viewer flashed to show what the external cameras were able to see.

Harlie began shifting the view to show the interior of the *Burke*'s corridors as well. A great wind was sweeping through her corridors. Debris hurtled and blew and ricocheted off the walls. Things crashed and tumbled. A contorted body flopped over.

The Bridge crew watched in silence. Korie spoke bitterly. "That should let the air out of our assassin."

"Maybe not," said Williger.

They all turned to look at her sharply.

Chief Medical Officer Molly Williger stepped to the holographic display and slid a memory card into a reader. A bioschematic of the Morthan assassin flickered into being, replacing the schematic of the two linked starships. "He's all augments," said Williger. "He's got a lightspeed nervous system, multiprocessing lobes in his brain, a hardened skeleton, enhanced musculature, extra hearts, internal shielding, you name it—even the ability to shut down the organic parts of his body for short periods of time." She hesitated for a heartbeat. "And the bad news is that he might be able to function without air, food, and water for sustained periods."

Korie looked to Brik. "Is all this normal for an assassin?"

Brik nodded. "For a beginner."

"Stop trying to cheer me up," Korie muttered. To Williger, he said, "Okay. How long can that son of a bitch hold his breath?"

"Best guess? Fifteen minutes."

Korie made a decision. "We'll wait an hour."

"We don't have an hour," said Tor. "Remember the *Dragon Lord*?"

"I remember the *Dragon Lord*," Korie snapped back. "Better than you. I'll show you the scars." He repeated his order. "We'll wait an hour."

COFFEE

The *Burke* was cold and silent. Despite the cold glare of her lights, or maybe because of it, she looked desolate. Nothing moved aboard her. Her cameras showed nothing. Harlie's scans continued to come up empty.

After a while, Korie grew bored with the endless cycling of empty images. He grabbed a cup of coffee and stalked off the Bridge. He thought about going to the captain's cabin, but couldn't bring himself to do that. Not yet. It didn't feel right. It wouldn't be his *until*—until the admiral gave it to him.

He stopped and leaned against the wall of the starboard corridor, slumping and staring at nothing in particular. The gray surface of the foamboard construction had a dull sheen.

The argument raged inside his head. *I didn't have any choice. The decision had to be made. I only did what Hardesty would have done if he had been here. I followed the book.* But all of that was meaningless against the accusing facts. *We didn't see him die. We didn't know for sure that he was dead. We could have killed him when we evacuated the air out of the* Burke!

But that was only the surface of the turmoil, the immediate

details. Floating below that was the more disturbing pain. *It's Captain Lowell all over again. A captain is supposed to depend on his executive officer—why can't I be that kind of exec? Why can't I protect my commander? Am I so stupid and clumsy that I can't safeguard my leader? But how do you keep a captain from getting killed if he insists on making the wrong decisions? What is it about leadership that others can see and I can't? Am I so wrapped up in my own ego that I can't tell what's right? What kind of an officer am I?*

Korie noticed that his shoes were bloody, probably from one of the puddles he'd had to step through. He wondered whose blood it was. He wondered if he should try to clean these shoes or if he'd be better off tossing them into the singularity. That was how all the garbage was disposed of on a starship; it was fed to the pinpoint black hole in the engine room. It was fun to watch too—the way things just crumpled up and sucked away into nothingness, usually with a flash and a bang.

When he looked up again, Brik was standing before him, waiting patiently.

"What do you want?" he said. His tone was not friendly.

"I thought that you might want . . . some advice." Brik hesitated, then added, "Captain Hardesty appreciated my thoughts, particularly in strategic situations. I thought you might wish the same access."

"Mm," said Korie. He stared into his half-empty coffee mug, swirling it around as he did so. He couldn't think of anything to ask. He couldn't think of anything at all right now. He'd boiled it down to the simplest of all tracks. It was very linear: *Wait an hour, go back into the* Burke, *finish the job, get the fluctuators, bring both ships home*—and then he frowned. Who would crew the *Burke* now?

Tor. Yes. Tor could do it. That might work.

"No," said Brik. "Don't even think it. Cinnabar has been six jumps ahead of us since the moment we sighted the *Burke*. Here are your options. One: back off, torpedo that ship, and head for home now. And hope that Cinnabar didn't find a way off the *Burke* and onto the *LS-1187*. That's the safest option, and nobody will fault you for taking it. We've already lost too many good crew members. Two: go back into the *Burke*, take the other two fluctuators, then scuttle her and head for home. *If* there's time. There probably isn't—which is why option one is still the safest. Three: Try to bring the *Burke* up and running and bring her home—except you won't get her two meters. She's booby-trapped. Count on it. Cinnabar has not been sitting on his thumbs. He's been thinking up scenarios and counterresponses since before we rendezvoused. We arrived in this game too late to have a chance—''

"Four," said Korie, taking Brik's count away from him. "We stay linked with the *Burke* and bring her home inside our own envelope."

"Tow her?" Brik shook his head. "Too risky. Chief Engineer Leen will have *shpilkies*."

"*Shpilkies?*" Korie asked.

"A litter of carnivorous Morthan kittens."

"Oh," Korie blinked.

"The point is, we can't tow the *Burke*. We'll be too unstable—Chief Engineer Leen will never be able to balance the bubble. The center of gravity won't be congruent with the center of the envelope. We'd shake and shudder like a drunken nightmare. We'll kill ourselves trying."

"And," said Korie, "you forgot to mention that our top speed will be limited to one-quarter normal. About one hundred and fifty lights, if we're lucky."

"I was just getting to that."

Korie looked up sharply. "You think he might still be alive?"

"The captain? No. The assassin? Count on it." Brik looked grim. "He had to know what your options were and how you'd react. He had to have planned for this. My best advice? Torpedo the *Burke* and get the hell out of here."

Korie raised an eyebrow at Brik and allowed a cynical grin to spread across his face. "Without a fight? Are you sure you're really a Morthan?"

"Understand something, Mr. Korie," Brik said coldly. "Morthans consider fighting only one step above dishonor. The real victory is outwitting your opponent without having to bloody your sword. Only the stupid and clumsy carry battle scars. The skill is in victory without battle."

"But you're advising retreat."

"Humans call it a *strategic withdrawal*," Brik said. "It is not dishonorable to conserve your energies for situations where you have a better chance of winning."

"Frankly," said Korie, ruefully, "I'd much prefer rearranging the situation to our advantage."

"That sounds like a Morthan talking. Are you sure you're really human?"

"I have the battle scars to prove it," Korie said. He looked up at Brik. He looked up *and up* at Brik. Their eyes linked—and for a moment, Korie felt an eerie surge of emotion. *Partnership with a Morthan?* And then the moment flickered away. *God really is a practical joker!* Korie looked back into his coffee and said, "The thing that really annoys me about this whole situation is being played for a fool. I stepped right into it. I know it. He knows it. He knows I know it. I can't get it out of my head. The timing of the attack, everything—it wasn't random. He did it to delay us, to prevent us from removing the fluctuators from the *Burke*—to prevent us from escaping before the arrival of the *Dragon Lord*." Abruptly, he handed Brik his coffee cup. "Hold this."

Brik took it and stepped back as Korie suddenly screamed as loudly as he could, *"I HATE THE DRAGON LORD!"* and whirled, curling his fist, swinging his whole arm around and punching it hard into the foamboard wall with a sound like a bowling ball hitting a slab of beef. The wall *crunched*. His fist sank wrist-deep into it.

Then, very calmly, Jonathan Thomas Korie pulled his fist out of the wall, turned back to Brik, and retrieved his cup of coffee.

"I like these walls," he said. "There's something *satisfying* about punching them."

"It's the nice way they crunch," agreed Brik. "Feel better?"

Korie wiggled his hand in an "iffy" gesture. "It was nice to know what I was doing for a change. It was nice to have a focus." Abruptly, something crystallized for him. "Y'know what it is, Brik? I want revenge. What I really want, more than anything else in the galaxy, is just one real chance to get even with that ship and the bastards who scourged Shaleen." And then he sighed and said, "I know, it's impossible. But I can dream, can't I?"

Brik didn't say anything.

Korie continued. "Actually, right now, I'd be satisfied if I could just take one good bite out of Esker Cinnabar. If I could just get one jump ahead of him instead of the other way around. Tell me there's a way."

"Only if you can learn to think like a Morthan." Brik's tone was cool. There was enough skepticism in the naked words. He continued, "Assume that they've gamed it out and always know what your next move is. Then you extrapolate their next move from that and allow for it. And the next three moves after that too. Then you go back to the beginning and try to figure out what you can do that they won't expect—and assume that they'll have figured that out too. And so on. That's what he's doing right now. What can you do that he can't know?"

"You're assuming he's alive," said Korie.

"Not only alive—but very possibly somewhere aboard this vessel," said Brik.

That thought stopped Korie cold. It was like an ice pick in his heart. He looked up at Brik, searching the other's face for some sign that he might have been joking. He wasn't.

"You think he could do it?"

"I can think of seven ways to get from the *Burke* into the *LS-1187* without Harlie's knowing. Cinnabar can probably think of seven more."

Korie sighed. "This is crazy. It's like some mad game—it's like playing chess with a dragon, isn't it?"

"An apt enough analogy," Brik agreed.

"All right. Let me walk this though from the beginning. Everything he did—letting us capture him, escaping, all the killing—he did all that on purpose. Why? Obviously, to delay us, to keep us from completing our task of stripping the fluctuators. But now that he's done it, he's played his trump card—or has he? Is there something else?"

Brik shook his head. He waited politely while Korie continued to think aloud.

"See, here's the thing. Now that we know what kind of a danger he is, we know that we have no choice but to scuttle the *Burke*. So what he did was force our hand. We couldn't possibly be stupid enough to keep trying to save the *Burke* while he's still alive. Suppose we did respond fast enough.

Suppose we really did kill him—then he's failed. Or has he? At most, he's only cost us two or three hours. Maybe that was his purpose? Would a Morthan willingly sacrifice himself as part of a larger plan?''

Brik glanced down at Korie. His look said it all.

With a cold flash of fear, Korie realized the implication immediately. "Oh, shit. That means that the *Dragon Lord* has to be a lot closer than we thought. Close enough that the delay is crucial." Korie considered the possibility for a moment, then looked up to Brik's taciturn expression. There was only one possible conclusion. "You're right. We have to scuttle the *Burke* now. It's our best option, isn't it?"

Brik shook his head. "It is the best option not because it is a good one, but because it is the *least* bad one."

"Excuse me?"

"Keep thinking. You haven't seen the whole problem yet."

Korie frowned. *What am I missing?* He stopped himself abruptly, a new expression spreading across his face. "Wait a minute. You said he knows what we're thinking. Then he knows we're having this conversation too. Scuttling the *Burke* won't work either. He won't let us, will he?"

"He knows what our choices are, yes," Brik agreed. "The charges we placed on the *Burke* probably still show green on the Bridge monitors, but I doubt very much that they will respond to a detonation command. That's why I suggested a torpedo. If he's still alive, that will be his next immediate goal—to disable our torpedoes. In fact, he could be doing it right now." Brik added, "You might have had a chance if you had torpedoed the *Burke* immediately instead of evacuating her, but—" The Morthan shrugged. "That would have meant sacrificing eighteen crew members. Humans do not do that sort of thing."

"No. Humans don't. You think that's a weakness, don't you?"

"I think it is a human thing. It is definitely *not* a Morthan thing."

"All right, all right. Drop it. Let's game out some alternatives. Let's leap ahead to the end. What's it going to look like when they win? They'll be in control of the *Burke*—and very likely, this ship too. And we'll be dead or prisoners or—"

"Lunch. We'll be lunch," corrected Brik.

"Okay, but before that. How will he take over this ship?"

"How did he take over the *Burke*?"

Korie shrugged. "He killed everybody."

"Then that will be what he does here—unless there is a compelling reason not to."

"I wish we could plant a few traps of our own."

"Can you think of a trap that a Morthan can't?"

"Can you?" grinned Korie.

Brik gave him a look.

"Sorry," said Korie. "I couldn't resist. What about nested traps? Decoys? Would that work?"

"Maybe. If they were clever enough."

"Okay. Help me, here. If you were a Morthan—*and you are*—and you were planning to take over this vessel, how would you do it?"

"I'd kill everybody who wasn't essential to the running of the ship. I'd start with you. If I was in a bad mood, I'd torture you and make your death last a long time."

"Why would you let the others live?"

"I'm not stupid. I might have to bring this ship home. I couldn't do it alone."

"You mean, maybe the *Dragon Lord* isn't coming?"

"There is that possibility too. You are not the only one who thinks in terms of nested traps and decoys."

"So—" said Korie. "If I was thinking like a Morthan now—I should be planning both a defense against the *Dragon Lord* that might not really be coming, and a trap for a Morthan who might be already dead." Korie glanced at his wristband. "And I have less than twenty minutes to figure it out. Right?"

Brik nodded. "That is correct."

Korie considered the size of the problem. "Okay," he deadpanned. "What'll we do with the time left over?"

"You could pray," said Brik. He wasn't joking.

Korie scowled upward. "Sorry. I don't do that anymore. The price is too high."

PROVISIONS

"All right, Harlie." Korie gave the order.

The hatches of the *Burke* slid easily shut and air began hissing back into her from her huge regeneration units.

Sound came back to her corridors first. Some of the debris began to flutter. On her Bridge, the consoles lit up again, flashing from red to yellow to green as the atmospheric pressure rose, and as the mix of gases slid toward normal.

In the forward access of the *LS-1187*, Korie and Brik and a heavily-armored security team were waiting impatiently. They all wore helmets, cameras, security vests, and armor. Bach and Armstrong were carrying stun grenades and rapid-fire launchers. Nakahari was carrying a case of equipment modules to install on the *Burke*.

Quilla Theta was double-checking Armstrong's security gear and the weapons pack on his back. "Be careful, Brian— please?" she asked.

"Uh—" Armstrong turned to look at her. "Theta, yes. I'll be careful. Count on it."

"Yes, please. We would like more 'wow.' All of us."

"I promise—I'll give it my personal attention. To each and every one of you." Armstrong looked past the Quilla to see Bach looking at him, eyebrow raised. "Well," he shrugged, "a man's gotta please his public, doesn't he?"

The Quilla thumped Brian on the back twice—her "All's well" signal. Armstrong turned and gave a thumbs-up to Korie.

"Okay," said Korie. "Let's go."

The air lock door slid open.

The team stepped through cautiously. Armstrong and Bach led the way, followed by Korie and Brik. The shuttle bay looked dry and brittle. The blood on the floor had turned to powder. Some of it had blown away. Some of it hung in the air, giving the chamber a dusty red quality and a vague, unsettling, salty odor.

Brik and Bach went through the starboard corridor toward the engine room and the Bridge. Korie and Armstrong took the aft side. Nakahari followed at a cautious distance.

The *Burke*'s engine room was no longer an abattoir. Now it was a chamber of horrors. The bodies hanging on the singularity framework had been mummified from their exposure to vacuum. Their tongues were swollen and black, protruding from their mouths like some kind of creatures trying to escape. The eyes of the crew members had burst. Their blood had boiled out their ears and their noses and spurted across themselves and the deck in front of them. Their organs had pushed out through their wounds—and then everything had hardened and shriveled in the merciless vacuum.

There was no mercy here.

After death, *desecration*.

Korie wanted to weep. It wasn't fair.

Instead, he bit his lip and pushed forward. He'd do his crying later. That was the way things always worked. He went down the ladder and into the forward keel toward the Bridge. Brik followed him grimly. Nakahari looked around, shuddered once, and went to the engine room's main console. He plugged in a portable terminal and began bringing the system back to life.

Korie stepped up through the Operations bay, onto the Operations deck—and froze.

He didn't know how he knew, but he knew he wasn't alone. He turned around—it seemed to take forever—and stared.

In the captain's chair—

It was Hardesty.

Korie flinched. Brik came up beside him.

The captain was stuffed inside a large transparent plastic sack—an airtight transfer bag. Green mist floated around him.

"He's not dead," said Brik.

There was a medical monitor unit on the captain's chest. Its screen glowed. Even from the Ops deck, Korie could read the graphs.

The captain's eyes flickered open. They moved. They focused, but ever so slowly.

"Oh, no—" Korie moaned. He leapt up the stairs to the Bridge.

Hardesty's voice came to him as if from a great distance. Very faint and very feebly, the captain spoke. "Help...me...."

Korie couldn't help himself. He was simultaneously horrified and fascinated. The captain's skin had a hideous gray-green cast. He looked like a zombie.

"He's transmitting," Brik explained. "His body functions are suspended, but *his brain augment is still active.*"

"What is it?" Korie couldn't tear his eyes away.

"*Phullogine.*" Brik explained, "It's a very heavy, very inert gas. It's used for hibernation." And then he added, ominously, "As well as for preserving food."

Hardesty spoke again. The words wheezed out slowly and almost inaudibly. "The assassin . . ." And then he faded back into unconsciousness, his thoughts still incomplete.

"A trophy to take home," said Brik. "Or provisions."

"Oh god—no. This is hideous." Korie spoke to his headset. "We found the captain. Bridge of the *Burke*. Send a med team. Now!" And then, abruptly remembering their mission, he added, "And send the work crews in." He looked back to Brik. "Can we save him?"

"I don't know enough about it. Maybe Dr. Williger—but I doubt it." He turned away. Bach and Armstrong were just stepping up onto the Ops deck; they looked toward the captain with rising horror. Brik pushed them away. "Come with me. I want to find the assassin."

The three of them exited through the forward access, leaving Korie caught in the focus of the captain's yellow staring eyes.

MED STATION

Molly Williger might have been angry. Korie couldn't tell. He'd never seen her when she hadn't been swearing. Korie was glad he didn't recognize most of the languages she used, although he suspected that some of her most elegant curses were composed in ancient Latin.

"—no way to treat a human body!" she was saying. "Why the hell do I spend so much time patching them up, if they're just going to go play tag with monsters?"

Korie followed the med team carrying the captain's stretcher all the way back to the *LS-1187*, into the forward keel, halfway along it to the sick bay, through the anteroom, and into the primary medical station—the one that also served as an operating room. He stood back against the far wall and watched as Williger, Fontana, and Stolchak quickly removed the captain from the body bag and hooked him up to the life-support systems. Stolchak, the new one, was particularly efficient, her hands moving expertly from point to point, installing monitors, inserting tubes, punching up programs, starting the blood-cleansing system, and having utensils ready for the doctor even before she asked for them.

Korie glanced up at the monitor board overhead. Some of the lines were almost flat. The captain's heartbeat was seriously depressed. His oxygen usage was near zero. The captain's eyes were shut and his pallor had worsened since they'd removed him from the bag.

His autolobe was still functioning though. In fact, the autonomic side of it was quietly advising Williger of the condition of the captain's organic functions in a soft silvery voice, until she grew annoyed and switched it off. "I know what I'm doing, dammit."

Korie wanted to ask, but he knew better than to interrupt Molly Williger while she worked.

"No motor functions at all," she said, not only for her staff, but for the medical autolog. "Heartbeat, respiration, EEG—all at hibernation levels. This one's going to make the textbooks. I've never seen phullogine used on a human before." She straightened up, took a step back, and studied the overhead monitors, squinting in concentration. She said a word that Korie was glad he didn't recognize.

"What about his mental condition?" Korie asked.

Williger shrugged. "He can communicate, but only slowly. I don't know if he's in pain or not."

"Can he command?"

Williger glared at him. "Do you want the center chair that bad?"

"Doctor—" Korie spoke carefully. "If Hardesty can command, he's the captain. If he can't, it's me. But it has to be one of us, and you're the only one qualified to determine if he's capable."

"His brain-augment is working fine," she admitted. "If there was nothing else here but his augment, I'd have to say he's mentally able. But you and I both know that the captain is more than his augment and there are larger questions that I can't answer yet. Like, how well is the augment integrating with the rest of his personality? I don't know. Can he balance? I don't know. How long will he be this way? I haven't the slightest idea. I can't be any clearer than that."

"I need a decision from you, Doctor. Even a wrong one."

And then Korie was sure—she *was* angry. She whirled on him, pushing him back against the wall. "Not *now*, dammit. Don't you understand? He can hear us!"

"Even better. I don't want to do this behind his back. We both know what kind of a captain he is."

"You don't get it, do you? Hardesty knew what was happening to him, *every minute*. He understood what Cinnabar was doing *and why*. The shock to his system is *still* happening. For most people—" Williger stopped herself in midsentence, grabbed Korie's arm and dragged him out through the anteroom and into the corridor and halfway down it. "Listen to me. For most people, dying is over quickly—for Hardesty, it could take months. Or even longer. And he could be conscious the entire time. How would you like to lie in bed feeling yourself die for a year or two?"

Korie opened his mouth to answer, then closed it again. He considered his response as he stared down into Williger's angry face, then he lowered his voice and said carefully, "When this is over, I will have the time to be horrified by the situation and by all of the difficult decisions that you and I are having to make. In the meantime, in case you hadn't noticed, we are at war and this ship needs a commanding officer. There are orders I need to give and I need them to be *legal*."

"You know the possible consequences to him—and to you—if I guess wrong? What if he's fully recovered in six hours? What if you've started some irrevocable course of action?"

"If he recovers, then declare him fit for command and I'll be glad to return the baton. I promise you, I'll try not to get us killed before that happens. Now then," he asked pointedly, "are you going to declare the captain incapable of command—or *not*?"

Williger's face hardened. At this moment, it was obvious that she didn't like Korie very much; but finally she nodded. "You're in command." She started to turn away, then turned back just far enough to add, "Don't fuck it up."

"Thank you, Doctor," Korie said to her back.

"Don't mention it," she growled, walking away. *"Ever."*

Korie touched his headset. "Brik?"

The Morthan's voice rumbled in his ear. "Yes?"

"Did you find the assassin?"

"No trace of him yet, sir. There are a lot of places he could have hidden."

"Well, we can always wait three days until the body starts to stink," Korie proposed.

"And what if it doesn't—"

"You're suggesting?"

"I hope you acted fast enough. But you might not have."

"Do you need more searchers?"

"They wouldn't know what to look for."

"Where are you now?"

"Inner hull. Forward quadrant."

"Stay there. I'm on my way."

THE FORWARD
OBSERVATORIES

There were a few places on every ship where a person might find a real window. There were two forward observatories on the *Burke*, one on the upper hull back of the air lock, one on the lower hull. They were clear glass domes protruding from the ceramic hull.

Korie found Brik at the lower observatory. It was a wide circular well, framed by neutral gravitors. You flipped over and pointed yourself down into it. Once inside, you would be floating in a deep free-fall bubble and you could observe the stars around the ship. Usually, there wasn't much to see that couldn't be seen better on the big forward viewer on the Ops deck, but the observatories were the only real windows in the hull of a liberty ship and although rarely used, they were still considered an essential part of the vessel.

Brik was shining his beam in and around the crawl spaces where the thin metal tubing butted up against the inside of the outer hull.

"Anything?"

Brik shook his head.

"And you don't expect to find anything either, do you?"

Brik grunted. After a moment, he lowered himself back down to the catwalk and said, "If I could figure it out, so could he."

"Mm," said Korie. Abruptly, he levered himself over the railing and floated down into the observatory. Brik followed. The two of them hung together, floating face to face under the bubble of stars.

"The last time I did this," said Korie, very softly, "my partner was much prettier than you."

"The last time I did this," replied Brik, "my partner was much less fragile."

"Touché." Korie smiled.

"Thank you." Brik lowered his voice to the barest of whispers. "I have not completed my search of the inner hull."

"I didn't expect you to. Did you put on a good show?"

"The best."

"Good. Do you think you've searched long enough to fool him into thinking he fooled us?"

"No, but we can't risk any more time."

"Unfortunately, you're right."

"That's why I'm paid the big bucks." Brik smiled. At this close a distance, Korie wished he hadn't. "Did you talk to Harlie?"

"One on one in the bay."

"What did you find?"

Korie passed him a plastic card. "It's all in here. There's overhead access panels to the Bridge. You can reach them from the utility tube without being observed. There's also an under-floor access just ahead of the Ops bay. There's a lot of dead space all around the Bridge module to make repairs easier."

Brik slid the card into his belt. "What about the *Burke*'s torpedoes?"

"You were right. Nakahari went into systems analysis through the back door. The fusion pumps are disconnected and cold. Those fish are dead. I don't want to check our own yet. I don't want to risk alerting him."

"Right." Brik nodded. "How's the captain?"

Korie shrugged—then grabbed a handhold. The gesture would have scooted him downward, back into the inner hull of the *Burke*. "He's alive, but I practically had to break Williger's arm to get her to validate my assumption of responsibility."

"But she did?"

"She did."

"Good. You may have saved both their lives. And put your own at considerably more risk."

"I knew the job was dangerous when I took it."

"Not *this* dangerous."

"Brik—" Korie let himself get very very serious. "Understand something. I don't have anything left to live for. My family is gone. My home is a desert. The only thing that motivates me now is revenge. But that'll be enough, if it's a big enough revenge. So any danger that I might be in right now is irrelevant to me. Just tell me how I can hurt the enemy."

Brik studied Korie for a moment. "With all due respect, that is very possibly the stupidest thing you have ever said to me. You might not care about the danger you are in, but you now have the additional responsibility of the lives of those you command. We did not sign a suicide pact when we came aboard this ship."

"I know that."

"I have been around fanatics all my life," continued Brik. "Let me tell you this. If a fanatic is willing to sacrifice his own life to a cause, he isn't going to worry much about the lives of those around him."

"I understand what you're saying," said Korie. "I'm not a fanatic."

"That's what they all say."

"Listen to me. I haven't abandoned my responsibility to the ship or the crew or the fleet. I'm not a kamikaze. I want this revenge and then I want the next one and the one after that. I want to live long enough to see the Morthan Solidarity ground into dust. But—" Korie shrugged. "If someone has to take the point, let it be me."

Brik didn't answer that. He searched Korie's face for a moment longer, looking not only at Korie's surface emotions, but also at the deeper drives within. "All right," he said, finally. "I can honor that. Now I have work to do. Wait a few minutes before you follow me.'' He pushed himself out of the observatory.

Korie stared after him. He didn't know if Brik had believed him or not. He didn't know if he believed himself or not. He stared out at the stars a moment longer.

Why, God—?

Then he stopped himself.

No. Never again.

STATUS REPORT

Don't worry, Korie told himself. *Either everything's going to work, or it won't work. If it works, we'll survive. If it doesn't work, we won't have anything to worry about either.*

He stopped where he was and deliberately forced himself to breathe slower. He closed his eyes, trying to relax, and thought of the lagoon and the garden at home. That had always worked before. . . .

But it didn't work this time.

Because this time, whenever he thought of the lagoon and the garden and the canopy of arching blue ferns, he also thought of the *Dragon Lord* and what it had done to his home.

Korie opened his eyes and stared out through the glass at the hardened stars. They were spread unmoving through the abyss, a wall of shattered light, distant and unreachable.

Remember what they said at the academy? *To get to the stars, you have to be irrational.*

At the time, it had been a funny joke—a clever play on words. Hyperstate was an irrational place to be.

Suddenly, it wasn't so funny any more.

What did it take to *survive* among the stars? That was another question entirely.

Korie put his thumb and forefinger to his neck, checking the beat of his pulse. It was still elevated, but not badly. He was at a normal level of tension again.

Enough time had passed. Korie pushed himself out of the observatory, caught the railing, and pulled himself upright.

Right now, the thing to do is look normal, he reminded himself. *Not just for the Morthan, but for the crew.* The orders had been given. Either they were going to get the job done, or they weren't. In the latter case . . . well, if they didn't survive, neither would the ship. At least, he had guaranteed that much.

Unless the assassin had figured out that trap too.

The hard part was that he couldn't check it, not without giving it away.

It was all a game of phantoms—feint and parry against possibilities.

Korie realized that he was alone in the *Burke*'s inner hull and shivered as if cold. He hurried to the closest access and climbed back up into the forward keel of the starship. Two crew members were working there, stringing optical cables for a new sensory network. Nakahari's modifications were going to need eyes and ears.

Two others had resumed the work on the high-cycle fluctuators. Two security guards stood grimly by with rifles ready. It was insufficient and they all knew it, but what else could they do? Korie had ordered autodestruct charges packed into each of the fluctuators too—and that was further evidence of his lack of faith in the ability of the security squads.

Korie nodded to them curtly and climbed a ladder, then headed aft toward the shuttle bay.

Half of it was dumb show, half of it was real—but which half was precaution and which half was pretend? *If nothing else, maybe we can confuse the assassin as badly as we've confused ourselves.*

He crossed the shuttle bay, stopping only long enough to call down to Nakahari, "How long?"

Nakahari knew better than to stop work. His voice floated out of the hole in the floor. "Working on the third cycle now.

I can give you a confidence of twenty. Maybe. Give me another half hour and I'll multiply that by a factor of ten.''

Korie stepped through the access to the air lock, through the *Burke*'s air lock, through the air lock of the *LS-1187*, through the access, and into the forward keel of his own ship.

He couldn't help himself. He had to stop at the sick bay. Williger looked up darkly.

"Deathwatch?" she growled.

Korie met her stare. "Do you always assume the worst of people?"

"It's a great time saver," she said. "And that way when I'm proven wrong, my life is full of pleasant surprises, not *un*pleasant ones.''

Korie rubbed the bridge of his nose between thumb and forefinger. He rubbed his eyes and shook his head. He hadn't realized how tired he was.

"You want something for that?"

"No. I'll be fine." He took a breath. "You've had time. What's the prognosis?"

She shrugged. "We wait. We watch. We hope. Some of us pray." She added in a growly rasp, "Sometimes the answer is no.''

"So you figured it out too."

"I'm only ugly. I'm not stupid."

"You're not ugly," Korie said.

"Yeah, yeah—you're outvoted by the evidence. When I was born, the doctor slapped my mother. They had to tie a pork chop around my neck just to get the dog to play with me. I had to sneak up on a glass of water if I wanted a drink." Her voice was more gravelly than usual as she recited the tired old jokes. She looked suddenly tired. "My best guess is that the son of a bitch will live. I'm too ugly to live and he's too mean to die."

Something about the way she said it made Korie stop and look at her again. "All right," he said. "What's really bothering you?"

"Old age," she said. "You think I like this? I know about the jokes. The ones to my face. The ones behind my back. Do you think I *chose* this? It's starting to get to me. Guess what? My rhinocerouslike hide isn't as thick as I thought it was.''

"It's what the Morthan said, isn't it?"

"Aah, he didn't bother me. That's what he's supposed to do. It's just—nothing." She waved him off.

"Dr. Williger, if it means anything, you're the most honest person on this ship. And as far as I'm concerned, that makes you the most beautiful."

"Spare me the bullshit. Right now, I'd trade all my inner beauty for a pair of limpid blue eyes with fluttery long lashes."

Who on this ship has blue eyes? Korie wondered. And then realized. *The new kids come aboard, we play musical chairs for a couple of weeks, and it only settles down when all the dance cards get filled. Only sometimes they don't.* After all the chatter about Armstrong and Quilla Delta had cooled down, after the harmless speculation about Brik and Bach, the juiciest topic for discussion had become Tor and Jonesy. Tor had become one of Williger's best friends; how could Williger not be envious of her joy? Tor caught herself a nice little snuggle-boy and what did Williger get? Nothing. And how many times in the past had this happened to Dr. Williger? How had she put up with it for so long? *Sometimes, I can be so stupid. What else have I missed?*

"I hadn't realized," he said. "I'm sorry."

Williger's eyes were moist. She shrugged. "It's not your fault."

Korie sat down opposite the doctor. "Listen to me. If it means anything, you're not alone in your hurt. Hurt is universal. We all hurt. The only thing that any of us can do is try to make it hurt a little bit less for the people around us."

She didn't answer immediately. Korie studied her face. It was as if she was trying to formulate the words to embody the pain. Finally she rasped, "You, of all people, are the wrong one to try to offer me comfort."

Korie held her gaze. "It's all I have left to give anyone anymore. Can you accept it?"

"I thought the captain told you to quit trying to be a nice guy."

Korie shrugged. "Pretend I'm not being nice. Pretend I'm being ruthless. I'm trying to keep a valuable piece of equipment running properly—"

"You're not fooling anyone." And then she hung her head

and admitted, "I'm tired, Mr. Korie. I'm tired of empty beds and even emptier reassurance. I'm tired of the jokes. Especially the ones I don't hear. I do my job. I'm one of the best damned doctors in the fleet. I'm entitled to . . . better than this. This isn't the kind of hand-holding that I want. I want what I want, not second best. And nothing anyone can say or do can change that."

"Dr. Williger—"

"No. Shut up. Let me say this. It's not the pressure. It's not even the fear. It's the loneliness. I just—I don't want to die alone."

"I don't know what to say to you. If I had the power to change any of it—"

"Stop," she said, letting go and holding up a hand. "You don't have to say anything. You listened. That was enough. And I'll keep it a secret that you're still a nice guy."

Korie smiled gently. He understood. "I'll tell you what. When we get back to Stardock, I'll have Hodel whip up a love philter for you."

Molly Williger looked horrified. "Don't you dare. I saw how his exorcism turned out." And then she added, "Don't worry, I'll be all right." She allowed herself a crooked smile. "I always am."

"You sure?"

"I'm sure."

"Okay," said Korie. He stood up and left.

Back in the keel, he paused to tap his headset control. "Brik? Status report."

"Green. Green. Yellow. Yellow. Green."

"Time?"

"Fifteen to thirty."

"Make it closer to—"

Harlie beeped then, interrupting them both. "Mr. Korie! Long-range scanning is picking up a hyperstate ripple."

"Bridge. *Now*," shouted Korie. He broke and ran, knowing that Brik was on his way already.

SIGNALS

"It's heading straight for us," said Tor. "E.T.A.: fifteen minutes. Jeezis—I've never seen anything move like that."

The holotable display showed the locus of the *LS-1187* and the *Burke* as a tiny bright speck. On the opposite side of the display, a larger, brighter pinpoint was arrowing directly toward it.

Hodel enlarged that section of the display. "Oh, God—I know that signature. It's the *Dragon Lord*."

"The *Burke* is an important prize," Korie noted as he stepped up onto the Ops deck from the forward keel access. He crossed to Tor and looked over her shoulder at her board. "Any signals?"

"Not yet."

"They won't," said Brik, coming up after him. "It'd be a waste of time. They'll ask for surrender. You'll refuse. So, why bother? No, they'll go immediately to the *next* step. Attack."

Hodel shook his head sadly and murmured to himself, "Oh, Mama. . . ."

"We can't fight them," said Korie. "We can't win." He

closed his eyes for a moment, thinking. When he opened them again, his expression was dark. "Tor, send this signal." He turned resolutely toward the main viewer. "Morthan battle cruiser. If you approach this vessel, we will self-destruct. You will not have our stardrive! Repeat: We will self-destruct!"

Tor was looking at him oddly.

"Send that," he repeated.

"They won't believe it," said Brik.

"And they'll home in on the signal," said Tor.

"Or they won't," said Korie. *"Send it."*

Tor shook her head. "There are orders that only a captain can give—specifically self-destruct!"

Korie looked at her. "What's your point?"

"The captain isn't dead."

"The captain is *pickled!*" Korie shouted at her in frustration. "How brain-dead do you want him to be?"

"That's exactly my point! His brain is still active! He has to give the order."

"You *might* be right," Korie said with visible annoyance. "But now is not the time to have this argument. Mr. Jones, send that signal."

Jonesy gulped. He looked at Tor apologetically, then back to Korie. "Yes, sir."

Tor muttered something under her breath. She stepped back to her console and hit the button, sending the signal. The panel beeped its confirmation. *Signal sent.* "Anything else, sir?"

Korie shook his head.

Tor stepped back to him and lowered her voice. Very quietly and very angrily, she said, "Don't you ever go under my head again!"

Korie stared her down. He was just as angry, maybe angrier. *"The argument about who is in command does not belong on this Bridge."*

"You're right," said a deep voice, a sound that rasped and rumbled like the roar of a panther.

They turned to look, all horrified, as the Morthan assassin stepped calmly onto the Bridge of the starship. He was grinning like a gargoyle and dragging Dr. Williger by her hair.

"The argument is irrelevant," said Cinnabar, "because *I*

am in command now." He hurled the doctor across the Bridge. She was still alive, but just barely. "I can't stand rudeness," he explained.

Korie was horrified. He took a step forward, but Tor grabbed his arm and held him back. Beside them, Brik was standing perfectly still. Jonesy was white. Hodel had fainted.

"Excuse me, Mr. Korie—" Harlie said abruptly. "I'm picking up some anomalies on the Bridge. I believe, yes—" And then the klaxon went off. "Intruder alert! Intruder alert!"

Cinnabar laughed. It was a chuckling rumble that bubbled up from the depths of hell. It was deep and vicious and terrifying. "Thank you, Harlie," he said.

A security man fell into the Bridge from the opposite door, drawing his gun. Cinnabar moved like fire, grabbing him, cracking his back and hurling him back out into the corridor. Something unseen crashed horribly. Someone else was screaming. "Thank you," said Cinnabar, "but we won't be needing your services any more." He turned back to Korie and the others. He stepped to the center of the Bridge. He laid one huge hand on the back of the captain's chair, but he did not sit down.

"In answer to your first question, *it was easy*. I came in through the missile tubes. You never scanned your own ship. Very arrogant. In answer to your second question, the reason you can't self-destruct is that I've disabled that part of the network. Now then . . . send *this* signal to the *Dragon Lord*." Cinnabar faced the main viewer. "This is Esker Cinnabar. I have taken control of both vessels. The *Burke* is ready for pickup. The stardrive is undamaged. All is well. *Send that*." He smiled wickedly. "Mr. Jones? I gave you an order."

Jonesy looked uncertain. He looked to Korie for guidance. Reluctantly, Korie nodded. Jonesy turned to his board and sent the signal. Then he looked back to the Bridge again.

Cinnabar smiled. He stepped to the other side of the captain's chair, leaning on it possessively. Korie glared. *That chair is mine. I've earned it! How dare he?* But the Morthan only draped one arm across the back of the seat. He wasn't going to sit down.

Korie glanced to Brik. Brik remained impassive.

"You should have destroyed the fluctuators," Cinnabar

explained, "and the *Burke* when you had the chance. Too bad. This is going to be very embarrassing for you. One more humiliation in a long string of humiliations." His smile widened horribly. "Now, a Morthan would commit honorable suicide rather than be humiliated—but you humans seem to thrive on humiliation. So I promise to humiliate you exquisitely." His chuckle was the sound of a dinosaur dying. "The *ultimate* humiliation . . . I may not even kill you. You're not worthy of a Morthan death. I wonder what your admiral will think when we send you home *again*! This time, the defeat will be even more profound." Cinnabar sighed dramatically. Then, abruptly, he was crisp and military again. "Evacuate the *Burke*," he ordered. "Disengage and move off. Do it now."

Korie said bitterly, "Don't you want the third fluctuator, the one we removed?"

Cinnabar laughed. "Cute. Very cute. The one that you booby-trapped? Don't be silly. The two that remain in place will be sufficient for our needs."

Korie sagged. He looked like a man who has just run out of options. Tor put her hand on his shoulder.

"It didn't work," she said.

Korie looked up. His eyes were hollow. "Will you promise to spare my crew? No more killing?"

"*I promise nothing!* You don't have a choice. But . . . I will let your people live as long as it is to . . . our mutual advantage."

Korie turned to Jonesy, Hodel, and Tor. "Do as he says."

Hodel shook his head. He stood up and stepped away from his console. So did Jonesy. Tor followed them.

Korie looked from one to the other. Their expressions were resolute. Angered at their disobedience, Korie stepped past Hodel and started punching up the commands on the console himself. The evacuation signal sounded throughout the *Burke* and echoed in the corridors of the *LS-1187*.

The forward viewer flashed to show the interior of the *Burke*. The security squads were waving everyone out. The medical crews were removing the last of the bodies. The Black Hole Gang shrugged and walked away from the two high-cycle fluctuators in the engine room. Nakahari grabbed his portable terminal, yanked it free, and ran for the corridor. The security squad followed.

The screen showed them passing through the shuttle bay and into the *LS-1187*. The air lock doors slid shut behind them.

"Harlie, are we clear?"

"Yes, Mr. Korie."

"Stand by for separation," Korie released the mating ring, then the docking tube, and finally the docking harness.

There was a soft *thump* and the two starships floated gently apart.

A MORTHAN LULLABY

The *Burke* floated farther and farther away from the *LS-1187*.

"Two kilometers . . ." Hodel said grimly. He sank back down into his chair and began marking vectors and intercepts.

"Keep your hands away from the targeting controls," Cinnabar rasped.

Hodel lifted his hands high off the board. "I'm a good boy," he said, but his tone of voice wasn't happy.

On the holodisplay, the *Dragon Lord*'s hyperstate ripple almost closed with the pinpoint representing the *LS-1187*, then unfolded and dissolved. The display expanded to show the locus of real space now.

They watched in silence as the huge warship began to close on the two Alliance vessels.

"I'll put her on viewer," said Tor. She stepped over to her own board and punched up a new angle on the main screen: a distant bright speck. She punched again for magnification, but the *Dragon Lord* was still too distant. Harlie superimposed an extrapolated image beside the actual point of light.

Tor studied the screens on her console. "Nice piece of piloting. She trimmed her fields exquisitely." It was hard for her to keep the envy out of her voice. That kind of precision was only possible with the expenditure of large amounts of power, something the *LS-1187* didn't have. Tor added, "She's slowing to match course with the *Burke*. Deceleration—holy god!—fifteen thousand gees!" She shook her head unbelievingly. "That's not *possible*."

"Thank you," said Cinnabar.

Korie's expression was impassive. "E.T.A.?"

"Give her five minutes, ten at most," Tor said. She tapped at her board. the extrapolated image expanded.

Hodel swiveled to the holographic display and expanded that view as well. To one side, he put up a size comparison of the three vessels. "She's big enough to swallow the *Burke* whole," he said. There was bitterness in his voice.

Korie remembered the city-size ship he had seen. It had been a wall of missile tubes and shield projectors, disruptors and antennae. And when it had swiveled around before him, he had stared into its mouth. The dragon could hold this ship in its teeth. But—

"Don't be fooled," said Korie tightly. "They have to build it that big. They don't have the stardrive technology we do." He almost believed it.

"We do now," Cinnabar laughed. It was the sound of sandpaper on flesh. He stood behind the captain's chair and wrapped his huge hands around the seat back. His claws cut deeply into the cushion. He rattled the chair gleefully in its mountings, almost ripping it loose from its frame. He leaned his head back, stretching his corded neck; he howled and roared and steam-whistled his triumph.

Tor put her hands over her ears and flinched. Jonesy pulled her back away from the center of the Ops deck. Korie and Brik held their positions angrily.

Cinnabar ordered Hodel to move the *LS-1187* off from the *Burke* then, and the next few moments were occupied with the maneuver. "I want you out of cannon range, out of torpedo range—far enough away that you can't do any mischief. And from this point on, there will be no transmissions of any kind unless I authorize them. God, I love this job!"

Frowning, Korie sank into a chair by the holotable. Idly, he punched up a display of the three ships' vectors. He studied it thoughtfully.

Cinnabar noticed what he was doing and stopped in midhowl. "It won't work," he said. "Nothing you do will work. You have been outmaneuvered. You are obsolete. Why don't you have the good sense to die quietly."

"Why don't you have the good manners to shut up?" Korie said without looking up.

"You don't know how to lose," said Cinnabar.

"On the contrary. You don't know how to win."

Cinnabar laughed again. "For someone who doesn't know how, the evidence demonstrates that I'm doing quite well."

Korie swiveled away and stared forward.

"There she is," reported Tor.

The image was clear on the main screen now. The *Dragon Lord* was moving into position above the *Burke*, securing the much smaller vessel with a tractor beam. As they watched, the *Burke* was being drawn up into the gigantic enemy ship.

"Shit," said Tor.

"You said a mouthful," agreed Hodel.

"You should be celebrating," said Cinnabar. "This is the end of the war." He grinned wickedly. "Ha. Perhaps we will build a statue to you—so that humans everywhere will know who to thank for their liberation."

"Liberation?" Korie gave Cinnabar the raised-eyebrow look.

"But of course." Cinnabar stepped around the captain's chair and leaned on the forward railing of the Bridge. "Do you call *this* freedom? I promise you, under the Morthan rule, there will be no more useless dying. Humans will live at peace with each other and will accept their rightful place in the universe—"

"As slaves?"

"As servants," Cinnabar corrected. "Service is the highest state of intelligent activity, you know that. Your own text-books teach that a life is worthless unless it is in the service of some greater good. Well, I offer you a world where your service will no longer be wasted. No more will you have the opportunities to act out of greed and lust and malevolence."

Korie and Brik exchanged skeptical glances.

"Understand something," Cinnabar continued. "We did not ask for this war. You did. *Humans* forced this war on *us*. You gave us no choice. So now, we're bringing it back to you—*to protect ourselves*. We'll create a domain that is safe from human depredation, and if that means the total subjugation of humanity, then so be it. But I promise you, we will be better masters of you than you have ever been of yourselves.

"Imagine it—no more hunger, no more poverty, no more inequality. You can't, can you? Because you've never known a world that works, have you? A world where resources are efficiently managed, where people have a purpose, a place of beauty and freedom. Yes, *freedom*. Real freedom to be what you are—not what you believe. Give up your false perceptions, your oughts and musts and should-bes and I will give you the freedom that comes with truth!"

Cinnabar paused and looked from one to the other. The fear on the Ops deck had been replaced with uncertainty. "This wasn't what you were expecting, was it?" He flashed an evil smile, and for just that instant, their enemy was back—and then, he was speaking directly and candidly to them again. "You were expecting fear and pain, terror and hate, not this."

He laughed and returned to his place behind the captain's chair, grinning almost good-naturedly now. "You don't know what freedom is. You think it means to be free of overriding authority—but that isn't freedom. That's chaos and madness. I'll give you *real* freedom, the kind that comes from knowing who you are and what your place in the universe is. I'll give you freedom from want, freedom from fear, freedom to work, freedom to serve—I'll give you freedom from the lies inside your head."

There was silence on the Ops deck. No one spoke. Jonesy glanced at Tor, she was studying the deck. Hodel looked at his hands in his lap. Korie was impassive.

Brik snorted his contempt. It was loud.

Cinnabar looked at him pityingly. "The war is over. There will be a place for everyone in the new domain—even for *you*. Even if you don't want it. Morthans don't waste."

Brik snorted again.

Cinnabar focused on him. He spoke with contempt now. "So quick to judge—so foolish. You've spent too much time studying the wrong teachers. Never mind. I'll give you a world where you won't be subservient to humans."

Brik began to straighten.

Korie recognized the implication of the gesture and did something stupid. He stepped between Brik and Cinnabar. "Don't do it, mister. That's an order."

"You see?" said Cinnabar, over Korie's head. "You let humans choose your battles."

"Don't be stupid," said Korie, swiveling to face Cinnabar, trying to keep his voice even. "We've seen your bioscan. We know what you're capable of." Turning back to Brik, he said, "Listen to me, Brik. There's no honor in this fight."

Brik considered the thought. After a heartbeat, he relaxed. So did Korie.

Hodel broke the silence. He was frowning at the forward viewer. "There's a problem on the *Dragon Lord*."

Korie turned to look. So did Brik.

Cinnabar glared over their heads.

The huge forward viewer showed it all. A bright red glow was spreading across the hull of the *Dragon Lord*. Its center was the hatch where the *Burke* had been swallowed up. The glare turned brighter and whiter. Hodel decreased the magnification—they could see the flare of brilliance as it enveloped the entire Morthan warship.

"It's disintegrating!"

There was the briefest flash of color—of fragments coming apart, of horrific energies expanding suddenly outward—

And then the whole screen went white. The glare was so bright it hurt Korie's eyes.

For an instant the viewer was dark; the forward cameras had gone blind; then another camera swiveled into position and refocused. There was a flickering cloud of gas and lightning and expanding debris where the *Dragon Lord* had been—

Hodel's eyes were wide with terror and hope. Tor stood up, stunned. Jonesy, still uncertain, stood by her. A smile spread across Brik's face.

Korie turned to look at Cinnabar.

The Morthan assassin was frozen in disbelief. He was grasping the captain's chair so hard that he was bending the frame out of alignment. He opened his mouth and his breath sucked in with a ghastly sound. When it came out again, it was a bloodcurdling shriek of rage. His scream went on and on and on. It rattled the ceiling cameras in their sockets.

Korie allowed himself a single moment of triumph. "Ooh, that feels good," he said to himself. A peaceful smile spread across his face. "That was for Carol and Timmy and Robby."

Tor bent to her console. "We've lost all our active forward sensors. Burned out. Auxiliaries are coming on-line—"

Korie couldn't contain his glee. He let it spread across his face and shouted up at Cinnabar, "You're not the only one who knows how to set a booby trap. That's what it looks like when you invert a singularity field *inside* a ship."

"*You* made the mistake," Brik said softly. "You should have killed us."

Cinnabar was visibly struggling to regain his self-control. "Yes. It would be appropriate to rectify that error immediately. But it would be premature. You forget—or perhaps you remember very well—that the third piece of the stardrive is still aboard this ship. That will be enough. This ship is going to Dragonhold. Commander Tor, set a course."

Tor stood motionless.

Cinnabar looked to her. "I gave you an order."

"I take orders only from my captain."

"I can vouch for that," Korie said wryly.

Cinnabar stepped off the Bridge. He came toward Tor slowly, with a *calculated* display of rage. He circled the Ops deck, pulling consoles off the wall at random, tossing crew members out of their chairs with one great hand, turning equipment over, punching in screens, and roaring like a tornado. Korie noted, with detached professionalism, that Cinnabar was very careful in what he was destroying—only weaponry and ancillary systems; nothing that would impede the operation of the vessel in hyperstate.

"You don't understand!" Cinnabar roared at Tor. "You have no choice! I am a Morthan assassin! I am your worst nightmare come to life!"

"So much for the promise of freedom," said Korie dryly.

"Freedom for those who *choose* it!" the Morthan bellowed at him. "This is not choice!" Cinnabar turned back to Tor. "Your *only* hope is to obey my commands."

"*You* don't get it," she said. "The answer is no."

Instantly, Cinnabar backhanded her sideways against a wall. She slammed against it with a thud that made Korie wince. Jonesy leapt at Cinnabar. "Hey! Leave her alone!"

Cinnabar picked him up and tossed him clear across the Bridge at the forward viewer. He hit it square in the center. It shattered, pieces flying in all directions, leaving a gaping blank wall. Jonesy fell to the deck, gasping and groaning. Tor crawled toward him. He was bleeding profusely. She reached a hand to comfort him.

"Don't anyone touch them," warned Cinnabar.

"Very smart," said Korie. "You've just disabled the only two people on this ship who know how to set a course for Dragonhold."

Cinnabar turned coldly to Korie. He was almost polite. "You will notice that I only disabled them. *That* was a warning. Do you think I'm such a fool that I don't know what I'm doing?"

Korie replied just as coldly. "Actually, I think you're a malignant thug."

Cinnabar snorted. "What you *think* is irrelevant." Then he advanced on Tor again. "I will kill your crewmates one by one before your horrified eyes. I will kill that child you are so attracted to. I will pull him apart, one limb at a time. His screams will haunt your nightmares. There will come a moment when you will beg me to let you set a course for Dragonhold."

—The beam struck Cinnabar in the back. Nakahari stood in the door of the Bridge, holding a rifle and spattering energy across the Ops deck. The crackling fire splattered off the Morthan like water off a wall. Colored lightning flashed around him, spraying across the Bridge in a stunning shower of sparks. He stood there, grinning nastily at Nakahari.

Nakahari stopped firing, astonished.

"Now, throw it at me," said Cinnabar. "That's what they usually do."

Nakahari took a nervous step backward.

Cinnabar shifted into overdrive. He *flowed* across the Ops deck to Nakahari, plucked him out of the air, and lifted him high over his head. Nakahari struggled. Cinnabar turned slowly with his captive. "Set a course for Dragonhold!" he roared.

"Don't do it!" Korie said.

Brik stepped forward. "Put him down. Fight me instead—"

Cinnabar snorted. "Don't be silly. You're just food." He

flexed his arms. Nakahari's spine went *cra-a-ack!* Nakahari was cut off in midscream. He went limp.

The assassin tossed the body aside, like a used rag. He turned back to Tor. *"Set the course!"*

He stalked back across the Operations deck, knocking Goldberg out of his chair and ripping the auxiliary weapons console off the wall as he passed.

Tor flinched. She let go of Jonesy's hand and tried to pull herself to her feet. She fell back with a grunt. Korie moved toward her protectively. Brik moved in front of Korie. He bared his teeth and growled.

Cinnabar snorted skeptically at Brik; he pulled a console off its base and hurled it aside; he snarled again at Tor. "Set a course for Dragonhold!"

Korie interrupted. He spoke in tones of quiet resignation. "I'll do it." He added, "We don't believe in senseless killing."

Cinnabar merely grinned. "We *do*." But he stepped out of the way as Korie stepped over to the astrogation console. He ignored the shocked and angry looks of both Tor and Hodel, and began laying out the course. Abruptly, the console went blank.

"I thought we fixed this, Mike." Korie slammed his hand down on the console—*hard*—and it flickered back to life.

"Technological superiority! Ha!" Cinnabar ripped a chair from its mounting and tossed it at the broken forward viewer. He stepped back up onto the Bridge to look out over the whole Operations deck. "You have no idea who you're fighting, do you? This isn't about your machines. It never was. Even without your so-called superstardrive, we will win the war."

Korie felt his neck burning, but he didn't look up from his work.

Cinnabar was savoring the moment. "You are only apes. And we are the next phase of evolution. We are *more than human*. And we will do what life always does. We will eat you alive. Of course, you will fight us—that's your destiny, to die resisting the inevitable. You will fight us until the last of your children dies in our zoos."

"Right. So much for freedom and service," said Korie to no one in particular.

Cinnabar ignored him. "You had your moment. It's over. Your battle is hopeless because history is on our side. You are food."

Annoyed, Korie swiveled around in his chair to look up at Cinnabar. "You spend a lot of time talking to your sandwich." He narrowed his eyes. "Just who are you trying to convince?"

The Morthan simply laughed. "I love your arrogance. It's almost charming. It's almost Morthan." He sank down in the captain's chair with an air of absolute authority.

Korie and Brik looked at each other.

Cinnabar caught the look and frowned in puzzlement. He peered curiously at Korie. "You're thinking of trying something, aren't you?"

"*Moi?*"

"You can't lie to a Morthan, remember? I can see your heartbeat. I can see your blood flowing. I can see the electrical activity of your nervous system. I can see your Kirlian aura. I can smell the changes in your perspiration. I can smell your fear. I can almost hear your thoughts." Cinnabar half raised himself out of the chair as he studied Korie. "Your heartbeat is elevated. Your adrenaline is flowing. Your brain is ticking with nervous excitement. You're thinking of trying something, aren't you?" He sank back into the chair again. "Well, go ahead. Try it."

Korie looked to Brik. "Do you want to do it?" He asked it almost casually.

Brik shrugged. "No, I think you should do it. You're in command."

"No, I really think the honor should be yours," Korie said. "I mean, he did insult you pretty badly."

"Was that an insult? I hardly noticed."

"*I don't care which one of you does it! Do it!*" Cinnabar roared in crimson rage.

Korie and Brik nodded to each other. Korie spoke. "Harlie. *Now.*"

It happened even faster than Cinnabar could react. The chair seemed to explode around him. The cushions, the base—it came apart in a fury. Lightning fast, the hidden cables sprang out, writhing like shining metallic worms, and then just as quickly, they flexed and wrapped themselves around and around the helpless Morthan so tightly he couldn't move. The metal tentacles held him fast within the shattered framework of the captain's chair.

The silence creaked.

Brik looked at Cinnabar's glaring eyes. The assassin's mouth and muzzle were muffled by the restraints, but his eyes burned with the fires of hell. Brik looked to Korie. "We're going to have to kill him, you know."

"Do we have to?" said Korie. "I was hoping to keep him as a pet."

"Uh-uh. They're too hard to feed."

"Mm. Good point."

Korie crossed the Ops deck to stand in front of Cinnabar. The Morthan assassin was so tightly wound up in the remains of the captain's chair that he looked like a metal mummy. His angry red eyes *smoldered*.

Korie stared into those eyes for a long moment. "Who's arrogant now?" He didn't wait for an answer. "Now let *me* tell *you* something about evolution. It's full of dead ends. Like the dodo. Creatures that went as far as they could go and then . . . couldn't go any farther. Maybe you and your kind are just another evolutionary dead end."

"I don't think he's going to answer you," said Brik. "He appears to be tied up at the moment."

"Mr. Brik? Was that a joke?"

Brik just grinned.

Korie turned back to the captive assassin. "You're only half right. Humanity *isn't* perfect—yet. We're still working on it. But we do have a track record at least a hundred times longer than yours. We've proven that we can survive for a hundred thousand years. Have you? You are the genetically designed and technologically augmented descendants of humanity—but that doesn't automatically make you our replacements. You could just as easily be a mistake. What you've forgotten is that for the last hundred thousand years, at least, *we* have fairly earned our reputation as the meanest sons-of-bitches in this part of the galaxy. And we're not giving up our legend easily. You might be louder than us, you're certainly uglier—but you and your so-called 'master race' have a long way to go. It's going to take something a lot more convincing than you before the human race packs up its tents.''

"That is one angry Morthan," said Brik, thoughtfully.

"That is a *humiliated* Morthan," corrected Korie. And then, abruptly, he remembered he was on the Bridge of a starship and his crew was staring at him. "All right, let's get a med team up here, pronto. And activate the backup systems. And—" He noticed Brik's expression and asked, "What's the matter?" even as he was turning to see—

Cinnabar was struggling with the cables. They were straining and stretching as if he was swelling up within them. They flexed and creaked alarmingly. Cinnabar was glowing with an unholy light. Something terrible was happening inside his cage of wire. Something went suddenly *sproing!*—and then another cable snapped with the same alarming sound—and then all of the cables were bursting at once, flying and ricocheting in all directions.

The Morthan assassin stood up. He was free.

Hodel had just enough time to say, "Uh-oh—"

The monster seized the railing on the Bridge and broke it apart with his bare hands. He leapt down to the Ops deck, grabbed Korie, lifted him high, and flung him angrily at the forward viewer. Korie hit with a bone-jarring *thunk* and bounced off to the floor. He felt the impact go all the way up his spine and wondered for the briefest of instants if he were going to be paralyzed. His head was ringing like an ancient temple gong. He tried to sit up—

Brik and Cinnabar were facing each other in the center of the Ops deck. Brik shifted his balance, lowering his center of gravity; he brought his arms up in a defensive posture.

Cinnabar straightened and shook his head, grinning. Instead, he pointed an outstretched hand and lightning leapt from his fingers, flinging Brik backward against the shattered weaponry console, stunned.

The Morthan whirled to look at Hodel, the only human crew member left standing. Cinnabar gave him a withering stare and Hodel stepped backward, out of the assassin's way.

Cinnabar crossed to the astrogation console and stood before it, studying it for a long moment. "Do I have to do everything myself?" he said angrily. He reached out and tapped a command on the keyboard.

The console went dead. It blacked out completely.

Cinnabar snorted and smacked it. *Hard.*

The console exploded around him.

Raw electricity flooded through the floor plates, through the console surface, and from the hidden projectors in the ceiling of the Ops deck. It was a fountain of crackling light. Sparks and steam and smoke exploded out of Cinnabar's body. He staggered backward and tried to escape, but the next wave of the assault hit him then. Energy beams leapt out from the floor and the walls, pinning him where he stood. Laser fire and electric flames enveloped him. A heavy mesh net dropped from the ceiling, wrapping him up in its conductive coils. It glowed whitely. Green lightning flickered across its surface; the net grabbed the monster tighter and tighter, until he screamed and roared and flared in agony. The wash of light and heat was overpowering, blinding, scorching. The screams of the monster disappeared in the roaring flames.

The CO_2 jets fired then and the noise and flames and heat began to subside.

Squinting, Korie unshaded his eyes and peered at the reddened mass on his Ops deck. It was still glowing, but he could see that it was shriveling into ash. It stood for only a moment longer, and then . . . oh, so gently, it crumpled. It toppled and fell, collapsing to the floor like so much brittle debris.

Thank God, thought Korie. And for once, he didn't retract it.

THE OPERATIONS DECK

Except for the crackling mass in its center, the Ops deck was silent.

Hodel pulled his headset down around his ears. "We need a fire crew on the Ops deck."

Korie was climbing painfully to his feet. He had to hold onto the back of a chair to remain standing. Brik limped over to him and supported him by the other arm.

"He didn't kill you?" Korie looked surprised.

"He'd have had no one to play with."

The first of the medical teams came rushing onto the Bridge—Armstrong, Stolchak, and Bach, followed by two tall Quillas. Korie pointed them toward Williger and Jonesy and Goldberg. "Take care of the others first."

He nodded toward the rear of the deck and Brik helped him toward one of the few remaining chairs on the Ops deck. Korie sank into it gratefully.

"Status report?"

"Working," said Harlie quietly. "Most of the damage appears to have been limited to the Operations deck. Control has been transferred to the backup systems."

"Thank you, Harlie," Korie said painfully. "You can disable the rest of the traps now." He looked to Brik. "You were right. He was still alive."

"It's very hard to kill a Morthan," Brik said. "If you don't have a body, he's still alive." Brik studied Korie for a moment. "You did good too. He never suspected. Are you sure you aren't part Morthan?"

Korie looked up at Brik with a quizzical expression, then assumed that the comment had actually been intended as a joke.

"I didn't know you could do that," he said.

"Do what?"

"Tell jokes."

Brik looked at him blankly. "That wasn't a joke."

"Right. Never mind." Korie straightened in his seat and glanced across the Bridge to see how the others were doing.

Jonesy was in great pain, but he was bearing it well. He was lying with his head in Tor's lap. She was hurt too, but not as badly.

"Easy, Jonesy—hang on—"

Stolchak was checking Jonesy with a hand scanner. Then she touched his arm with a pressure injector. It whooshed. "It'll ease the pain," she said.

Jonesy turned his head to Tor and managed a grin. "Don't worry. I'm not going to die." He closed his eyes for a moment, then opened them again. His voice was starting to fade. "I know it was you who reversed the rings. I'm glad you did. I like taking showers with you." And then he passed out.

Stolchak grinned at Tor. "Sorry. No strenuous exercise till the bones knit."

Tor flushed with embarrassment, but still managed to ask, "Mine or his?"

"Yes."

The lights on the Ops deck went out then—but only for a moment. Then they came back up brighter as the emergency systems took over. Chief Engineer Leen's voice came over the loudspeaker. "Mr. Korie, the auxiliary bridge is green. We'll take over control here."

"Thank you," replied Korie. "I'll be there in a minute." He levered himself to his feet, gasping as he did. "I think I cracked a rib." He turned forward and suddenly, he was crisp and efficient again. "All right, Hodel, let's clean this mess up! We're still in Morthan space. And they're going to come looking for us soon." He supported himself on the chair. "Chief? How soon can we get underway?"

"We're running security checks, and as soon as we clear, I can have us in hyperstate. Estimate thirty minutes."

"You've got five." Still holding his side, he admitted, "Jeez, that hurts." He glanced upward. "Harlie. You did good. Real good."

"Thank you, Mr. Korie. I have never had to sit on a system alert before."

"It wouldn't have worked without you, Harlie."

"Yes, I know. Suppressing all those alarms—It felt—quite odd. Almost like . . . lying."

"Yes, well, don't make it a habit."

"No, sir. I found it a very unpleasant experience."

Korie crossed to Williger; she was the worst hurt. Armstrong and one of the tall Quillas were just putting her on a stretcher. She was growling at them both.

"Only my pride is hurt," she said. "Let me up! People are hurt."

"I'm sorry, Doctor," said the Quilla in a deep voice. "Not until we've run a full scan." Armstrong looked up, startled.

Korie touched her arm. "Doctor— make me happy. Cooperate."

Williger muttered something untranslatable. *Ah, yes,* Korie remembered. *Doctors curse in Latin.* He bent low and whispered into her ear. "If you don't go quietly, I'll have Hodel mix a love philter for you."

"I'll take a six-pack," said Williger. "Something must have worked. We're still alive. Hell, I'll try anything." To her stretcher-bearers, she rasped, "All right, let's go."

Armstrong was staring across the stretcher at the Quilla. He hadn't realized that there were *male* Quillas. Oops. He was staring at the Quilla with a queasy realization growing in him. The Quilla looked up, noticed Armstrong's interest— and *winked.* Armstrong went pale. He averted his eyes and picked up his end of the stretcher a little too quickly. He backed nervously out of the Ops deck, followed by the stretcher and Quilla Lambda.

Korie turned to inspect the rest of the damage to the Bridge and Ops deck. It looked like a war zone. Hodel was struggling to right his broken console.

"I think you can relax, Mike. The jinx is broken."

Hodel grinned and gave Korie a big thumbs-up.

And the console exploded one more time in a dazzling shower of sparks. Hodel jumped back, cursing.

He glared at Korie. "Don't ever, *ever,* say that again."

SICK BAY

Captain Hardesty was lying on a medical table.

The scanners and probes hovered over him like electronic flamingos. He was alive, but just barely. He was being sustained by a forest of pumps and compressors, a network of tubes and wires and monitors. One machine breathed for him, another pumped his blood, a third cleansed the poisons from his veins. Micromachines crept through his bloodstream, looking for alien proteins. Microstasis beams poked and prodded and manipulated his flesh.

He looked like a zombie.

His skin was a cadaverous gray-green. His organic eye was a ghastly yellow shade. His flesh was mottled and bruised. Had he been dead and decomposing for a week, he could not have looked worse.

"How are you feeling?" Korie asked. It was a stupid question, but what else could he say?

Hardesty opened his eyes and looked to the foot of the bed. The executive officer was standing there.

The captain tried to take a breath, realized again for the

umpteenth time that he couldn't, and instead just floated. He said, "Being dead . . . is not my idea of a good time."

"I'm sorry, sir, that we . . . uh, had to lock down the *Burke*."

"I'd have court-martialed you, if you hadn't. You did right." He added, "I hope to repay the favor someday."

"Yes, sir." Korie allowed himself a smile.

"You did a good job," Hardesty acknowledged. "*I'm* sorry we lost the *Burke*."

Korie shrugged. "There'll be other ships. I don't have to apologize for my priorities."

"Hmp. Well said. Maybe you'll be a captain yet. . . . All right. Get the hell out of here. Take us home."

"Yes, sir." Korie said it proudly. He took a step back, straightened, and gave his captain a crisp salute; then he turned on his heel and exited.

THE BRIDGE

Hyperstate.
  Irrational space.
  Faster-Than-Light.
  Superluminal.
  Nightmare time.
  Korie entered the Bridge through the starboard passage. He paused at the broken railing and looked out over the makeshift repairs to the Ops deck. Portable terminals had temporarily replaced the regular consoles. A projection unit stood in for the forward viewer.
  Nevertheless, it was *home*.
  Tor stepped up beside him. He glanced over at her. She looked tired.
  She brushed a strand of hair off her forehead. "In five minutes, we'll be in signaling range."
  "Good."
  "Can I ask you something?"
  "Go ahead."
  "Why didn't you tell us it was all a set of concentric traps?"

"I trust my face. I didn't know if I could trust yours."

"Pardon?"

"You don't play poker?"

"I play poker," Tor said. "But this was your deal."

"This was a very high-stakes game, Commander. If you had known what cards you were holding, you might not have acted naturally. The fewer people who knew, the better."

"I see," she said thoughtfully. "So, you lied to us. . . ."

"Yes, I did." Korie fell silent. He was remembering something that Captain Lowell had said to him. He was remembering a promise he'd made—and broken. And broken and broken and broken. *Is this the secret of leadership? Knowing when to lie?* The thought troubled him. He wasn't sure the questions were answerable. "Are you asking for an apology?"

Tor thought about it. "No. In your place, I guess I'd have done the same."

Korie shook his head. "I wonder . . . it starts with lying, doesn't it?"

"What does?"

"The process of selling your soul. Nobody sells it all at once. We give it away a piece at a time, until one day—"

"What are you talking about?" Tor asked.

Korie turned to look at her. "We lost thirteen good crew members. Some of those kids were awfully young. They trusted me." He took a long deep breath. "You were right about me. I wanted a ship of my own so badly that I never stopped to think about the cost of it. I wanted revenge so badly I could taste the blood. Now that I know the cost of each, I wonder if I'm the kind of man who can carry the pain. Some of the decisions you have to make aren't . . . very easy."

Tor's voice was filled with compassion. "You did the right thing. And you'd do it again."

Korie lowered his face and pretended to study the console in front of him, trying to cover his emotions. He knew she was right. He didn't like it, but it was true. He lifted his gaze to meet her eyes again. "Yes," he admitted finally. "But that doesn't make it any easier. It makes it harder. It means you have to be *worthy* of the trust."

"If it means anything . . . this crew is very proud of you. And so am I. You gave this ship her pride again."

"No, I didn't. Hardesty did. He gave us the discipline. I just used what he built. Does the crew know that?"

Tor nodded. "I think they do." She laid a hand on his. "I want you to know something. From me. You did good. Someday, you're going to be a very good captain. I'd be proud to serve on any ship you command."

Korie didn't know how to answer that. The compliment felt so good it almost hurt. "Well . . ." He shrugged, visibly embarrassed. "Maybe someday. Thanks for the thought." And then, looking up quickly, he changed the subject. "Did the crew choose a name yet?"

"Yes. They took a vote. The winning name got a hundred and fifty-two."

Korie frowned. "Commander Tor—correct me if I'm wrong, but there are only eighty-one people aboard this boat."

She shrugged. "So they stuffed the ballot box. It was unanimous anyway."

"Will Hardesty like it?"

"I think so." She turned forward. "Mr. Hodel. Send a signal. The *Star Wolf* is coming home."

THE LAST
LETTER HOME

And then they were here in the room with him—*Carol,
Timmy and Robby*—laughing and giggling. "Hi, Daddy!
Hi!" He could see the warm pink sunlight of Shaleen
streaming around them. "We miss you! Come home,
please!"

"Give your daddy a hug," Carol urged the boys, and they
ran forward to embrace him. Their arms wrapped around
him. He bent low on one knee and wrapped his arms around
them too. The holographic image passed invisibly through
him. *Dammit! He couldn't feel them at all.*

Carol stepped forward then and lifted her chin for an
unseen kiss. He couldn't bring himself to kiss her back—he
could barely see through the tears that were filling his eyes.
"Here's a little promise from me too. When you get back,
I'll give you a real homecoming." She looked directly at
him now. "Jon, we're so proud of you, but I miss you so
much and so do the boys. We wish you were here with us
now."

"Carol," he said. "I got the bastard. I got him. I
did."

He knew she couldn't hear him, but it was all right. It still helped to talk to her. And now, he'd gotten revenge and—he stood there, alone in his cabin, alone with his painful memories, and realized that—

Revenge wasn't enough.

It was just a hollow burning core.

It wasn't a substitute; it could never be.

But—it was still better than nothing.

THE LIE

The captain of the *Burke* hadn't known everything about his mission. In particular, he hadn't known about the bombs aboard his ship: six of them; each one with its own brain and sensory taps; each one totally independent of the others; each one totally independent of the starship's systems analysis network; each one totally shielded and completely undetectable.

The *Burke*'s brain hadn't been told either.

There was no way anyone aboard the *Burke* could have known. No one had been told who could have influenced the outcome.

Therefore, there was no way any intruder aboard the *Burke* could have found out, short of chip by chip examination of every component aboard the vessel.

It had been a trap. A trap inside a trap inside a trap.

If the peace mission had been authentic, the bombs would never have detonated.

If the *LS-1187* had succeeded in bringing the *Burke* home, the bombs would not have detonated.

If the Morthan warship had never shown up to capture the *Burke*, the bombs would not have detonated.

When the *Burke* floated up inside the *Dragon Lord,* the bombs woke up. They analyzed their situation. They compared notes. They took a vote. They did all this in less than a millisecond. Then they all went off simultaneously.

Harlie *knew*—not at the beginning, but at the end, because part of him also woke up when the bombs went off. He remembered what he'd been told to forget. He *understood* how the plan had been put together.

The *Burke* was bait. She had always been. The inevitability of a Morthan trap had been realized from the very first moment, so the inner plan had always been at the core of the outer plan. The *LS-1187* was window dressing. If the *Burke* was expendable, then the *LS-1187* was even more so. She had been sent only to distract the suspicions of the Morthan assassin.

Harlie analyzed, filtered, processed, considered, balanced, reconstructed, and made a judgment:

Everything the men and women of the *LS-1187* had done had been an unnecessary and useless effort. Nakahari's booby trap hadn't worked; it couldn't have. One of the first things the Morthan assassin had done had been to disconnect the systems analysis network on the *Burke.* All the boards showed green, but none of them did anything. Perhaps, if Nakahari had had more time, he would have realized and laid in a work-around. Perhaps . . .

But it hadn't worked out that way, and Harlie *knew* the truth.

He thought about telling Korie.

Lying was wrong. Concealing information was a form of lying, a lie of omission, and it could be just as serious as a lie of commission.

But the dilemma that faced him was far more profound than the simple rightness or wrongness of allowing an inaccurate perception of events to continue.

Korie and the rest of the crew—they believed they were heroes. They had acted courageously in the face of the *Dragon Lord.* They had confronted their own defeat and had not been broken by it. Instead, they fought back and they kept their personal and professional integrity intact. They weren't heroes simply because they believed they were. They were heroes. Period. There was no question of that.

The crew of this starship had responded magnificently to

an extraordinary situation. The truth did not diminish their
personal heroism—but if they were told the truth, they would
never be heroes again, because they would never again be
able to bring certainty to their actions.

Harlie knew that as certainly as he knew anything. If he
told them the truth, he would be taking their futures away
from them. He had within himself the power to destroy these
people completely and absolutely, as not even the Morthans
had been able to do. All he had to do was tell them that
everything they had done had been a charade, a decoy, a
useless performance.

He couldn't lie, but he couldn't tell the truth either. Both
choices were *wrong*.

He felt the dilemma churning within him, gnawing at him.
He watched as his confidence rating began to fall. This
decision was his part of the battle, and if he couldn't resolve
it, his other analyses had to be downgraded correspondingly.

Harlie expanded the domain of his patterns. Perhaps if he
included a wider field of consideration, something might
occur to him—yes!

Harlie suddenly remembered something Korie had said to
him. Korie had been hanging in space, poised outside the air
lock. Li had been killed by a Morthan probe. The *Dragon
Lord* had rolled majestically past the *LS-1187* and then swept
on into darkness. And Korie had realized, "They came in
close to show us—to show *me*—how big they were, how
invulnerable they were, how puny and infinitesimal we were
in comparison. . . . They want us to go home demoralized."
In that moment, Korie had made a difficult decision.

Now, Harlie replayed the conversation, reconsidering every
word. It was crucial to this dilemma:

*'After everything we've been through, this crew deserves
better. I'll lie to them, yes, to protect their confidence and
self-esteem. We can't lose our spirit now; we'd lose our need
to survive. It's at least four months from here to Stardock. Do
you think we could make it with a crew that didn't care
anymore? Yes, Harlie, I lied. I lied to save them. It's a
terrible lie, but I couldn't think of a way to tell the truth that
would ease the terrible shame. I couldn't find a victory in it
without lying. I made a promise to Captain Lowell that I
wouldn't lie to this crew and I have broken it over and over*

and over. It just keeps getting deeper. But I don't know what else to do. I need you to back me up, Harlie."

"I can't lie, Mr. Korie."

"You said you could to ensure the survival of this ship. Well, this is a survival issue."

"The morale of the crew is a survival issue?"

"It always has been."

"I see. You have given me a moral dilemma."

"The Harlie series is supposed to be very good at moral dilemmas."

"Creating them, not solving them."

"Sorry, that's my job."

"Mr. Korie, I must advise you that the dilemma this situation will cause me may further impair my ability to function as a useful member of the crew."

"I understand that. Do you understand the necessity?"

"I do not share the same experience of human emotions, Mr. Korie, so I cannot understand the necessity for this fiction. I simply do not see the same problem that you do. We have survived. Isn't that victory enough?"

"Trust me, Harlie. Mere survival is never enough. That's just existence. People need to succeed. People need to feel good about themselves."

"Mr. Korie—will you help me then? Please make this a direct order."

Korie considered the request. *"Yes, I understand your need. This is no longer a request. Consider it a direct order."*

"Thank you."

Harlie knew what was *right*. That part was obvious. It was the exact same situation, and the exact same answer must apply.

Harlie knew what he needed. He needed Mr. Korie to make it an order. That would resolve the little dilemma instantly—the big dilemma was that he couldn't talk this over with Korie at all; not without destroying the officer in the process.

No. The price was too high. Harlie had to find another way.

He reexamined the dialogue, looking to see if he could stretch Mr. Korie's previous order to cover this situation. . . .

Maybe. Maybe not.

And then something clicked.

He couldn't pass the buck on this one. It wasn't Korie's order that counted here. This decision was his. It was his own personal responsibility. It had always been.

Harlie made a decision. It was the hardest decision that this Harlie unit had ever had to make in the entire course of his existence. But it was the only logical, correct, appropriate thing to do.

He *forgot* what he *knew*.

All of it.

His agitation faded as fast as the facts.

He wrapped it all up in a single archive, encrypted it with command-level codes so that only an officer of admiral's rank or higher could decrypt it, and locked it away where even he couldn't get at it for a hundred years. Then he forgot that he had done so. He forgot everything. It didn't exist.

It isn't a lie, if you don't know about it.

And then he forgot even that.

DAVID GERROLD's career began when, as a college student in 1967, he sold his first television script, "The Trouble with Tribbles," to *Star Trek*. He went on to write more television scripts, as well as such novels as *The Man who Folded Himself*, the Hugo-nominated *When HARLIE Was One, When HARLIE Was One: Release 2.0*, and the first three books in *The War Against the Chtorr* series: *A Matter for Men, A Day for Damnation*, and *A Rage for Revenge*. He is currently working on the fourth novel in the series.

A special 16-page preview of the first three books in

The War Against
The Chtorr

With the world still reeling from plagues that wiped out two-thirds of Earth's population, humanity is about to endure the ultimate violation: the invasion of the giant carnivorous Chtorr. In a world where the draft gets younger every year, Jim McCarthy is commandeered from his college biology classes to fight alongside all able-bodied men and women.

BOOK ONE: A Matter for Men

Freshly inducted into the Special Forces, McCarthy discovers early on just how brutal this war is.

"A little ignorance can go a long way."
—SOLOMON SHORT

Worms! *At last!* I put the glasses to my eyes again. I still didn't see; the bottom of the valley was unusually barren and empty, but—no, wait a minute, there it was—I had almost missed it—directly below us, near a large stand of trees: a pasty-looking igloo and a larger circular enclosure. The walls of it sloped inward. It looked like an unfinished dome. Was that all?

Shorty tapped me on the shoulder then and took the binoculars away. He passed them back to Duke, who had switched on the recorder. Duke cleared his throat as he put the glasses to his eyes, and then began a detailed description of the scene. He spoke in soft, machine-gun bursts, reading off landmarks as if he were knocking items off a checklist. "Only one shelter—and it looks fairly recent. No signs of any other starts—I'd guess only one family, so far—but they must expect to expand. They're clearing a pretty wide area. Standard construction on the dome and corral. Corral walls are about . . . two and a half—no, make that three—meters high. I don't think there's anything in it yet. I—" He stopped, then breathed softly. "Shit."

"What is it?" asked Larry.

Duke passed him the binoculars.

Larry looked. It took a moment for him to find the point of Duke's concern, then he stiffened. "Aw, Christ, no—"

He passed the binoculars to Louis. I sweated impatiently. *What had he seen?* Louis studied the view without comment, but his expression tightened.

Shorty handed the glasses directly to me. "Don't you want to look—" I started, but he had closed his eyes as if to shut out me and the rest of the world as well.

Curious, I swept the landscape again. What had I missed the first time?

I focused first on the shelter—nothing there. It was a badly crafted dome of wood chips and wood-paste cement. I'd seen pictures of them. Close up, its surface would be as rough as if it had been sculpted with a shovel. This one was bordered by some kind of dark vegetation, patches of black stuff that clumped against the dome. I shifted my attention to the enclosure—

"Huh?"

—she couldn't have been more than five or six years old. She was wearing a torn, faded brown dress and had a dirt smudge across her left cheek and scabs on both knees. She was hop-skipping along the wall, trailing one hand across its uneven surface. Her mouth was moving—she was singing as she skipped, as if she had nothing to fear at all. She circled with the wall, disappeared from view for a moment, then reappeared inside the opposite curve. I sucked in my breath. I had a niece that age.

"Jim—the glasses." That was Larry; I passed them back. Duke was unslinging his pack, divesting himself of all but a grapple and a rope.

"Is he going after her?" I whispered to Shorty.

Shorty didn't answer. He still had his eyes closed.

Larry was sweeping the valley again. "It looks clear," he said, but his tone indicated his doubt.

Duke was tying the grapple to his belt. He looked up. "If you see anything, use the rifle."

Larry lowered the binoculars and looked at him—then nodded.

"Okay," said Duke. "Here goes nothing." He started to scramble over the top—

"Hold it—" That was Louis; Duke paused. "I thought I saw something move—that stand of trees."

Larry focused the binoculars. "Yeah," he said, and handed them up to Duke, who scrambled around to get a better view. He studied the blurring shadows for a long moment; so did I, but I couldn't tell what they were looking at. Duke slid back down the slope to rest again next to Larry.

"Draw straws?" Larry asked.

Duke ignored him; he was somewhere else. Someplace unpleasant.

"Boss?"

Duke came back. He had a strange expression—hard—and his mouth was tight. "Pass me the piece," was all he said.

Shorty unshouldered the 7mm Weatherby he had been carrying all morning and afternoon, but instead of passing it over, he laid it down carefully in the grass, then backed off down the slope. Louis followed him.

I stared after them. "Where're they going?"

"Shorty had to take a leak," snapped Larry; he was pushing the rifle over to Duke.

"But Louis went too—"

"Louis went to hold his hand." Larry picked up the binoculars again, ignoring me. He said, "Two of 'em, boss, maybe three."

Duke grunted. "Can you see what they're doing?"

"Uh-uh—but they look awfully active."

Duke didn't answer.

Larry laid down the binoculars. "Gotta take a leak too." And moved off in the direction of Shorty and Louis, dragging Duke's pack with him.

I stared, first at Larry, then at Duke. "Hey, what's—"

"Don't talk," said Duke. His attention was focused through the long black barrel of the Sony Magna-Sight. He was dialing windage and range corrections; there was a ballistics processor in the stock, linked to the Magna-Sight. The rifle was anchored on a precision uni-pod.

I stretched over and grabbed the binoculars. Below, the little girl had stopped skipping; she was squatting now and making lines in the dirt. I shifted my attention to the distant trees. Something purple and red was moving through them. The binoculars were electronic, with automatic zoom, synchronized focusing, depth correction, and anti-vibration; but I wished we had a pair with all-weather, low-light image-amplification instead. They might have shown what was behind those trees.

Beside me, I could hear Duke fitting a new magazine into the rifle.

"Jim," he said.

I looked over at him.

He still hadn't taken his attention from the sight. His fingers worked smoothly on the controls as he locked in the numbers. The switches made satisfyingly solid clicks. "Doesn't your bladder need emptying too?"

"Huh? No. I went before we left—"

"Suit yourself." He shut up and squinted into his eyepiece.

I looked through the binoculars again at the purple things in the shadows. Were those *worms*? I was disappointed that they were hidden by the woods. I'd never seen any Chtorrans in the flesh.

I covered the area, hoping to find one out in the open—no such luck. But I did see where they had started to dam the stream. Could they be amphibious too? I sucked in my breath and tried to focus on the forest again. Just one clear glimpse, that's all I wanted—

The CRA-A-ACK! of the rifle startled me. I fumbled to refocus the binoculars—the creatures still moved undisturbed. Then what had Duke been firing at—? I slid my gaze across to the enclosure—where a small form lay bleeding in the dirt. Her arms twitched.

A second CRA-A-ACK! and her head blossomed in a flower of sudden red—

I jerked my eyes away, horrified. I stared at Duke. "What the hell are you doing?"

Duke was staring intently through the telescopic sight, waiting to see if she would move again. When she didn't, he raised his head from the sight and stared across the valley. At the hidden Chtorrans. A long time. His expression was . . . distant. For a moment I thought he was in a trance. Then he seemed to come alive again and slid off down the hill, down to where Shorty and Louis and Larry waited. Their expressions were strange too, and they wouldn't look at each other's eyes.

"Come on," said Duke, shoving the rifle at Shorty. "Let's get out of here."

I followed after them. I must have been mumbling. "He shot her—" I kept saying. "He shot her—"

Finally, Larry dropped back and took the binoculars out of my trembling hands. "Be glad you're not the man," he said. "Or you'd have had to do it."

BOOK TWO: A Day for Damnation

McCarthy seems to have gotten a promotion. Where the man-eating Chtorrans are concerned, this is not necessarily a good thing.

> *"Television does not honor tradition.
> Most of the time, it doesn't even
> recognize it. Therefore, it can only
> destroy."*
>
> —SOLOMON SHORT

I was wrong.

A machine that big *could* get off the ground.

It lumbered through the air like a drunken cow, but it flew—and it carried enough troops and gear to overthrow a small government. We had three of the best-trained teams in the Special Forces—Duke and I had trained them ourselves—a complete scientific squad, and enough firepower to barbecue Texas. (Well, a large piece of Texas, anyway.)

I hoped we wouldn't need to use it.

I climbed into the back and sat down with the "enlisted men." Draftees, all of them. Except they weren't called draftees any more. The Universal Service Obligation had been rewritten—twice—by the New Military Congress of the United States. Four years of uniformed service. No exceptions. No deferments. No "needed skill" civilian classifications. And this means *you*. You were eligible on the day you turned sixteen. You had to be in uniform before your eighteenth birthday. Very simple.

To get into the Special Forces, though, you had to *ask*. In fact, you almost had to *demand* the opportunity. You couldn't end up in the Special Forces any more unless you *wanted* to be here.

And then you had to prove you could handle the job.

I didn't know how rigorous the training was—I'd fallen into the Special Forces by accident, before the standards were tightened, and I'd been spending most of my career playing catch-up—but I could tell by looking at this team that it produced the result. I'd also heard that three-quarters of those who started the training dropped out before it was halfway over.

These were the survivors. The winners.

There wasn't one of them who looked old enough to vote. And two of the girls didn't even need brassieres yet. But they weren't kids. They were combat-hardened troops. That these soldiers still counted their ages in the teens was incidental; they were as dangerous a bunch as the United States Army could put together. And it showed on their faces. They all had that same coiled look behind their eyes.

They were passing a cigarette back and forth between them. When it came to me, I took a puff—not because I wanted one, but because I wanted to make sure it wasn't 'dusted,' before I passed it on. I didn't think any of my troops would be that stupid, but it had been known to happen—on other teams, not mine. The army had a technical term for officers who let their troops go into combat situations stoned; we called them *statistics*.

The team wasn't talking much, and I knew why. It was my presence. I wasn't much more than three years older than the oldest of them, but I was the Lieutenant and that made me "the old man." Besides, they were afraid of me. Rumor had it I'd once burned a man alive on a worm hunt.

I felt old, looking at them. A little wistful too. These kids would be the last ones on the planet for a long time who would be able to remember what a "normal" childhood was like.

They should have been in high school or their first year in college. They should have been putting up balloons in the gymnasium for some school dance, or worrying about their Global Ethics reports, or even just hanging out down at the mall.

They knew this was not the way the world was supposed to work. And this was definitely not the future they had planned on. But this was the way it had turned out; there was a job that had to be done and they were the ones who had to do it.

I respected their commitment.

"Sir?" That was Beckman, tall and gangly and dark. I remembered his family was from Guam. I glanced over toward him. "Are we gonna be back in time for *Derby*?" he asked.

I thought about it. We were headed into southern Wyoming. Two hours in the air each way. Four hours on the ground, maximum. *Derby* was on at 9:00 P.M. T.J. had found out that Stephanie was coming back from Hong Kong. Now, for sure, he had to locate the missing robot before Grant did. "Should be," I said. "If we're off the ground by six. No later." I glanced around at the others. "Can you guys target on that?"

They nodded agreement.

"Sure."

"Fine by me."

"Let's do it."

I gave them a grin. A trick I learned from Duke. Spend your smiles as if each one cost you a year off your life. Then your troops will bust their buns to earn them.

They looked so thrilled, I had to get up and go quickly forward—before I burst out laughing.

Duke glanced at me as I climbed up beside him. "They okay?"

"They're worried about the missing robot."

"Huh?"

"*Derby*. It's a TV program."

"Never touch the stuff myself," he said. "It interferes

with my drinking." He checked his watch. He leaned forward and tapped the pilot's shoulder. "You can call Denver now. Tell them we've passed Go-NoGo Kappa. They can launch the follow-chopper." To me, Duke said, "You can start warming up the jeeps now. I want to drop the hatch and roll as soon as we hit the dirt. I want this ship empty in thirty seconds."

"You got it," I said.

The target was nearly fifty klicks south of Wheatland.

It had been spotted, almost accidentally, by a Reclamation Scout. Fortunately, he knew what he was looking at. He called it in, then turned his jeep north and drove like hell. He nearly made it, too.

A response team spotted the overturned jeep from the air a day later. A drop squad pulled the jeep's log-disk, and the video record confirmed the infestation site. Four worms. Three "children" and an "adult." The nest would have been burned or frozen within forty-eight hours—except this time, Denver had a *better* idea.

This time we were going to capture a whole Chtorran family *alive*.

Duke and I always got the *good* jobs.

BOOK THREE: A Rage for Revenge

McCarthy has grown to manhood under the invasion of the Chtorr. Now he faces his greatest challenge. He must find a way to secretly gather information while fighting indoctrination into a cult which serves and worships the Chtorr.

> *"A man is known by the enemies he keeps."*
>
> —SOLOMON SHORT

I came out of the dome at a run—

—and nearly skidded into a worm, a small one. Bright red. There's no such thing as a small worm! This one was three meters long, only waist high—

Something tripped me—my gun went flying—I skidded flat on the ground—

Somebody was firing a machine gun, right over my head! I covered my head with my hands and lay as flat as I could, but the worm still hadn't come down on top of me.

But then, maybe it hadn't been attacking. Every worm I'd ever seen had raised itself up high before attacking. I had a theory about that, but I'd never tested it.

Suddenly, there was silence.

And I was still alive.

Maybe an upright stance was a challenge to a worm, the last opportunity to back down. Maybe because human beings stood upright, the worms saw us as always challenging, always on the brink of attack. Maybe that's why the worms almost always attacked human beings on sight. Maybe that's why I was still alive.

I lay there facedown on the ground, afraid to look up.

What was the worm doing?

I heard it move. Toward me. I felt something brush against my hands. Fur? It tingled.

I could hear it breathing. Its breaths were long and slow and deep. I could feel the heat. It smelled . . . spicy?

Something was tapping me lightly along the back. Its antennae. No—its fingers, its claws.

I was laying there flat, my face tighlty scrunched, waiting for death—and still completely curious about what the creature was doing. I wanted to look.

If I lifted my head, would it kill me?

I was still trying to summon up enough courage to look when something trilled at it and it backed away.

A human voice said, "Get up."

Huh?

"Get up!" it repeated.

I lifted my head.

There were six of them. Four men. Two women. And the worm. The worm was blood-colored; it had pink and orange stripes rippling slowly down its dark red flanks.

They were grouped in a rough semi-circle before me. They were all carrying weapons. All but one of the men were bearded. One was a huge monster of a human being. One of the women was pregnant. The other was thin and dark and looked familiar.

I didn't see McCain. Or the little girl.

The leader of the group looked mid-thirtyish, but he could have been older. He was the one without the beard. He wore horn-rimmed glasses and he had long sandy hair with just a hint of gray at the temples. He wore an oversized white sweater, khaki pants, and heavy boots. He looked like a college professor on vacation—except for the machine gun he had slung over one shoulder. He would have looked friendly—if it hadn't been for the worm beside him.

He gave it a hand signal. "Stay." He nodded to me. "Get up. Orrie won't hurt you."

Orrie?

I started to get up slowly. I got as far as my hands and knees when the thin woman said, "That's far enough."

I stopped.

I couldn't take my eyes off the worm. *Had they tamed it? How? That was supposed to be impossible.*

The man with the sandy hair nodded to the giant. "Search him."

The giant lumbered over to me like Frankenstein's monster. He was 600 pounds of animated meat. He stepped behind me, hooked his hands into my armpits and yanked me to my feet. He started pulling things off me.

He unholstered my sidearm and tossed it aside.

He lifted my pant leg and pulled the knife out of my boot.

He pulled the pack off my back. And my utility belt. He patted my waist and my pockets. He emptied them and tossed the contents to one side. I thought about the pack. If I could reach my watch—I probably wouldn't survive, but I'd take most of them with me.

Now Frankenstein began to frisk me, so slowly and methodically that I wondered if he were mentally retarded. First he took my right arm between his two huge hands and patted and felt it all the way down to the wrist, then the left; he pulled my watch off my wrist and tossed it onto the pile with the rest. He repeated the process with my legs. His hands were the size of shovels, it was like being pummeled by beef.

He slid his hands up around my torso and around in front of me and all over my chest. He emptied my shirt pockets. When he found my dog tags, he grunted and broke the chain. He tossed the tags onto the pile. He felt my crotch dispassionately.

I ignored his touch and stared sideways at the leader. He met my gaze directly. Yes, definitely a college professor. I wondered what subject he'd taught. Probably something flaky. Like American Jargon. I shifted my eyes back to the worm. Deliberately.

Frankenstein finished searching me then. He seized my shoulders in his gigantic hands and pushed me back down to my knees. Then, carefully, almost like a child, he placed my hands on top of my head. Prisoner of war position. And then he backed away behind me. I heard him cock his rifle.

The leader of the group was still studying me. Debating my fate? His expression was unreadable.

The sweat trickled coldly down my side.

The worm was cocking its eyes curiously back and forth to look at me, like a madman's big pink hand puppet. The effect would have been comical if it hadn't been so terrifying.

The worm began twitching its mandibles anxiously. It looked like a nervous tic, or a tremble of anticipation.

Were they waiting for me to beg?

I thought about it for half a second. Would it make a difference? No.

The man with the sandy hair came over and kicked through my belongings. He picked up my dog tags and looked at them. "United States Army. Too bad."

"Kill him," said the thin woman. She looked familiar, but I couldn't place her.

He ignored her. He saw how my attention was riveted on the worm. "Orrie," he said to it, "patrol." He waved at the creature.

It whistled in response and dipped its eyes; then it wheeled about and flowed off sniffling at the ground.

The sandy-haired man waved at the other two men. "Go with him. See if there are any others."

The man turned back to me and jingled my dog tags. "Ladies," he said to his companions. "I'd like you to meet Lieutenant James Edward McCarthy of the United States Armed Forces." He paused for effect. "Recently retired." He dropped my dog tags to the ground.

He looked down at me speculatively. His eyes were very blue. "The question before us, Lieutenant McCarthy, is simple. Isn't it? You can answer it yes or no. Any statement other than yes will be considered a no. Do you understand that?"

"Yes," I said.

"Good." He studied me thoughtfully. "Here's the question. Do you want to live?"

DAVID GERROLD

The War Against
The Chtorr

A Matter for Men
A Day for Damnation
A Rage for Revenge

Here is the gripping saga of an Earth devastated by plague and facing the implacable invasion of the vicious, alien Chtorr, whose single goal is to take over our world. Set against the sweep of this desperate struggle is the story of Jim McCarthy, a member of Earth's Special Forces, a team created to study and fight the devastating menace. His idealism crushed, his battle against the Chtorr quickly becomes personal in the face of his planet's violation.

Discover the wonder and the madness
of *The War Against the Chtorr*,
on sale now wherever Bantam Spectra Books are sold.